T0024914

The Colour
of Murder

The Colour of Murder

With an introduction
by Martin Edwards

Julian Symons

Poisoned Pen Press

Originally published in 1957 by Collins, London

©2018 The Estate of Julian Symons

Introduction Copyright © 2018 by Martin Edwards
Published by Poisoned Pen Press in association with
the British Library

First U.S. Edition 2019

10 9 8 7 6 5 4 3 2 1

Library of Congress Control Number: 2018956094

ISBN: 9781464210891   Trade Paperback
ISBN: 9781464210907   Ebook

Poisoned Pen Press
4014 N. Goldwater Blvd., #201
Scottsdale, AZ 85251
www.poisonedpenpress.com
info@poisonedpenpress.com

Printed in the United States of America

*For Michael Evelyn
with much gratitude for his patient guidance
through the legal maze*

Introduction

The Colour of Murder was one of the most acclaimed British crime novels of the 1950s. On publication, it received a rapturous reception from the critics, and it won the prize given by the Crime Writers' Association for the best crime novel of the year in 1957; then called the Crossed Red Herring prize, it is now known as the CWA Gold Dagger.

At that time, the book seemed highly contemporary, with its focus on the psychological make-up of a man accused of murder. Today, more than sixty years later, it is also of interest in the way it documents British social history. *The Colour of Murder* remains a crisply written and highly readable novel, with a clever plot, even if it is very different from the cerebral whodunits that were in vogue during the Golden Age of Murder between the world wars.

The first part of the book comprises a lengthy statement given by John Wilkins to a consulting psychiatrist. He describes his early years, his less than exciting job in a complaints department in an Oxford Street store, his troubled marriage to a wife desperate for respectability and social status, and his infatuation with an attractive young librarian. And he mentions his disturbing tendency to have blackouts.

Wilkins' world is recognisable to a twenty-first century reader, yet different from our own in innumerable ways, great and small. It's a world, for instance, of "television parties"; I hadn't even realised there ever were such things, but evidently for some people they formed part of 1950s social life. It's also a world where racist attitudes are commonplace, as is clear from the account of a murder committed by a Jamaican bus conductor. The bus conductor is sympathetically presented in the narrative; the relevance of the crime is that Wilkins takes an interest in it. Before long, he is asking his uncle how he'd go about it if he wanted to kill someone.

Readers will presume from the outset that a murder has been committed, and also suspect that Wilkins stands accused of it. But who is the victim? One aspect of the plot is that the first part of the book is a "whowasdunin" story, of the type which came to the fore in the 1930s thanks to novels such as Anthony Berkeley's *Murder in the Basement*, which was taken forward by American writers such as Patricia McGerr and Anita Boutell, and interests novelists to this day; a recent example of this kind of story is Mark Lawson's *The Deaths*.

The second part of the book covers the discovery of a crime, a trial, and the verdict. Symons handles the courtroom scenes splendidly, and in this part of the book it becomes clear that he wants to explore the nature of justice. *The Colour of Murder* is in the tradition of earlier crime novels which explored the quirks and ironies of the British justice system and which Symons much admired: examples include Berkeley's *Trial and Error*, Raymond Postgate's *Verdict of Twelve*, and Edward Grierson's *Reputation for a Song*. But Symons' approach, with its emphasis on Wilkins' psychological profile, was in its day strikingly fresh.

The novel is dedicated to Michael Evelyn, "with much

gratitude for his patient guidance through the legal maze". Evelyn, a senior figure in the office of the Director of Public Prosecutions, was not only a close friend of Symons but also himself a crime novelist who wrote under the name Michael Underwood; the first Underwood novel appeared in 1954, and he became a prolific author of sound, low-key mysteries, often with a legal setting.

Symons' presentation of the barrister Magnus Newton owed much to the insight he gained from Evelyn, and he enjoyed writing about Newton so much that he returned to the character in his Edgar-winning novel *The Progress of a Crime*, and also in *The End of Solomon Grundy* and the excellent *The Man Whose Dreams Came True*. In notes included in his bibliography, compiled by John J. Walsdorf, Symons forgot that Newton appeared in the last of these four books, and said that *The End of Solomon Grundy* marked his final appearance: he was "in danger of becoming my abomination, a series character".

Symons' lean writing style was always one of his strengths, and *The Colour of Murder* illustrates his ability to cover a good deal of ground without wasting words. Even fans of forensic detection are catered for, since the trial features discussion of the benzidine test for blood, relevant in the days before DNA profiling. The final section of the book is an Epilogue, which delivers—through Newton—an ironic plot twist of which a leading Golden Age novelist such as Berkeley would have been proud. This novel, with its focus on post-war society, and sexual desire and repression, is very different from many of the British Library Crime Classics dating back from the 1930s, but it shares some of their virtues.

Julian Gustave Symons was one of the most influential British crime novelists and critics of the twentieth century.

Born in 1912, he was the youngest of seven children, the son of a Jewish immigrant whose real name he never discovered. He left school at fourteen, and in effect educated himself. He enjoyed writing poetry, and founded a magazine called *Twentieth Century Verse*, running it singlehandedly until the war came.

He and a friend, Ruthven Todd (who later wrote a handful of detective stories as R.T. Campbell), planned a jokey murder mystery, which Symons wrote up. Six years later, in 1945, the story was published as *The Immaterial Murder Case*, but although it appeared as a green Penguin paperback, Symons later decided it should not be reprinted again. He became equally dissatisfied with his next two novels, but with *The Narrowing Circle*, he felt he'd made a breakthrough, in terms of character development and "saying something about the form and shape of society".

The success of *The Colour of Murder* and *The Progress of a Crime* cemented his reputation as a crime novelist, and he also became a highly respected critic. In addition, he was a biographer and historian of distinction; indeed, the book for which he is best remembered today is *Bloody Murder* (*Mortal Consequences* in the U.S.), his splendidly pithy history of the crime genre. Since his death in 1994, his work as a novelist has fallen into regrettable neglect. As a long-term admirer of his work, I cannot help hoping that the British Library's reissue of this novel, and *The Belting Inheritance*, will lead to a revival of interest in his fiction.

Martin Edwards
www.martinedwardsbooks.com

Note

The benzidine test for blood described in the second half of this book is a real test, and there is some dispute about its value, on the lines that I have suggested. No reference to any real murder case is intended, however, and all the characters in the story are imaginary.

—J. S.

Part One

BEFORE

John Wilkins's Statement
to Dr. Max Andreadis,
CONSULTING PSYCHIATRIST

I

It all began one day in April when I went round to change a library book. At least, that is the time when it seemed to me to begin, though I know you people trace things a lot farther back, and I'd like to say that I don't believe in all that. Whatever a man does, he's got to take responsibility for his own actions, that's what I believe. I don't see how the world can run any other way. I have to say that, even though I know it may be against me.

When I got home from work that evening May had one of her migraine headaches. She was lying down in the bedroom with the curtains drawn, said she'd had nothing to eat all day, but the first thing she asked me was to change her library book. That seems queer, doesn't it, when she didn't want to read, but it was just like May. You see, the library book was due back that day, and if we hadn't returned it there would have been a twopenny fine. May never forgot things like that. She was—is, I ought to say, but life with her seems so far away—a good housewife, looking after the pennies.

I ate my supper, corned beef and potato salad and part of a tin of fruit, went to the library, handed over the book. The girl who took it was new, a pretty dark girl, rather plump, and she smiled at me. It isn't very often that women smile at me, you know. I'm not attractive to women. Not that there's anything wrong with my looks, mother always said I was good-looking when I was a boy, and at school I used to get on pretty well with girls. But since I've been about twenty-one I've noticed that most girls don't want to talk to me for long. It's not bad breath or B.O. or anything like that, it's—well, I'm nervous with women, talk too fast when I'm with them, and get excited. I can't get nearer than that to what it is.

Anyway, this girl smiled at me, and I asked her if she was new, and she said she was. Then, when I was looking at the books, she came out wheeling a trolley with the books on it that had just come back, and I spoke to her, asked if they had any books by Moira Mauleverer, that was the slushy romantic novelist May particularly liked. She smiled again.

"I'm not sure, Mr. Wilkins. Do *you* read Moira Mauleverer?"

"Oh no," I said, and then I went on, "They're for my sister. She's an invalid, you know, confined to the house, and she reads that kind of book. I like Somerset Maugham myself."

"He's a fine author."

"He's a man of the world. Very sophisticated."

"Yes. Will you excuse me a moment?" She put the books from the trolley up on the shelves and I noticed that she had very pretty finger-nails. Then a couple of minutes later she came back to me. "Has your sister read this one? It's new, we haven't put it on the shelves yet." She held out the book in its glossy jacket, *Princess Make Believe* by Moira Mauleverer.

As I took it our hands touched, and I felt a kind of thrill go up my arm.

Then I began to thank her and perhaps I went on too long because she began to seem a little embarrassed and said she must go back to the issuing counter now. So I took the book and went home. That was the first time I met Sheila, and that very first time I told her a lie, saying that May was an invalid and pretending that she was my sister instead of my wife. I don't know now why I did it.

II

The next day May was better, up in the morning to get breakfast, and pleased about the book. She said she would be well enough to go to work—she had a part-time job at a local stationer's shop—and I went off feeling more cheerful than usual. We were going round to see mother that evening, we always went there on Wednesdays, and I arranged that we would meet there.

At work, though, things didn't go smoothly that day. You know my job, assistant manager of the Complaints Department in Palings, the big Oxford Street store. It's an important position, you know, I carry a great deal of responsibility, although the pay isn't very high, five hundred and fifty a year. That morning the manager of the department, my immediate superior, Mr. Gimball, called me in.

"How are you this morning, Mr. Wilkins?" he asked.

"I'm fine, sir," I said heartily.

"No more of those blackouts, I hope."

"Not a trace." I'd had two or three blackouts during the past year. I mean by blackouts that I'd gone out for lunch, had a couple of drinks, and apparently not returned in the afternoon. I was never quite sure that Mr. Gimball believed my explanation that I didn't know what had happened, although it was perfectly true. The last blackout had been just before Christmas, and after it Mr. Gimball had suggested that I should take a couple of days off.

"You aren't feeling the strain of overwork or anything like that?"

I thought about the way the girl in the library had smiled at me, and laughed confidently. "Oh no, Mr. Gimball."

"Then how do you explain *these*?" He pushed three letters across the desk at me, and I read them. They were complaints letters, one about a pair of stockings, another about a pullover, and the third a complaint from a woman that one of the assistants in the soda fountain had insulted her. Mr. Gimball tapped this letter. "A week old. We've had another letter from her to-day threatening to take legal action against the firm."

"This is the first I've seen of these letters, Mr. Gimball."

"They all have our date stamp of receipt. They have been on your desk since they came in."

"Oh no." I simply had to say it. "That's not true."

"Are you calling me a liar, Mr. Wilkins?" I always thought of Mr. Gimball as a frosty man—his hair was like frosty powder, little gleams of frosty light twinkled off his spectacles, he always wore a gleaming pearl tie-pin. I suddenly realised that to-day he was even frostier than usual.

"Of course not, sir. I only mean that I know I should have seen these letters if they'd been on my desk. You know I've always adhered faithfully to the Gimball system. We Turn Complaints to Compliments, I never forget that." That was one of Mr. Gimball's slogans, and it was stuck up all round the department.

"I'm glad of that. So you've never seen these letters before."

Something about the way he spoke made me say, "Not to the best of my knowledge."

He lifted his telephone and asked for Miss Murchison.

She was a long-nosed, red-eyed girl who looked after the filing, and I knew she didn't like me. When she came in he asked, "Where did you find these letters, Miss Murchison?"

"On Mr. Wilkins's desk, sir, under a lot of other papers. I mentioned them to him, sir, two days ago. He said not to bother him now, he was too busy." I stared at her, astonished. Her hangdog look, the way she mumbled her words, convinced me that she was speaking the truth. Yet I could remember nothing about it. Or could I? Distantly, somewhere in the haze of memory, I seemed to recall Miss Murchison speaking words like these. Then why had I paid no attention to them, what had I been doing? I thought about this, and suddenly became aware that Gimball was talking to me and that Miss Murchison had gone.

"What were you doing that was of greater importance than our proper business of turning complaints to compliments, Mr. Wilkins?"

"It is true that we've been very busy lately—"

"You informed me five minutes ago, however, that you were not overworked."

I felt sweat on the palms of my hands. I knew I was gabbling. "I know, but we are sometimes very busy, you know yourself these things go in waves. You know I wouldn't let a thing like this slip by unless there were exceptional circumstances. I frankly don't recall Miss Murchison speaking to me about this, although I accept that she did. If you'll let me have that letter from the lady who's written twice—"

"I have already replied to it. The letter was brought to me only because it was a second communication and the first had not been answered. I am wondering how many other cases of delay have occurred which have not been drawn to my attention."

"None at all," I said eagerly. "I'm sure of that."

"What I can't understand, Mr. Wilkins, is how you came to overlook these. That is really incomprehensible to me."

He seemed to expect an answer. "I shall see it doesn't happen again."

"Perhaps a transfer to another department—"

"I hope you won't think that necessary, Mr. Gimball." This was really a threat. Transfer to another department meant that I should be downgraded to some kind of clerk's job. I thought that would be the end of it, but he talked for another ten minutes before he let me go.

I went back and dictated letters at once, sending a pair of new stockings to the woman, and asking the man to return his pullover. I looked at everything else on my desk and dealt with all the items that had any urgency at all about them. I went through the rest of the day in a kind of daze.

Because, you see, while I had been talking to Gimball I *had* remembered those letters being on my desk, I remembered thinking that I must answer them. Why hadn't I done so? When I reached that question my mind became blank and at last, some time in the afternoon, I gave up trying to answer it and began to think again about the girl in the library.

III

May didn't much like going round to mother's place every Wednesday, she only did it because I insisted, and she often complained. There were several reasons for this, as far as I could make out. One was that we had a flat in Windover Close, a newish block overlooking the south side of Clapham Common, while mother lived in a small house in Baynard Road, one of the small roads between the Common and Wandsworth Road.

There was nothing wrong with this house, you understand, but when father died, that was when I was in the Army, mother hadn't much money. We moved out of the big house in Kincaid Square and she bought this one in Baynard Road. There was nothing wrong with the house as I've said, it was like all the others in Baynard Road to be sure, but it was respectable. I'd been living there myself when I first met May. I had a kind of affection for the place, even liked the little squeaking iron gate and the dust patch at the back that you couldn't call a garden.

May hated it. She'd been brought up herself in Nelson Terrace, which was much worse than Baynard Road, on the wrong side of Wandsworth Road, really in Battersea, not Clapham. Her own mother and father—well, May never wanted to be reminded about them or about that kind of life. I think Baynard Road did remind her. She was a great one for having nice young couples in to play bridge and drink coffee and eat little sandwiches cut into shapes of hearts, clubs, spades and diamonds and watch TV. She was always on at me to ask Gimball and his wife to dinner, and used to say I had no idea of improving my social position. It was funny she should be like that when she wanted to forget all about her own social background, but that's the way it was. And then she didn't like mother, and hated Uncle Dan, who lived in Baynard Road too, and—but I'd better get back to that evening, which was like all the other evenings and yet a little different.

The pattern of the evenings never changed much. We would have dinner, a good solid dinner of the kind I liked, the kind that May never cooked for me. Then there'd be a bit of talk, and we'd settle down to play cards, sevens or Newmarket or solo whist. May really only liked playing bridge, she said the games we played round at mother's were slow and old-fashioned.

That evening there was steak and kidney pie, plenty of kidney inside and a nice brown crust on top. When I passed up my plate for more, mother said, "I knew you'd be asking for a second helping. I don't forget my boy's favourites."

"You shouldn't have any more, John," May said. "It's gluttony, really. It's not good for you."

"Not good for him." Mother held up her hands in astonishment. "Steak and kidney pie never hurt anybody."

"It's delicious pie." May snapped off the word *pie* as though she were biting it. "But too much isn't good for John. He's getting fat."

It was a fact that I'd put on a bit of weight in the last few months. Doubtfully I said, "I don't know, perhaps May's right."

By now two great tablespoonfuls of pie were on my plate. "Can't take it back now," mother said. "It won't hurt him for once. After all, he doesn't get it very often." She didn't mean any harm but I could see from May's face that it was the wrong thing to say.

"Eat it up, boy. Be all the same in a hundred years," boomed Uncle Dan. He was my mother's brother, a big man with a fine shock of grey hair, who had done all sorts of things in his time—trading in a Chinese junk up the Yangtse, acting as agent for several British firms in the Far East, and finally running an insurance book in south-west London. He had given this up a few months back and now lived with my mother as a kind of lodger or paying guest.

After the pie came treacle pudding. Uncle Dan ate heartily, and so did I. May hardly touched her piece. Afterwards we had the usual argument about helping with the washing up, and as usual mother finally agreed to let us wipe the plates. May never let guests help with the washing up at home. When it was done she said she was too tired to play cards. Mother had just got down the pack from its place on the mantelpiece. Now she paused.

"Too tired to play cards," Uncle Dan said incredulously. "Why, girl, I've sat up all night playing solo, drinking whisky, felt fresh as a daisy at the end of it. Nothing like a game of cards to take you out of yourself when you're feeling down."

"I'm not feeling down," May said. "Just too tired to play cards."

"Tell you what, we'll have a change." Uncle Dan took the cards and gave them what he called his cardsharp's shuffle. "We'll have a real little flutter to-night, a game of pontoon."

"Pontoon would be a nice change." That was my mother.

"Need to get the rules straight first. My experience is every school has its own different way of playing. Split on aces only, is that agreeable to all? Pay double for pontoons, treble for five-card tricks, maximum stake threepence, banker can double if he wants. A real gamble, eh?"

"I don't want to play cards," May said in a high voice.

"Have a little flutter and see if you can be the first lady to break the bank at Monte Carlo," said Uncle Dan. "Wonder if I've got enough money for this gambling school now, where are my coppers?"

Mother said in the very quiet voice she uses when she feels hurt, "May said she didn't want to play cards, Dan."

Uncle Dan looked quickly at my mother and at May, then he put the cards away again in their case. We spent the rest of the evening talking about the weather and the neighbours and whether it was better to own your house or rent it. Mother kissed my cheek with an extra pressure when she said good night. Uncle Dan asked why I didn't join the tennis club this year. I said I would think about it. I had been a pretty good player, but I'd given it up when I got married because May didn't like the game.

Walking back home over the Common, May and I didn't talk to each other. When we'd got into the flat, though, she said, "That's over for another week, thank goodness."

"You upset mother."

"She knows I don't like to play cards. Why does she produce them every time we go over as if she were giving us a treat?"

"You play bridge."

"That's a *real* card game."

"Just once a week doesn't hurt, surely."

May was off on a new tack. "Don't think I didn't notice what your mother said about the steak and kidney pie. Won't hurt him for once, doesn't get it very often, I know just what she means. And that awful vulgar old man with his bad jokes. It's not just once a week, it's been once a week for years."

"What's the matter with Uncle Dan? I must say I'm surprised to hear you talking about vulgarity. I don't think it comes very well from you."

She turned to me. Her face was flushed, but her long nose was quite white. "That's a mean thing to say. Just because my father was a workman—"

"A street bookie," I said. "When he wasn't drunk or in prison."

She sat down in a chair and began to cry. Phrases came through the tears about having made a good home for me, my family always having been against her, I was ashamed of her, and so on.

"Stop it," I said, and then I shouted, "*Stop it.* It's all nonsense."

"Your mother hates me. I took away the baby boy she used to make steak and kidney puddings for."

I hit May then. It was the first time I'd ever hit her. I struck her with the palm of my hand across the cheek, not very hard but enough to make a mark. She put her hand to her cheek, stopped crying, and looked surprised.

Immediately I'd done that, I was terribly sorry and ashamed. I had never struck a woman before, and I had been brought up to believe that nobody who is decent does that kind of thing. I can remember that once, when we lived in the Kincaid Square house, before father died and we moved to Baynard Road, I looked out of the window one night and saw a man hitting a woman in the square. I was perhaps eight years old at the time, and the noise outside must have wakened me from sleep. The linoleum was cold under my feet as I went to the window, pulled aside the curtain and looked out.

A man was shouting at a woman, then they were locked together and he had pushed her over to the pavement. Another man came up and they began shouting and then hitting at each other. The woman got to her knees and was pushed over again. It all seemed to me a joke, grown-up people playing the same kind of games that we played at school. Rain was falling, the pavements gleamed in the lamplight, and I can remember that what impressed me most vividly was that grown-ups apparently did not mind getting their clothes dirty. My excitement and interest must have made me move about, for my mother came in and exclaimed with dismay as she saw me standing by the window. She bundled me back to bed, and would not answer my questions except to say that the people outside were behaving in a beastly way, that they were drunk, and that drink was a terrible thing. I remember wondering why when children did that kind of thing it should be called play, and when grown people did it they were behaving like beasts. I did not forget the scene when I grew older, but of course I understood it and came to think of it with horror, as some adults think of films that frightened them long ago. Now I had behaved like that man in the square and I was ashamed. I hadn't even the excuse of drink. I wondered what my mother would have said.

I went down on my knees to May and asked her to forgive me, told her I had had a difficult day at the office, she shouldn't have spoken as she had of my mother, but I was wrong, too, much more wrong. I had my arms round her legs and when she suddenly stood up I nearly fell over. She said she was going to bed. She went to the bathroom while I undressed and put on my dressing-gown. Then I went to the bathroom, washed, and brushed my teeth. I took a long time about this because I knew that May did not like me to see her undressing. When I got back to the bedroom the light was out. I got into bed and put my hand on her side, but she pushed it away.

I lay on my back and began to think about the girl in the library. I used to be a good runner, good at most games as a matter of fact, although I gave them up when I got married because May wasn't interested. Now I was running in the half mile, which was always my best distance, and she was in the crowd, I saw her before the race and her eyes widened in surprise. "I didn't know you were a runner," she said. "You looked so much like a student, a real literary man, the other day in the library. Are you going to win?" I smiled and answered confidently, "You'll see." When I made my spurt as I came into the straight, legs pounding away like pistons, gathering speed in a way which took me yards beyond the pacemaker and allowed me safely to look over my shoulder before I breasted the tape, I saw her looking at me with lips parted, white teeth showing. And when I went up to receive my prize she was there on the platform. She gave me the little silver cup and then said, "There's another prize, too, you know." She put her arms round me and kissed me full on the lips…

IV

How did I come to marry May? It's very hard for me to think back, and understand the state of mind in which I got married. My father died early in 1945, he was killed by one of the V2's as he was going out to lunch one day. He was fifty years old. I was just old enough to be in the Army, doing my preliminary training, and I came home for the funeral. Mother was very brave, I remember, but she broke down at the graveside.

I had a week's compassionate leave to clear up father's affairs, and I soon found out that there weren't many affairs to clear up. In my grandfather's time, Wilkins Engineering Distributors had been a flourishing little firm. Grandfather had bought the house in Kincaid Square, which was one of the best parts of Clapham, and had brought father up into the business. Father had never really liked engineering or even been interested in it, but he had done what grandfather told him. He was the only son, and when grandfather died he got the business and the house in Kincaid Square. There were two daughters as well, Ellen and Gertrude, who got a thousand pounds each. Both of them were married. Ellen to a dentist in Manchester and Gertrude to a farmer up in Scotland. We had always stayed on good terms with Ellen, and mother and she wrote to each other quite often, but my father had had a great row with Gertrude at the time of grandfather's death, and they hadn't seen each other for years. The Kincaid Square house was much too big for us, as I was an only child, but father would never consider letting any of it, any more than he would consider having a partner in the business. It was a family business, he said, and it was going to stay that way. He wanted me to apply for exemption from military service so that I could stay and help him, but I wouldn't do that. It was one of the things, and there were a good many of them, about which we didn't see eye to eye.

Somehow I never seemed really to get to know father. He was a quiet, lonely man, and looking back now I think he always had it in mind that, without meaning to do so, I took mother away from him. He thought that she spoiled me and so he was determined that he wouldn't spoil me too. I don't mean that he was unkind, but he always kept his distance from me and never showed much interest in what I did. I was very good at running as I've told you, got in the first team at Cording Grammar School for football and cricket, and later on when they started a tennis team I was captain of tennis, but it never seemed to mean anything to father. He never meant much to me either, or that's the way I felt about him at the time. It is only since his death that I've come to realise how much he must have disliked most of the things he did and the life he led. Mother once told me that what father really wanted was to go on the stage, and he was very disappointed when grandfather wouldn't permit it.

As I've said, I went through father's affairs, with a lawyer to help and advise me. The position was that Wilkins Engineering Distributors was practically finished. Father had neglected it for years. The firm existed simply on little dribs and drabs of orders from people who'd dealt with it in grandfather's time and had gone on doing so out of habit. No new business came in because father never looked for any, and he lost a certain amount of old business each year because of slackness in filling orders. I had known something of this, because I worked at the office for a few months before going into the Army, but I was too young then to understand that behind father's grave attentive manner and his courteous way of speaking to clients on the telephone was simply laziness. For the past five years, we discovered, father had been drawing on his capital. There was nothing for it but to close down the firm, and sell the house in Kincaid Square. When that had been done and the house in Baynard Road bought, mother had just enough to live on, especially with the help of Uncle Dan.

I made another discovery at the office, one which shocked me a great deal. In the safe, to which in his lifetime only my father had had a key, were three bundles of letters. They were from a woman called Mrs. Meadows, a widow, and they showed conclusively that she had been, and in fact was up to the time of his death, his mistress. I couldn't imagine such a thing, a man like my father having a mistress, a man who always seemed to me the image of respectability. It was a betrayal of my mother, that was the way I felt about it. He had always come home at nights as far as I could remember, so he must have gone to see Mrs. Meadows in the afternoons. That was another reason, no doubt, for the decline of the business.

I burned the letters from Mrs. Meadows, and never mentioned them to my mother. I have wondered sometimes recently if mother knew about them all the time, or if Mrs. Meadows wrote to her after father's death. I don't suppose I shall ever know now.

All this happened while I was in the Army. I was very keen to get in, volunteered when I was still under age, but I was disappointed with Army life. Most of the men were so cynical, they seemed to regard the war and everything about it as a racket. They called me a bull-shitter because I tried to be smart and because I once asked the drill corporal for an extra hour's instruction. I didn't take much notice of them, but what did upset me was that I didn't seem to get on too well with the instructors either. I tried really hard and I was as good as most of them and a lot better than many, but even after I'd passed out as a driver-mechanic in the R.A.C. I wasn't quite satisfied. I won't say I felt there was a conspiracy against me, but people who hadn't got a quarter of my intelligence and enthusiasm got one stripe and even two stripes up while I remained a trooper.

One of the sergeants said to me, "You know, Wilkins, you try too hard." I said to him that I couldn't see there was such a thing as trying too hard. I simply wanted to be a good soldier. At that he just laughed and didn't say any more.

After I'd been in about three months I was ragged one night. There was a big tough fellow named Gibson who bunked next to me in the barrack room. He used to go out and drink a lot, and after he'd had a few drinks he was very quarrelsome. This night he came back to camp just before lights out and said to me, "Who's the biggest crawler in the squad? You are, Wilkins." I took no notice of him, and he came over and grinned at me. "Say it, Wilkins. Say 'I'm the biggest crawler in the squad.' Tell the truth for once in your life." I still said nothing, but when Gibson came up and put his hand on my shoulder I punched him on the jaw.

You might think that the other men would respect some-body who was prepared to stand up for himself, but what happened was that a whole pack of them, Gibson's friends, set on to me. I fought, but I was no match for the lot of them. I won't say what they did, it was humiliating more than painful, but it made me sick of the Army. It seemed you couldn't be a good soldier when you tried, the others wouldn't let you.

A couple of days afterwards I had the first of my blackouts. I got a pass out, went into town on my own and drank some beer, and didn't get back to camp until three o'clock in the morning. I got seven days C.B. for that.

A week or two after that the doctor found that I had an ear-drum injury which should have been noticed on my original medical examination. He downgraded me to B.1, I was made a permanent clerk, and I spent the rest of my time in the Army filling in forms and making up weekly returns. I came out early in 1947. The way I felt about the Army was that I had tried really hard, but it hadn't done any good. Soon after coming out I took a job in Palings. That was how I met May.

V

Like most big firms nowadays, Palings have a fine sports ground, with cricket and football teams, six good hard tennis courts and a pavilion where you can get snacks or hot lunches, and play table tennis or cards. I'd given up cricket by this time because you can't play cricket and tennis, and I was better at tennis. I played football in the winter, and used to spend most week-ends down at the ground, which was at Eltham, on the same side of London as Clapham but a kind of cross-country journey. There were dances every other Saturday, and I used to go to them, although I don't dance much. I don't flatter myself I'm all that good a dancer, but it seemed to me that others no better than I am were always on the floor. I don't see anything wrong when I look in the glass, but as I told you I'm not attractive to women.

It was a surprise to me when one day a girl came up and asked me to dance. She said, "If you're free would you like to dance this one with me?" So we danced. She wasn't a bad-looking girl, with a good figure and nice legs, although her nose was too long and her eyes were set rather close together. She told me she worked in the Accounts Department and that her name was May Colter.

At our second dance—I asked her this time—she said, "I've seen you before, I don't mean at the club. You live in

Clapham, don't you? So do I. Do you think it was awful of me to ask you to dance with me? I've never done that before."

I said I thought it was very brave.

"You live in one of those Kincaid Square houses, don't you?" I told her that we'd moved, and she seemed disconcerted, but not for long. "I've known you for years, seen you about," she said. I asked her where she lived, but she was vague, said with a laugh that it was not nearly so grand as Kincaid Square. I asked her if she played tennis, and she said she loved it. It seemed only natural to be seeing her home, although she wouldn't let me go all the way, said something about her mother not liking strange young men. When we parted we arranged to meet at the Plough and go down to the ground together on the following day.

That was how it began. May wasn't a good tennis player, nowhere near my class, but I got into the habit of partnering her in mixed doubles, and of playing mixed doubles a lot more than I had done. Then we met sometimes at lunchtime and took the same bus home quite often in the evenings. When it was wet we sometimes went to the pictures. Right from the start May wanted me to take her home and introduce her to mother. She didn't exactly ask me, but she was always saying that she couldn't wait to see what my home was like, and asking me to describe exactly what things stood where, and so on. I had my doubts about doing it, I'd never invited a girl home before, and I had a feeling mother and May wouldn't get on, but after a few weeks I gave way. I told mother that I had a girl-friend and I wanted to ask her home.

So May came in one evening to supper. It didn't go off very well. Mother and May both seemed to me to behave in such a funny way. Mother was very straight and starchy, as she sometimes is when things go wrong. She'd got out the

Doulton dinner service that we didn't use more than once a year. There were napkins and finger-bowls, which I'd never seen at our table before, and we had four courses, which was something in those days a couple of years after the war, and mother talked an awful lot about the weather.

As for May, she wore a very frilly white blouse which had no sleeves, so that you couldn't help seeing she had skinny arms, and she had had her hair done specially. She only ate a very little of each dish and she talked about what was on at different West End theatres. Of course mother knew nothing about them, and as far as I knew May had never seen any of the shows herself. I asked her if she'd seen one she was talking about and she said oh yes, and I asked who with. She giggled. "A friend. He mustn't be jealous, Mrs. Wilkins, must he?"

"I hope he's no need to be," my mother said. "Only a foolish woman tries to make a man jealous. I never gave your father cause for jealousy, nor he me, in the twenty-five years we were married." I couldn't help thinking of the letters in the office drawer.

"I think John needs to be made a teeny bit jealous. He might feel too sure of himself otherwise." May paddled her fingertips in the bowl.

"What an extraordinary idea."

"Honestly it was only a girl I went with, but it was an awfully good show. I did ask John to take me, but he wouldn't."

"John's a real home boy," my mother said. "And by the way, I've darned another pair of your grey socks, I know you never like wearing them more than two days. He's *so* particular," she said to May. "I really don't believe anybody but his mother would put up with him."

That was the way they went on talking to each other. I was glad when the evening was over and I was seeing May back to Melbourne Avenue, where she had a room. She'd explained to me that her mother and father had both been killed in a railway accident, and since she was seventeen she'd always lived by herself. May didn't say much about the evening, except when I asked what she thought of my home now she'd seen it. "It's awfully old-fashioned, isn't it, all that furniture and everything. And that dinner service, some of the pieces were a bit chipped, I couldn't help noticing."

"The dinner service was Royal Doulton. It's been in our family since grandfather's time, perhaps earlier."

Perhaps I sounded a bit stiff. She said at once, "I know, John, it's just that I like contemporary things. I expect it was much nicer at Kincaid Square."

At the end of Melbourne Avenue, which wasn't as grand as its name, just about like Baynard Road, I kissed May good night. She would never let me do more than that. "One thing leads to another, and I don't think people ought to do that kind of thing before they're married," she said. Sometimes in the cinema she would dig her nails into my palm, but generally it was just this momentary light pressure on the lips when we parted. I can't say I ever wanted much more at that time.

As for mother, she only said, "Arms like matchsticks, that girl's got. Doesn't eat proper food, I suppose." She must have been asking questions, though, because a day or two later she spoke to me casually. "Your friend Miss Colter doesn't live at home, does she?"

"No. Her mother and father died years ago."

"Her father's Barney Colter, and he's very much alive. In fact, he's only just come out of prison."

For a moment I couldn't think who Barney Colter was. Then I remembered that long ago, at Kincaid Square when I was a child, we'd had a gardener named Barney Colter and he'd been sacked for stealing some money. Since then I vaguely knew that he'd been in and out of prison for street bookmaking and petty theft.

"It can't be the same one."

My mother nodded. She looked very formidable. "No doubt at all about *that*. I thought it was odd she should have the same name, and I made some inquiries. The father a thief and the mother a habitual drunkard. Not a nice family, John."

Really I agreed with mother, but I felt bound to defend May. "That's not her fault."

"Perhaps not." My mother gave grudging agreement. "But she should have told you. I must say I consider it deceitful."

I didn't answer, because now I was remembering what must have been May herself, a very small pig-tailed girl who had come sometimes with big Barney Colter, and had played quietly on her own in the garden. Somehow the incident made me feel, for the first time, that I really loved her. It was as though she were a little girl again, somebody who looked up to me and was helpless, in need of protection. The next time I saw her I told her I knew about her mother and father. She went very red.

"Why did you say they were dead?"

"I was so ashamed. I hate them. They're—oh, you wouldn't understand—they're filthy. Disgusting. I never want to see them again." She burst into tears, I took her into my arms, and for the first time she kissed me of her own accord, a hard passionate kiss. I knew then that I was going to marry her.

Three months later we were married, very quietly, at a local registry office. I paid for the wedding breakfast afterwards, because May wouldn't even let her mother and father come to it. I could understand that, I was even rather glad in a kind of way because from what I'd heard May's parents were quite capable of making an awful scene, but at the same time I felt that she was rather hard about it. A telegram came from them and Uncle Dan, who was in charge of the proceedings, read it out. The telegram said: *Best of luck girlie don't let him get you down. Dad and Mum.* Uncle Dan thought it was a splendid joke and I didn't mind it, but May was very upset. I think from that time onwards she really hated Uncle Dan.

VI

When I married May I had a kind of idea in my head of what I expected marriage to be like. Not just our marriage, but all marriages. May was up first in the morning and always looked very crisp and neat in little check pinafore frocks, rather schoolgirlish you might say. Breakfast was ready for me, grapefruit, coffee, little squares of toast, marmalade. I went off to the office and came back in the evening to find her cooking something I specially liked.

"M'm, that smells good," I said as I came in. "What is it?" But May, who had changed her frock specially for my return, wouldn't tell me. She bustled about in and out of the kitchen, telling me to put on my slippers and warm my feet in front of the fire. Then after dinner, which would be steak and kidney pie or pork chops with a good suet pudding to follow, she sat by my slippered feet in front of the fire, while I ran my fingers through her hair and told her the events of the day. Sometimes there were difficulties and then she sympathised and told me to throw up the job if I wanted to, sometimes wonderful things happened like my promotion at Palings, and then she shared my pleasure but said it was certainly no more than I deserved. I saw us winning the mixed doubles tournament at the club, being chosen the most attractive young couple on the floor at the big annual dance. I suppose it was all pretty silly. I've always been rather a dreamer, and I was only twenty-one when we got married. May was a couple of years older, so my recollection of her as a little girl in pigtails can't have been quite right. I mean to say, if she was small I must have been smaller, although that's not the way I remember it.

We had a week's honeymoon at Brighton, and it was there I began to find out how different marriage was from the way I'd expected it to be. We had a fine send off, I must say. Most of the people at the wedding breakfast were from the firm, naturally, with a few of mother's friends as well. I was a clerk in Complaints then, and I was very honoured, and so was May, when Gimball came along. The firm gave us a handsome cheque as a wedding present, and there was a photograph of the wedding breakfast in *Palings' Quarterly*, the store magazine.

It was when we got to the hotel that things began to go wrong, or not wrong exactly but different. I didn't mind people knowing we were a honeymoon couple, and in fact I told the hotel manager. May was annoyed about that, it seemed she wanted it hidden as though it was something disgraceful. She liked to get up early for breakfast instead of having it in bed, and she wanted to dress in the evening for dinner—not dress really, I mean, but change from what we'd been wearing in the day. It was a small hotel and winter time—we got married early in 1948—so there weren't many people staying in the place. I couldn't see any reason to change our clothes, it seemed awfully silly to me, but May wanted it and that was what we did. At the hotel, too, we started playing bridge for the first time, with an elderly couple. The stakes were only a penny a hundred, but they were both very keen players and so was May. We played several rubbers during that week at times when I was longing, for one reason or another, to go to bed.

About all that, about going to bed, I found that May was very different from what I'd expected, or I suppose you might say dreamed. She was very shy about letting me see her, which was something that I could understand and respect at first, but then she never changed, or if she did it was to become even more modest. And when we were in bed together she shivered uncontrollably for the first night or two as if she were terrified. Later she lay like a marble block, quite still, and let me make love to her.

I found out something else too, and this was about myself. I had always been I suppose you might say an innocent young man. I had never thought much about girls, and as I've said I had not been successful with them, so that although I knew what to do I was inexperienced. What you have never had you don't miss, they say. I don't know about that, but I do know that now I had May I wanted her. What was more, even in that first week I became aware that I wanted her in special ways and wanted her to do certain things, unusual perhaps. At the time I was ashamed of this, and worried about it a lot. Later on I came to read psychologists and the Kinsey Report and realised that the kind of thing I wanted wasn't so very different from what a good many people want and do. In the few days of our honeymoon I didn't say anything to her about this. Later on I did speak to her but it was no good, she was disgusted and nothing more.

May never wanted children, and we made sure that she never had any. She said that we were too poor, but I think she was frightened.

This is a very delicate subject, but I know you psychiatrist people think it's important, and perhaps it is. I don't want to say any more about it. Don't think I blame May, although I did have that feeling of frustration. Although I said at the beginning that we all have to take responsibility for our actions, at the same time I think we can't help being the people we are. May and I should never have got married.

My ideas about home life were changed pretty quickly too. For a couple of months we lived with mother at Baynard Road, which was terrible because mother and May just didn't get on at all, and then we were lucky enough to get this flat in Windover Close. It was two rooms with a bathroom and kitchenette, all very compact and nice. "A flat can never be a home," mother said in her decisive way, but I liked the idea of a flat myself. It seemed such a clean, modern way to live, although it was more money than we could afford at that time. I suppose I had really known from the start that May would have to go on working, but still I didn't like it. Not only that there were no slippers by the fireside (we had all-electric heating) and no steak and kidney pie (May was very economical, good at making scratch meals out of bits of cold meat and some left-over vegetables—at times it seemed we had nothing day after day but bits of stuff left over, and I used to wonder what they could be left over from), but also I feel strongly that the husband should be the breadwinner in a family. At this time May got almost as much money as me.

What can you say about a marriage? You peel off the years, seven of them there had been, like the skin off an onion, and there's nothing inside. I got my promotions until I'd become assistant manager of the Complaints Department, May gave up the work at Palings and got a part-time job, we both grew older. We didn't go down much to Palings' sports club after the first year of our marriage, when I won the men's singles. For some reason or other May didn't like it, she said it was a long way to go and she'd got so bored with the people there, and anyway we saw enough of them in our working hours.

She joined a local Conservative group and the district Townswomen's and Housewives' Association, and made quite a lot of friends there who came in to play bridge. It seemed to me they were much the same sort of people who went down to the club, but May wouldn't have it. "Why, Moira Tateworthy's husband is a specialist, a consultant at Barts," she would say, or "I did like the Batesons, didn't you? Billy's got an influential position in a firm of stockbrokers, you know, he's almost a partner. I think they're worth cultivating." I wanted to join a tennis club nearby, but May wouldn't have it, said the subscription was too high. So we just went on the way we were, giving and going to little dinner parties or bridge parties or television parties. One of those parties, I remember, was at the home of some people named Lowman, who had a small house in Streatham. Lowman was a bank clerk ("next to the manager," May called him), a dried-up little man in his forties, and his wife Patricia was a few years younger, lush and overblown.

We had dinner and then watched the television, and then we had an argument about washing up. "Husbands and wives," Patricia Lowman said in her rather loud voice, "but not their own wives. Let's toss up for it." Her husband muttered something and she said, "Oh, come on, George, be a sport." So we tossed up and George Lowman and May lost, and went out to wash up. When they were out of the room Patricia Lowman said to me, "They can't hear a thing, you know, with the tap on out there and the plates clattering."

"Can't they?"

She looked at me. Her lips were wet. "George is no good to me, you know, no more use than a dry stick. And that wife of yours, she looks a frigid bitch. But not you. I seem to see something burning away below the surface, hidden fires, eh?"

"No." My voice was choked, I could hardly speak the word.

"I say yes. We could make wonderful music together." She had had a few cocktails that evening, but she was not drunk. She came up to me and pushed her body against mine, pushed her wet mouth against mine. It was revolting. She was a middle-aged woman, nearly forty, and I felt nothing but disgust. I pushed her violently away and she fell back, landing on the sofa. The kitchen door opened and Lowman pushed his head round it.

"I thought I heard something. Did you fall over, my dear?"

Patricia Lowman was sprawled on the sofa, and she was laughing. Behind Lowman I saw May's head. She looked from one to the other of us, frowning.

"Did you hurt yourself, dear?" Lowman asked.

"Only my feelings," said Patricia Lowman. "Do you know, Mrs. Wilkins, you've got a wonderful husband. I just assaulted his virtue and he repulsed me. Now I'm going to bed. Good night all."

Lowman laughed uncertainly as she went out of the room. "Patricia will have her joke. I expect you've got a headache, isn't that it, Patricia?"

"I expect so." Her voice came down the stairs.

"The television, you know, that screen does flicker—under the circumstances don't bother about the washing up—"

We said our good-byes. We never saw the Lowmans again. That night I had a blackout. We reached home at half past ten and I told May I should go for a short walk before coming to bed. I returned, so she told me, just after two o'clock. I had no idea where I had been.

This story about Mrs. Lowman may sound as if I considered myself a sort of Don Juan. That isn't the case at all, it was the only time such a thing happened to me, but I must say that although it was a small incident it was something I never forgot. For some time afterwards I used to lie awake at night wondering what would have happened if I hadn't said no to her. How would she have arranged meetings? She could have telephoned me at the office to say that Lowman was going out for the evening, and then I could have made some excuse to May. Or the other way round—I would have let her know that May was out at a meeting and she would have come to Windover Close, quickly, furtively, for an hour. I could see it all, the careful watch to make sure that no one knew it was our flat she was coming to, the door gently opened and closed, our embrace inside the hall, so furious that we could hardly wait to get into the bedroom. Slowly the real Mrs. Lowman, the wet-mouthed, sagging-bodied woman who had pressed herself against me, disappeared from my mind and was replaced by somebody much younger and more attractive, one of half a dozen cinema stars.

I said not long ago that May and I shouldn't have got married. That's what I think now, but I don't want to make it seem that I was really unhappy. If anyone had asked me I would have said that ours was a pretty average marriage, and as far as I know May felt the same. That was the way things were when I met Sheila.

VII

After that first meeting I used to go to the library fairly often. If May remarked it she didn't say anything. I went to get books out for myself, which I hadn't done for a long time, and I usually found the chance to say a few words to Sheila. She always smiled at me, but then she smiled at most people, I noticed, she was a friendly kind of girl. One day I got quite annoyed because she kept talking to somebody else while I was waiting to speak to her, to ask whether A. E. W. Mason's *Four Feathers* was in, and at last another attendant came up to me and asked if she could help me.

A few days later Mr. Gimball gave me two complimentary tickets for a West End theatre. A cousin of his worked in the box office, and often gave him tickets. He couldn't go this time, because his wife wasn't well, and he wondered if I could use the tickets. I thanked him and said I could. The next night I went to the library and asked Sheila (I had found out that her name was Sheila Morton) what she usually did in the evenings.

"In the evenings." She smiled. "It all depends. Sometimes I stay indoors, and sometimes I go out. If anyone asks me."

"I wondered if you were doing anything particular next Tuesday." I spoke very casually.

"Tuesday. I rather think I am going out on Tuesday. Yes, I'm sure I am. What a pity."

"Isn't it?" I tried to stay casual, although I felt desperate. I found myself saying, "I've got complimentary tickets for the show at the Princess, and it's supposed to be rather good. A relative of mine's a theatrical manager, and I often get tickets. Perhaps another time."

"That would be lovely. It's sweet of you to ask me, and I'd really love to come another time."

Why did I tell that lie? I think it must have been because I knew that in the future there would be nothing to stop me buying two tickets and saying they were complimentary. After all, Sheila wouldn't need to look at the tickets. So I went with May to the show at the Princess and the next time I saw Sheila asked her again. That was no good, but the third time I asked her she said she would love to come. I'd been able to find out what it was she particularly wanted to see, and it turned out to be a detective play at the Aldwych, so I bought two tickets in the dress circle.

It should have been one of May's nights at the Housewives' Association, but the meeting for that night had been cancelled. I had to think of a story to tell her, and it had to be a good story too because obviously we wouldn't be back till late. I said I had been asked to stay late by Mr. Lacey. He was one of Palings' directors, and in fact I had only spoken to him once or twice.

I aimed high to impress May, but I hadn't quite realised the effect of mentioning Mr. Lacey's name. She became very excited.

"But, John, that's wonderful. It must be something very important."

"Oh, I don't know. Probably he just wants to talk about office work."

"It must be much more than that. You say he told you it would take the whole evening."

"Yes, well, that's what he said."

"That means he must be taking you out to dinner. Do you think you ought to dress?"

"No, I don't think so. Now I come to think of it, he said we would be going to his club."

"You don't seem very excited. Didn't he say anything at all about why he wants to see you? He must have dropped some sort of hint, he can't just have said he'd like you to come out to dinner, just like that."

"It was like that—more or less, anyway. He's quite informal, you know, Mr. Lacey, always has been. I am excited about it, but I don't want to build up any hopes. It may be to do with my idea for reorganisation." Two years earlier I had put forward a scheme for the reorganisation of the Complaints Department so that it should be merged with the Service Department, but nothing had ever happened about it.

"I thought you said Gimball simply sat on that."

"That's what I thought," I said, exasperated. "But for goodness' sake I don't know, do I? Perhaps he suddenly changed his mind and passed it on to Lacey. We'll have to wait and see."

"Don't have too much to drink, you know drink brings on those fits of yours." May annoyed me by calling my blackouts fits. "And don't tell your mother about it when we go over there on Wednesday. You tell her everything."

I got very much worked up, looking forward to my meeting with Sheila, but it wasn't really an exciting evening. We met at six o'clock and had supper before the theatre, in a little restaurant. My idea had been that we should have one or two drinks beforehand and then have supper after the theatre, but Sheila said that she had to get home early because her father was more or less an invalid. The service was slow and we had to hurry a bit, but it was wonderful to see her sitting opposite me, wearing a blue silky kind of dress that showed off her wavy dark hair and was the colour of her blue eyes. I told her that her eyes were a deep deep blue, blue as the sea, and she laughed.

During dinner she told me about herself and her family. Her mother was dead and her father had been a timber merchant, but a few years ago he had retired after suffering a heart attack. Sheila was an only child. "As a matter of fact I haven't got many relatives at all. Mary, that's my second cousin up in Manchester, she's married to a doctor named Dansett, she's my best girl-friend, I suppose. And my cousin Bill, that's Bill Lonergan, he's doing some kind of engineering job in Birmingham."

"Bill Lonergan," I said. "I used to know a Bill Lonergan at school."

"That would be the one. He lived in Clapham till a couple of years ago. He's a mad boy, but sweet too. He was kind of an elder brother to me when I was a kid."

"I remember Bill Lonergan." For the rest of dinner we talked about him. I did remember him very well, a tough chubby boy a couple of years younger than I was, a good cricketer who opened the first eleven batting. I didn't remember anything particularly sweet about him but he was mad all right, had a terrible temper at times. I told Sheila about the time when I bowled Bill Lonergan for a duck and then said something or other which annoyed him, so that he suddenly picked up a chunk of iron railing that was lying around, and threw it at me. I can remember it whistling past my head now.

Sheila laughed, which wasn't exactly the reaction I had expected. "Yes, Bill used to be mad all right, I remember when he drove off in somebody's car just for a dare, they'd left the ignition key in, you know. Drove it around for an hour, then returned it, no damage done. And he hadn't even got a licence. But he's settled down a lot in the last few months. I say, were you in the cricket team then, Mr. Wilkins?"

"Call me John. Yes, cricket and football too."

"Funny, I used to watch most of the matches, but I don't remember you."

"I was a pretty useful bat and first change bowler, one year I took most wickets and another I headed the bowling averages. But I expect you were thinking about Bill Lonergan." I was beginning to feel a little jealous of Bill Lonergan and the way Sheila must have been watching him at the matches, although I knew that was silly.

So that was the way we passed the time, getting along pretty well, calling each other John and Sheila, and then we went to this detective play. After we sat down there was a bit of trouble because somebody thought we were in the wrong seats. To prove that it was all right I got out our counterfoils, and it turned out that the other people were in the wrong row.

"Extraordinary to me how people can make mistakes like that," I said.

"Oh, I don't know. Those aren't complimentary tickets."

"What do you mean?"

"Complimentary tickets always have the word stamped on."

She certainly had sharp eyes. I swallowed. "The tickets had it on, these are just the counterfoils."

"The counterfoils have it on too. You shouldn't have done it." She put her hand on mine for a moment. "But it was sweet of you."

Somehow that pat on the hand and being told I was sweet didn't please me very much. I found it hard to give much attention to the play, which was one of these things about how a man plans a perfect murder and then it all goes wrong. I was too conscious of Sheila sitting next to me, her bare arm touching mine occasionally in the darkness. I kept thinking of that, and wondering what she really felt about the theatre tickets.

In the second interval she wanted to smoke a cigarette, and we stood out in the corridor. Somebody tapped me on the shoulder. A woman's voice said, "Hallo, John, fancy seeing you here."

I turned round with a sick feeling. There stood an enormous shark-like woman, with a lopsided grin on her face, and her tiny pilot fish husband in tow. It was Mrs. Piddock, an old acquaintance of mother's. Her husband owned a chemist's shop and was a harmless little man, but Mrs. Piddock was one of the biggest gossips in Clapham. She used to go to mother's tea parties.

Mother had a liking for gossip which I could never understand. I always thought of her as a severe and reserved woman, devoted to her family, first her husband and then me. That was true enough, but there was this other side to her nature as well. I suppose most people who have lived for a long time in one place get absorbed in what happens there, and mother certainly kept tabs on everything that happened in her part of Clapham. Almost every week she gave or went to a couple of tea parties where she chattered away with half a dozen women like Mrs. Piddock. These tea parties constituted a kind of unofficial detective agency about affairs in the neighbourhood, and it was through a tea party that mother had learned about May's family. Then once a week what you might call a digest of this news was sent to Mrs. Vincent, who was the widow of a friend who had lived in Clapham. Nora Vincent now only came up to Clapham from her home in Wiltshire two or three times a year, but mother never failed to send her weekly budget of local news, and I suppose Nora Vincent read it as eagerly as mother wrote. I shall never understand women.

I said hallo and tried to get away, but it is not so easy to get away from Mrs. Piddock. She asked what we thought of the play and then if I'd seen mother lately, she kept the conversation going with very little help from me and none at all from Sheila, while I waited for the bell to call us back to our seats as a groggy boxer waits for the gong. Before it came, though, Mrs. Piddock gave up subtlety and came in with a direct frontal attack.

She said to Sheila, "We don't know each other, do we, my dear, and yet I'm sure I've seen you before." The shark jaws opened, revealing her very white false teeth.

"Perhaps you have. I work in Clapham Library."

"Oh, I'm not a reader." She gave a great guffaw and her husband, the little chemist, smiled in timid sympathy. "Not in the library. You're a local girl, I suppose."

"I live in Clapham, if that's what you mean."

Mrs. Piddock gave her lopsided grin, and was obviously about to move in for the kill when the bell rang. I quickly took Sheila's arm and steered her away, muttering goodbye. When we were back in our seats again I said how sorry I was. "That woman, her name's Mrs. Piddock and she's nothing but a menace, one of these women who has nothing better to do than tear other people's reputations to bits. I don't know why mother even speaks to her. You were wonderful, really you were."

"It's nothing. She's just a busybody."

"You must have felt you were being pestered and it's all my fault. I do apologise."

"It doesn't matter," she said, but I thought she spoke rather coolly.

After that, somehow the whole evening seemed to go wrong. The third act of the play was a flop, so that I was fidgeting in my seat by the end, and after it we just went back to Clapham on the Underground. I don't know exactly how I'd thought that the evening would end, really I hadn't thought about it, I suppose, but it was certainly not with the two of us sitting side by side in a rackety tube train, staring at our reflections opposite and reading the advertisements above them. When I'd been thinking about the end of the evening I'd sort of pictured myself with a car, and we'd driven out in it to one of those roadhouses on the Great West Road, danced and had something to eat there, and got back in the small hours of the morning. But I hadn't got a car, and when I suggested getting a taxi back to Clapham Sheila said no very firmly. It would be a job to get a taxi out to the suburbs at this time of night, she said, and it would cost the earth, she just wouldn't think of it. So we took the tube and walked back from the Plough to the house she and her father lived in, on the North Side.

When we were walking down Long Road I drew her into the shadows and tried, rather clumsily, to kiss her. My lips only touched her cheek. I tried again, but her head was turned away. She said in a low voice, "I'd like you to take me home."

After that we didn't speak until we reached her home, which faced the Common, a little slit of a house among the red brick Edwardian villas. There was a light showing, and she said her father would be sitting up.

"I promised him I wouldn't be late. He's really not at all well." She took my hand. "Thank you for a lovely evening. I did enjoy the play. I hope it wasn't—wasn't too much of a disappointment for you."

"Of course not." My voice had a strangled sound.

"I think really I shouldn't have come. But I did want to see it." Then she was gone, the iron gate opened and shut, her feet tapped up the narrow road, the front door closed decisively. I walked back across the Common to Windover Close, my mind blank yet (I can't put it any clearer than this) with thoughts whirling among the blankness. If I had been a little more forceful, if we had had more to drink at dinner, if we had not met Mrs. Piddock—and then I went on to think how things might have been if she had returned my kiss and we had actually gone on to the Common. Somehow it wouldn't focus, none of it would focus in my mind, I couldn't get my thoughts into any kind of shape.

When I went in May looked up from the mending in her lap. "You're late enough. It's a quarter past eleven."

"Is it?" I looked at my watch. Since I had planned to come back at two or three o'clock in the morning, it seemed to me positively early.

"He must have had a lot of interesting things to say to keep you this long."

"Who?"

"Really, John." The tip of May's nose began to quiver, a sure sign that she is annoyed. "Mr. Lacey."

"Oh, Lacey." Before I went out I had had a story all ready to tell her, but now I simply could not remember it.

"I hope you've not had too much to drink. You know you can't take it."

"Certainly not. A little wine at dinner, that's all."

"What was it, then? Just tell me what he wanted to see you about, if that's not too much to ask. After all, I am your wife."

I had to sit down and tell her something, I knew that. So I told her in detail about how Lacey had wanted to talk to me about the reorganisation idea, he was much impressed with it and wanted to congratulate me on it, we had had drinks and then dinner at his club, and talked about all kinds of things, Gimball's impending retirement (which had been impending for years), the possibility of streamlining the Complaints Department, using fewer staff after the merger, and so on. There was not a word of truth in any of it, and I think I did a good job of fabrication.

When I had finished May was quite excited. "It's wonderful. I don't know how you can take it so calmly."

"Nothing's happened yet, it's only words."

"I suppose it would mean quite a lot more money."

"Another two hundred a year, I should think. Less tax."

"Do you know what I should like to have after you've got the job, what we ought to save up for?"

"What's that?"

"A car. After all, as a department manager in Palings you'll have a certain position to keep up. Quite a lot of our friends have got cars, and I've really felt quite ashamed sometimes of the way we're always getting lifts."

At that I really couldn't restrain myself, I burst out laughing. "A car, oh yes, a car's just what we need. We must get a car on order straight away. If you knew how much I wished I had a car to-night." Tears came out of my eyes, tears of laughter, while May stared at me without understanding.

VIII

I've mentioned already that Uncle Dan had asked whether I was joining the tennis club. This was a local club in Clapham named Evesdale. Uncle Dan had been a member there for several years, and had been on at me to join for quite some time, but May always said there was too much backbiting and petty jealousy in tennis clubs, quite apart from the expense. After the evening with Sheila I finally made up my mind that I wanted to join Evesdale, and told May so. Naturally I suggested that she should join as well.

May listened to me with the considering kind of look on her face that she has when she's pricing something in a shop and discovers that it's more expensive than she had expected. At the same time there was something else in her manner, a sort of respect you might call it, which I couldn't understand until I suddenly realised that it was my story about Lacey that had done it.

"Your Uncle Dan's a member at Evesdale, isn't he?" She always called him *your Uncle Dan*, to make it clear that she had no rights in him. "That's nothing in its favour. All the same I will say it's a good class club."

"That's very important." I spoke sarcastically, but sarcasm was wasted on May.

"Naturally, especially for you now."

"I was just joining to get a game of tennis."

She said as if I were a child, "Yes, but who you play tennis *with* is important too. How many of the members at Evesdale could you introduce to Mr. Lacey? From what I know I should say that quite a number of them have good social standing. How much is the subscription?"

"Four guineas each for the summer." I didn't go on to say that what May knew about the members at Evesdale was very little indeed—perhaps she had met half a dozen of them and knew the backgrounds of half a dozen more. When I tried to pull May up in that way I only got involved in a long argument which somehow I always seemed to lose. In the same way I knew it was no good simply saying that I meant to join Evesdale, or I should never have heard the end of it. The whole thing had to be discussed with May.

She winced at mention of the money. "And I suppose you'll need some new clothes. Rackets. Balls." I felt that an invisible accounting was taking place in her mind. "I think it's worth your joining," she said at last.

I was surprised. "But you'll join too."

"No." The considering mood was over, balances had been totted up and agreed. "I don't think it's worth while. I don't play very well, and when you meet people who seem worth cultivating you can always ask them back here. You know I'm not all that keen on tennis."

Remembering those days at the sports club, which now seemed so long ago, I said, "You put up a good pretence at one time."

She actually laughed. "That was when I first knew you. You were very raw then, but I always thought you were the one for me. I want you to know that I'm proud of you, John. I always thought you'd get a good position."

I had to think a moment before I realised she was referring again to my imaginary conversation with Mr. Lacey. I said truthfully, "There's nothing to be proud of."

"You like playing tennis, all right, you go ahead and play." She was like a schoolmistress awarding an unexpected prize. "But don't forget, John, that there's another side to Evesdale. You can say what you like, knowing nice people *is* important."

That was how I joined Evesdale, and went down there one Saturday afternoon at the end of May for my first game. I had belonged to a suburban tennis club before, and I knew that they have a set of invisible rules, much more important than those posted up on the notice-board. New members may play with other new members, otherwise they should wait until they are asked if they would like a game. They should not go up to long-established members and invite them to play a single, they should not offer themselves eagerly for a game of doubles or mixed doubles that is just being arranged, and above all they should not make a direct approach for a game to a member of the club team. If they commit all or any of these social errors they are likely to have an uncomfortable time, and even if their behaviour is perfect it will probably be several weeks before they are thoroughly accepted.

My own way in to Evesdale was smoothed by Uncle Dan. It was an average kind of tennis club, with four hard courts and six grass, and a clubroom where you could get drinks and snacks. When I got there Uncle Dan introduced me to the club secretary and then fixed up a men's doubles, in which he and I just managed to beat a big blond man and a small dark one. Uncle Dan was not really good but he played a cunning, economical game which was especially useful in doubles, and I played pretty well for somebody out of practice. I noticed that the big blond man was not very pleased, and when the game was over Uncle Dan told me that his name was Jackson, and that he was in the team.

Uncle Dan went off to get a shower and I was sitting in the bar drinking iced orange squash when I heard voices behind me talking about getting a fourth for mixed doubles. A voice I recognised as Jackson's called out to someone outside the clubhouse if he would like to play. The answer came: "Sorry, Jacko, fixed up already."

Another voice said, "That's a pity, Bill, I'm feeling in good form." This was a voice I knew, Sheila's voice, yet I could not believe it was hers. I turned round slowly and saw her, standing in the doorway with another girl. She held a racket loosely in her hand, and she was smiling at Jackson.

Slowly I said, "I'm not fixed up. I'd like a game—very much, I'd like one very much—that is, if I'm not butting in."

There was silence while they looked at me, Jackson and Sheila and the other girl. They looked at me as they stood in the door of the clubhouse, and it seemed to me that they were a hostile group banded together there against me. Then Sheila smiled and spoke, and the impression was gone.

"Why John, I didn't know you were a member here, you're new, aren't you?" There was something so warm and welcoming in her voice, even though it was very much the voice she used to people taking out books at the library, that I could have cried.

Jackson had been frowning at me. Now he uncreased his eyebrows. "You know Wilkins, do you, Sheila?"

"Of course. And we need a fourth, don't we, Les?"

Rather grudgingly Jackson agreed that they did, and we went out into the sunshine. When we spun rackets for partners, Sheila's and mine came down rough so that we were together. It all seemed to me like a dream as we moved to our side of the court, like that dream of the runner and the prize that I'd had in bed, and I knew that I was going to play well, better than I'd ever played in my life before, I could see myself driving and smashing and cutting off shots at the net while Sheila just stood by watching in amazement. When she turned to me now and said, with her warm smile, "I hope you're in practice. Les is pretty good," I answered confidently, "Don't worry, everything is going to be all right." I picked up the balls and walked to the baseline to serve.

And it was all right. I have a really hard first service when it goes in, and this afternoon it went in all the time. I hit my drives for the corners and that was where they went, I came in to volley, dashed up to the net, ran back to retrieve lobs and came up again. Sheila was quite a useful player but she hardly touched the ball except when she was serving. I played the other two on my own.

It wasn't until we'd played a couple of games in the second set, after winning the first one six-two, that I noticed the strange atmosphere which had come into the game. I realised it when I ran and ran for a drive of Jackson's and just managed to lob it back, falling over as I did so. To my surprise he gathered the ball and when I asked whether there had been anything wrong with my return he simply said "Your point." After that he served a double fault, to give us the game.

Sheila said, "Don't try so hard."

I wiped my forehead, which was sweaty. "What?"

"Don't try so hard. This isn't the Davis Cup. And you might let me see the ball sometimes."

She said it nicely, with her usual smile, but that broke my dream. I knew that I'd been doing the wrong thing, had known it really, I suppose, all the time. I tried to tone my game down, but that's something I've never been able to do and I just went to pieces and was glad when, after we lost the second set, we didn't play a decider. After we'd finished Sheila thanked me quite sweetly, but Jackson just gave me a nod. Then I went and had a shower and joined Uncle Dan at the bar. I asked him what he was having.

"I'll take the Pope's telephone number." He pointed to a bottle of Vat 69.

"One day you're going to say that to a Catholic and he won't like it," said Jackson, who was standing beside him.

"All the Catholics I've ever met are men who can take a joke," said Uncle Dan, putting his narrow head on one side. "But if I ever met one who took offence at what I'd said, I'd certainly apologise to him and say I was deeply sorry he was so narrow-minded. Here's all the best to you, John my boy. I hear you electrified them on the court just now."

"He's a real dynamo." Jackson didn't say it in a friendly way. I asked him to have a drink, but he said he wasn't drinking. Beyond him I could see Sheila's profile, and I asked her.

"No, thank you." She turned towards me. "You didn't tell me you were married."

I should have been prepared for that, of course, as soon as I saw her in the club, but I wasn't. I could think of nothing to say.

"You might have mentioned it. There was no need to invent an invalid sister. But I suppose you had to think of some reason for taking out books by Moira Mauleverer."

IX

I can't express how I felt after that afternoon at the tennis club. I don't believe anybody can have any idea of it. I relived every moment of the afternoon, recounted over and over again the humiliation and the shame, the foolish eagerness that had made me too keen to win, the unnecessary lie in which I had been caught out. I tried to reconstruct these scenes so that they would be more acceptable, to imagine what might have happened had I restrained myself, but the reality was too strong. Turning in endless anguish on the bed, I relived the afternoon, and thought how Sheila's warm smile of welcome had been so quickly turned to the cold rejecting look which was the last thing I remembered of her. The hour hand of the clock showed two, three, four. Beside me May slept peacefully, unmoving, a statue in the bed. I slept for three hours then, sleep invaded by bad dreams of something coming towards me, pulling me and then letting go so that I whirled about in space.

At Palings' next day things were no better. I dealt with the work mechanically, in a kind of dream. The letters I dictated were coherent, but they seemed to be produced by an outer shell whose doings left untouched my own warm, sensitive inner being. I saw Miss Murchison looking at me once or twice rather curiously, but there was nothing I could do about that. At four o'clock I could endure it no longer. I put on my hat and coat and told her that I felt unwell and was going home.

Instead I wandered down Regent Street and into Soho, where I went to a little club to which Uncle Dan had once taken me, and drank several glasses of whisky. With the second glass it was as though a weight pressing on my mind had been removed, or as though the inner being, the one who hadn't been able to make contact with what was going on outside Palings, had been blended with the outer one. This sounds a ridiculous way to put it, no doubt, but it's what I felt.

I must have stayed drinking longer than I intended, because when I looked at my watch it was seven o'clock. The time meant something to me. I remembered suddenly that to-day was Wednesday, our day for going to see mother, and that seven o'clock was the time we were due to arrive. I bought a packet of those tablets that are supposed to take away the smell from your breath, and then jumped on to a bus. I got to Baynard Road just after half past seven, and mother opened the door.

"I'm sorry, Mother, extremely sorry, but I had to work late. All to do with the reorganisation of the department and then Mr. Lacey invited me in to have a drink with him. At his club. He's an important man in the firm, you know, not the kind of invitation you can refuse. Is May here?"

"Oh." My mother sounded uncommonly grim. I reflected that if I had decided in advance to tell this tale I need not have worried about taking the tablets, which had left in my mouth a taste both dry and bitter. "Yes, May is here. Would you like to go upstairs and wash?"

"What's that?" This was a very unusual thing for mother to say, she was not usually pernickety about that kind of thing.

"Go upstairs and wash." In her voice there was the ring of authority I remembered from childhood. I went obediently up the stairs, turned on the hot-water tap in the tiny bathroom and confronted myself in the glass. There I saw the visible reason for my mother's grimness. On my left cheek, smudged but still plainly to be seen for what it was, showed the mark of a pair of lips. I washed it off and went downstairs, much shaken. Of the occasion when those lips had stamped themselves upon my face I could remember nothing.

That evening passed uneasily. I revoked at sevens, kissed May savagely and against her will as we crossed the Common, and when we reached the flat collapsed on to the bed with my clothes still on, and fell asleep.

X

…the cost of living goes up and up, and the really poor people nowadays are the ones like me who have a fixed income. I see in the papers to-day the engineers, or is it the railwaymen, are asking for more money. No doubt about it who are well off now, do you know it was in the *Clapham Observer* that Billy Nichols—you remember him, the little man who kept the draper's on the Hill and then branched out and bought up two or three other firms—he's living in one of those houses in Larkspur Road that have rents controlled by the Council, twenty-five shillings a week and the ratepayers make up the difference, and Billy Nichols must make forty pounds a week. I don't know what things are coming to.

Polly Paget at number sixty has had her baby. Just seven months married. Premature they call it.

I am worried about John, he has been acting *most strangely*. He came to dinner last Wednesday with the strangest look in his eye and *lipstick* over his face. I sent him upstairs to wash and fortunately May knew nothing about it, but his manner was odd all the evening, as though he were somewhere else, not with us at all. I know John better than anybody, I should do being his mother, and I can tell that there is something wrong. He is building up for something, as I used to put it. I know the signs. Do you remember when we were all on holiday at Teignmouth when John was eleven, and there was a man named Bellerby who teased John about not being able to swim and finally, after *days and days* of bottling up what he felt, John attacked Bellerby with a cricket bat and broke his nose? He is rather like that now, like he was in the days before he attacked Bellerby, I mean. At the same time, although I hold no brief for May, as you know, putting on airs when she is Barney Colter's daughter, after all she is his wife and has a right to some consideration.

Last week I saw Mrs. Piddock at the Joneses' and she told me that she had seen John at the theatre with a girl. The girl *would not give her name*, but admitted that she worked at the library and of course Mrs. Piddock soon found who it was. Do you remember Morton, the timber merchant who had a big yard in Grayling Road? This is his daughter and from all I hear she is no better than she should be…

EXTRACT FROM LETTER WRITTEN BY
SHEILA MORTON TO MARY DANSETT,
17 RANGELY ROAD, MANCHESTER

…So life at the library is pretty humdrum, although I like it in a way. It's quite fun really choosing books for spinsters who want something that's a little bit exciting but perfectly respectable. I have to resist the temptation to give them *Lady Chatterley's Lover*. I always do resist it, too. You know me, always did see lame dogs across the road.

Just that very thing, feeling sorry for lame dogs, I mean, has landed me in a mess lately. A young man came into the library and asked for books by Moira Mauleverer for his invalid sister. You know the sort, doggy brown eyes, pinky face, very puppyish though not so young as all that. Not my type a bit, but I felt so sorry for him I hadn't the heart to brush him off even when he hung about waiting to ask me questions to which he already knew the answers. Went on feeling sorry to the point where I simply had to go to the theatre with him, he'd asked me so often and said he had a lot of complimentary tickets. That turned out not to be true, he'd really bought the tickets all the time. Pathetic, isn't it? But really, he sends shivers up my spine a little bit, I don't know why.

Then what does he do but turn up at Evesdale, push his way into a four, poach all my shots and bound about as if he thought he were playing in the Davis Cup or something. You should have seen him after the game, looking so upset because I hadn't appreciated his efforts. I might have started feeling sorry for him all over again, except that I learned he's married and the invalid sister is an invention. So I hardened my heart and said a few sharp words, though whether I shall be able to keep that up I don't know. He's really a very pathetic creature, and you know I'm as soft as soap.

Give my love to mad Bill, when you're writing to him. By the way, this admirer of mine, his name is John Wilkins, knows Bill, played in the school cricket team with him. Or so he says. He's such a romancer I shouldn't be surprised if he's made that up too.

And now I must tell you something really exciting. I really have got an admirer. Nobody you know, darling, so it's no good exercising your wits. Is he serious? Am I serious? I'm really beginning to think I am. But he hasn't said anything yet and even if he does (said Sheila, anticipating as usual) what am I to do about Dad? His heart is no better, never will be, and I couldn't possibly leave him, poor dear, he's got absolutely nobody else. It's really a terrible problem. But perhaps—I can just see you saying it, Miss Cat—the problem will never arise...

John Wilkins's Narrative resumed

XI

When I think of the past, the past that is so near yet seems so distant, it is all like a dream. I find it very hard to disentangle what really happened from what I wanted to happen, or hoped might happen, in the weeks before May and I went to Brighton. But I shall tell it as best I can, and I hope that what I am telling will be the truth. It seems to me that I have wanted to tell the truth all my life, yet so often truth has turned to a lie under my hand.

For some days after that terrible evening I didn't go back to Evesdale. May kept urging me to go there, she simply couldn't understand anybody not taking full advantage of what she considered the inordinately high subscription, and in the end she badgered me so much that I went again. I didn't see Sheila and got quite a good game of tennis. Shortly after that I had to go to the library, but I avoided Sheila, actually moved behind one of the rows of bookshelves when I saw her coming. I went to the club again and Sheila was there, but we just nodded to each other, didn't speak.

Then I began to ask myself what I had done, after all, that was so very wrong. I had told her a bit of a lie about having an invalid sister, certainly. I hadn't mentioned that I was married. I'd made a fool of myself—no, that was putting it too strongly—I'd behaved impetuously on the tennis court. I granted all that. But what was suddenly obvious to me—I couldn't think why I hadn't seen it before—was that *all these things had been done for Sheila*. She had seen that already, no doubt, and women are always prepared to understand and forgive a lie if it is told for their sake. Yet I couldn't deny that she had been cold, almost unfriendly, after our game of tennis.

That, I saw now—and if I hadn't been so dull I should have seen it before—was because of May. Sheila was a simple, honest and innocent young girl. She would never have anything to do with a man who was married. No matter what Sheila's feelings for me might be, she would never let them show while I was married to May. I saw that my marriage was the most important factor in the situation, and because of it I couldn't take anything Sheila said at its face value. If I were not married to May, now, everything would be different.

But I was married to May. I thought about our marriage and I had to admit, quite seriously, that it hadn't been a success. It's not the kind of thing a man likes to think about his wife, much less to say, but it did seem to me that May was not cut out for marriage. This was something I hadn't worried about for a long time, but now I began to feel very sharply a yearning for sex relations of the kind that were unattainable with May. I put Sheila in May's place, quite unconsciously, and the whole thing was different. I couldn't even imagine anything exciting with May any more, but with Sheila I got to a point where I could imagine nothing else.

All this time, mind you, I knew it was only imagination. For there was May, my wife, and it was absurd to think of any situation in which she wouldn't be my wife. May had got her teeth into me, into the son of a family that had lived in Kincaid Square, and she would never let go. I don't mean that there was really anything to living in Kincaid Square, but there was to May. She would never divorce me whatever I did, I knew that.

One morning at breakfast I said, "May, what do you think of divorce?"

She looked up from her cereal. "Is there a case in the paper?"

"No, I was reading somewhere the other day, I can't remember just where, a man who said when two people didn't love each other any more they ought to be able to get divorced."

It was one of the days when May went to the stationers' shop and she was in a hurry. She spooned the last mouthfuls of cereal into her mouth and frowned. "It sounds a Communistic idea to me."

"No, it isn't that at all. The thing is, don't you agree it would be a good idea? I read somewhere else the other day about a husband and wife who've been waiting three years for a Poor Person's Divorce. In the meantime they've both gone off with someone else."

"I shall be late." May snapped her handbag decisively. "And you ought to be going too. You don't want to get into Mr. Lacey's bad books."

I came back to the subject that evening. "May, you remember we were talking about divorce."

"No, were we?"

"Yes, I'd been reading something about easier divorce, you know, when people don't love each other any more."

"Oh yes, I remember." May looked at me out of her close-set eyes. "What are you trying to tell me, John?"

"Nothing. I'm not necessarily trying to tell you anything."

"You've been unfaithful to me, is that what you mean?"

"Of course I don't." I dare say I said it unconvincingly, although in spirit it was perfectly true.

"It wouldn't make any difference." She looked at me, and then round the neat room in which I knew she took such a pride, at the shell-shaped wall brackets and the matching occasional tables, the three-piece suite and the paper frill in front of the fireplace. "I love you," she said, and I couldn't be certain whether she was referring to me or to the furnishings.

"And I love you too. I only meant—"

"I should never give you up." Again it seemed to me that she was not really speaking to me. "No matter what happened, I should never give you up."

There was no use in going on with the conversation. From that time onwards, though, I found myself increasingly replacing May by Sheila in my mind, thinking what Sheila would be like in the morning at the breakfast table, what Sheila and I would talk about in the evening, the way Sheila would furnish the flat, and so on. And I became very critical of May, and noticed more and more all the things about her that I found irritating. These things aren't important, except in the way that they show what I felt about May, so I'll only mention one of them, her way of eating toast and marmalade. There are two ways of eating toast and marmalade. The way I did it was to spread butter over a piece of toast, put marmalade on the butter, and eat. What May did was to put butter and marmalade on her plate, add a little of each to a small piece of toast, eat this piece, and then repeat the process. Silly to be annoyed about such a little thing, wasn't it, silly even to notice it, but I couldn't help it, couldn't even help mentioning it.

"May," I said one morning, "why do you eat like that?"

She looked at me in astonishment. "Like what?"

"Why don't you eat your toast in the same way that I do?"

"Do you eat it in a special way? I'd never noticed."

I felt my voice rising a little, but I kept the tone of it firmly conversational. "It's just a piece of affectation, that's all. I suppose you've seen somebody at the cinema eating like that or read it in one of those silly little articles on etiquette you're always studying."

"I just don't know what you mean."

"You know perfectly well what I mean. You did it to irritate me, and you've succeeded." I felt slightly ashamed of myself as I left the flat, and that evening I told May I was sorry. But that didn't make any difference to my feelings, and it didn't make any difference to May, who still went on eating her toast and marmalade in the same way.

At about that time, the end of May, the McKenna case was taking up quite a bit of space in the papers, and I found myself becoming very interested in it. You'll remember that Gregory McKenna was a Jamaican who murdered his English wife when she found out about an affair he was having with a young Jamaican girl. There was no doubt about McKenna's guilt, but there was quite a lot of sympathy for him. He was a bus conductor who was very well liked by his mates because of his cheerfulness and the way he kept his temper under the most trying circumstances.

His wife, on the other hand, was a slut who spent the housekeeping money on drink and was always telling McKenna he was a dirty nigger who should be thankful he was allowed to live in England. The neighbours heard her, and said his patience with her was something more than human. The Jamaican girl worked at a local café and McKenna met her there when he had to go out one evening to get some food because his wife was drinking. They became friendly, and he took her to one or two dances, without telling her he was married. Mrs. McKenna found out about it, went to see the Jamaican girl, called her a whore and made a scene in the café so that the girl lost her job. The girl refused to see McKenna any more. He went home and asked his wife to give him his freedom. She shrieked with laughter and asked what kind of a fool he took her for.

"You're going to bleedin' well make money and I'm going to bleedin' well spend it," the woman next door heard her say. "And if I hear any more of you going about with that little tart I'll go to the next place where she gets a job and tell them a few things like I did before." At that point McKenna hit his wife on the head several times with a rolling-pin, and went on beating her about the face and body after she was dead.

The McKenna case was a good deal in my mind when I went up to the North Clapham Chess Club one evening on Uncle Dan's invitation. Uncle Dan had been a member of the club for years, and sometimes played on one of the lower boards for the team. He wasn't all that good a player, but he had a very quick eye for a variation in the opening gambit, and often used to fluster opponents in matches by making his early moves at great speed, banging the clock very emphatically as he did so. Upset by the speed of Uncle Dan's moves, his clock-banging and his occasional snorts of well-simulated disgust, the opponent frequently made an elementary error which would be pounced on mercilessly. In a friendly game, played without benefit of the time clock and against somebody who knew him, Uncle Dan was less formidable, although he still had to be watched in the early stages.

That night he opened with a variation on the Allgaier gambit, and I almost lost a knight in trying to match his moves for speed. As often happened with Uncle Dan, however, he left himself in a bad position when his original surprise attack had failed. He hadn't the patience to play a long end game, and after an hour agreed to a draw even though he had an advantage in the pawns.

During the game the McKenna case had been in the back of my mind. Now, as we drank coffee at the table—the club met in a little restaurant—I said, "If you were going to kill somebody, Uncle Dan, how would you do it?"

Uncle Dan put his narrow head on one side and said with his foxy look, "And why should I give you the benefit of my experience?"

"No," I said. "Be serious."

"All right. Who do you want to kill?"

"Take the case of this man McKenna. His wife was somebody who, well, you might say she deserved to die. Reading the accounts of it you can see she was a bitch of the first water, no redeeming features about her. If McKenna could have killed her and got away with it I'd have said good luck to him and I expect you would too. As it was, just hitting her on the head with a rolling-pin, he hadn't a chance. But supposing you were McKenna, how would you have set about it?"

"I've been wise enough not to get married." Uncle Dan picked up the white queen, ran his fingers round her crown. "You're tired of life with May, is that it?"

"Of course not." I could feel my face getting hot. "There's no need to be personal."

"Isn't there?" He pushed over the white queen, took her off the board. "Play you a game of fox and hounds. You take the fox."

You play fox and hounds with four pawns for the hounds, one for the fox. The fox tries to break through the cordon of hounds. If he succeeds he is free. If the hounds pin the fox into a corner he is captured. The game had its usual ending. "You see," said Uncle Dan.

"What?"

"The fox hasn't got a chance. Same thing with murder. The police get you every time—if they know it's murder." Uncle Dan wagged a long dirty finger at me. "Only one safe way. Don't let them know. Take an Underground platform in the rush hour. People standing six deep, eight deep, ten deep. Somebody at the front gets pushed over in front of a train. Must have been a sudden attack of vertigo or pushing from the back of the crowd, nobody suspects murder or if they suspect can't prove it. Somebody nervous about heights falling off a cliff, non-swimmer drowning out of their depth in swimming pool, old lady with arthritis drowning in her bath because the bell won't work, yachting accident, faulty gas tap, so on and so on. Nobody can prove it's murder although they may guess. Any help to you?"

"Not very much, no."

"Didn't think it would be." Everything about Uncle Dan was somehow crooked, from his lopsided head and smile to the way he stuck out one foot sideways. "You want a straight answer, ask a straight question."

"Supposing you were McKenna, what would you have done?"

"Soaked that wife of his in booze until she died of alcoholic poisoning," Uncle Dan said promptly. His face took on a yearning expression that I knew of old, one that had always seemed to me peculiarly false. "Your mother's worried about you, Johnny boy."

I stared down at the chess-board, black squares on white. "There's no need."

"She seems to think there is. Some interfering old faggot saw you at the theatre with Sheila Morton, that right? Then you turned up to supper with her cupid's bow printed on your face—"

"It wasn't hers."

Uncle Dan stared. "So much the worse. A real Lothario. Wish I could carve a slice off the same joint. Point is, your mother's worried about you and May. Not out of any love for May, you know that. But you know how she feels about marriage. Never a cross word in her own marriage, faithful unto death, you know the sort of thing."

"That's not true," I said savagely. I told him about the bundles of letters in the safe at the office.

"The sly old devil," said Uncle Dan, delighted. "He was a deep one, your father, and no mistake. You've never told your mother any of this? Of course not. What a sanctimonious old rogue your dad was, to be sure, when you get right down to it. The way he looked down on the rest of us poor harmless sinners." He blew his nose loudly on a coloured handkerchief and returned with an effort to the business in hand. "You seem to be following in father's footsteps, Johnny boy. What are you doing, keeping a harem?"

I began to laugh, not happily. "I wish I were."

"You come in with lipstick all over your face, whose lipstick was it?"

"I don't know." When he stared I repeated, "I don't know. Those blackouts of mine, I've been having them again. The day I came in to supper I'd been drinking in that club you took me to, what's it called—"

"The Five O'Clock Shadow." Uncle Dan smirked. "Nice little place. Usually find one or two smart pieces there."

"One of them must have kissed me. I just can't remember it, that's all."

"Seen a doctor?"

I moved uneasily. "No. I—I just don't see what they can do for me."

Head on one side, Uncle Dan stared at me, then swept the chessmen back into their box. "If I were you I'd go and have a talk to one of the old mumbo jumbo men, you know, trick cyclists. Chap I know—" He fumbled in his pockets, looked at various dirty old scraps of paper. "Here we are. Glenister, Doctor Bowen Glenister. Matter of fact, I met him in the Five O'Clock Shadow. Real man of the world. Not exactly Harley Street, I dare say, but none the worse for that probably. Here you are."

He pushed the piece of paper at me. I put it in my pocket without looking at it.

We got up to go. "Another thing," Uncle Dan said casually, "I shouldn't think too much about that Sheila Morton if I were you. From all I hear, she's been a bit of a sheila in her time. Remember a kid called Bill Lonergan, who was at school with you? She went around with him for quite a while. Then there have been one or two others from what I hear, Charlie Main at the tennis club and Len Pilkington who plays soccer for Dulwich Hamlet. See what I mean?"

"All right."

He followed me out into the night. "Shouldn't think too hard about the McKenna case, either, if I were you."

"*All right*," I said. "Thanks for the game. Good night."

"Love to May." He began to walk briskly away from me, a tall thin figure leaning into the night wind.

XII

I went to the library again a couple of times and saw Sheila, but didn't speak to her. Then one day she was at the reception counter when I handed in my book. She smiled and said, "Hallo."

"Hallo." I could feel my heart throbbing hard.

"If you want any Moira Mauleverers there are a couple in." She smiled again. "Your invalid sister may not have read them."

"Sorry about that," I mumbled. "Don't know what made me—"

She laughed. She was looking beautiful, and terribly happy. "I was annoyed, but do you know a thing about me? I can never be annoyed for long. Shall I show you where the Moira Mauleverers are? They're with the new returns, not on the shelves."

"You're looking very pleased about something." Was it accident that as she stood beside me her leg moved for a moment against mine? It was removed almost instantly, but had I imagined a faint pressure?

Now she laughed, showing white teeth. "I am, rather. Just fixed up our summer holiday, daddy's and mine. I was afraid he might not be well enough to travel, but the doctor says he can as long as the hotel's got a lift."

"Where are you going?"

"Good old Doctor Brighton. I *am* looking forward to it, just booked up at the Langland, a room on the first floor facing the sea for daddy. I'm thrilled to death and I really think he's pleased, poor old thing. Only snag is, we're going at the end of May and beginning of June so it won't be awfully hot. I love to sunbathe, don't you?"

"Yes," I said, although I didn't. I could see a vision of myself and Sheila lying together on Brighton beach. She lay on her stomach. I knelt above her with a bottle of oil, dropped some in my palm and began slowly to spread it over her back and shoulders. "Won't you be lonely?"

"I expect I shall find something to occupy the time." She smiled. "One or two people waiting. See you at the club one of these days. Good-bye for now."

She left me. Was I wrong in thinking that I had received an almost open invitation to come down to Brighton at the time she took her holiday?

XIII

It was three days later that the internal telephone in my room rang. When I picked it up a voice said, "Lacey. Can you spare me five minutes, Wilkins?"

"Now, Mr. Lacey?"

"If you please."

There sounded something infinitely menacing about that *If you please*. I looked in the glass and straightened my tie, then walked out of my office and up the twenty stairs to the floor above. This was a floor I hardly ever visited, for it was the home of the directors and their secretaries. I tapped on a door that said *Mr. J. M. R. Lacey* and opened it.

Miss Stubbs, Lacey's secretary, sat at a typewriter filing her nails. If I had been in Lacey's position I should have had a pretty secretary, but Miss Stubbs was an almost completely shapeless woman who wore heavy horn-rimmed spectacles and used very little make-up. She nodded at me now, to show that I could go straight in. I opened another door, a heavy oak one, and advanced across thick carpet. I don't know what I expected, but it was nothing good.

Lacey was a tall handsome man with grey hair parted in the middle. He had a deep, rich voice, and I always thought of him as being like an actor.

"Wilkins," he said, looking at me without a smile. "Sit down."

I sat down in a chair on the other side of the desk. The chair did not seem very low, but it was somehow a good deal lower than the chair in which Lacey was sitting. The effect was that he looked down at me over his desk, or at least he would have looked down if he had been looking at me. In fact he was reading some papers, and although I knew this was an old trick that important people often use in the presence of subordinates, I felt myself beginning to fidget.

I don't suppose he kept me waiting more than a couple of minutes. Then he did look down at me, and spoke. "Wilkins, some time ago you prepared a scheme for the linking together of the Complaints Department and the Service Department."

I found a frog in my throat, coughed it out, and said, "That's right."

"That was a piece of initiative on your part which I much appreciated. Your scheme contained some—ah—some interesting ideas. Not all of them were practicable, but they were interesting, yes, very. I thought I would let you know that."

"Thank you, Mr. Lacey."

Rather hawk-like seen from below, Lacey's face gazed down at me. "I did not put your scheme forward because it so happened that a scheme similar in some details, although of somewhat broader scope, had been in my own mind for some time. This scheme of mine was put forward recently, and I am happy to say the board has approved it."

"Does it allow, like my scheme, for a complete merger of the two departments' work?"

"Ah—yes." Lacey frowned down at the papers. "There are some differences, many differences, of detail. It is the details that are important in these things. I have been able to streamline many of your original ideas so that a considerable economy will be effected. The other members of the board are delighted."

"I'm glad to hear it, sir."

"Yes. Now, as regards your own position, Wilkins. I am right in thinking you have been assistant to Gimball for some time. And you know the work of the department thoroughly, I suppose."

"I hope so."

"How do you get on with Gimball?" I hesitated. A smile touched the corners of Lacey's mouth. "That was hardly a fair question. He's not an easy man to know, I can believe that, although he has given us years of fine loyal service. A great man for the firm. We shall be sorry to lose him."

"To lose him, Mr. Lacey?"

"Gimball is retiring in August. I propose to recommend your name to the board as his successor. I should mention that the post will carry rather more, ah, weight than Gimball's, as it will entail control of the combined Service and Complaints Departments. There will be an, um, commensurate increase in salary." Lacey peered down benevolently. "I do not think there is any doubt that the board will accept my recommendation."

Silence. My mind was a whirl of thoughts, confused and confusing, a riot of thoughts about May and Sheila and my mother, as well as about my reorganisation ideas and the way they had been used.

"Have you anything else to say, Wilkins? Anything you wish to ask me?"

Silence. I found myself stammering slightly. "It's a complete surprise to me, Mr. Lacey. Thank you very much."

Lacey raised a hand, and I saw how smooth and beautiful

was its pink palm. "No thanks, Wilkins. You wouldn't have got the job unless I'd been sure you were the best man for it. That reorganisation scheme helped a lot." He said these words emphatically, and gave me a stare that was almost grim. Then his manner lightened. "I have told Gimball the news, and I am sure you will find him most co-operative in every way. Between now and August he will introduce you to your new duties, although I expect you know them by heart already."

Silence again. Lacey rose. "No queries? Congratulations, then, and good luck in your new position. Although I'm quite sure you won't need it."

When I went out Miss Stubbs was still filing her nails. She smiled at me as I passed her, a smile which said that she had known about the whole thing all the time.

XIV

"Did you have a satisfactory interview with Mr. Lacey?" Gimball twinkled at me frostily.

"Yes. It came as a great shock to me, Mr. Gimball, to know that you were retiring, I mean."

"The old ticker isn't what it was. And then I've given the firm thirty years' service, and that's enough for any man. I shan't be sorry to cultivate my garden, Wilkins. I dare say you may feel the same when you've been sitting in this chair for a few years." I realised that he was treating me as an equal, for the first time. Now he said almost archly, "I'm sure you'll do very well, as long as you don't have any more of those blackouts."

I mumbled something.

"I haven't mentioned those to Mr. Lacey. I thought it would be unwise. I did put forward your memorandum, however, with my warmest recommendations. Very happy to know that it's being acted upon."

"I'm grateful, very grateful, Mr. Gimball."

"Not at all, my boy. It's a duty, and a pleasure, too, to give a helping hand to those who deserve it. Now I think this calls for a little celebration." From a golden chain on his hip Mr. Gimball selected a key. He walked over to a cupboard at one side of the room, unlocked it, and drew out a bottle of port, two small glasses and a duster. He wiped the glasses with the duster, poured wine into both and handed one to me. This was a ritual I had heard of but never seen, since it was normally performed only in the presence of customers whose complaints had been turned into compliments.

As though he had been following my thoughts, Gimball spoke. "Fine old tawny port this, Wilkins, generally reserved for clients. And a word of advice. Always pour up to the pretty, never beyond it. The bottle lasts a third as long again. A small point, but worth remembering." I saw that my own glass was filled exactly up to the point where the decorative markings on it ended. "Here's wishing you every success, my boy. And all the good luck you won't need."

I drank. "Mr. Lacey said he'd prepared a scheme of his own which was very similar to mine."

"Did he now?" Gimball looked down at his glass.

"It is sometimes necessary to take such statements with, shall I say, a grain of salt."

"I don't understand."

Gimball gave a little superior smile. "Mr. Lacey is of course in general control of this department. But, quite confidentially, he would not have the detailed knowledge necessary for the kind of scheme that you suggested."

I said I saw, although I was not at all sure that I did.

"We have to take the rough with the smooth, you know." Rather more emphatically than seemed necessary he added, "You've got a promotion out of it which was totally unexpected. Let it rest at that."

I looked at my empty glass. Gimball rose, put the bottle back in the cupboard, and relocked it. The celebration was over.

XV

I was a little annoyed because May didn't show more surprise at the news. The annoyance was illogical, I know, because I had prepared her for it by my stories about seeing Lacey at his club. She was bewildered also by my anger at the trick which, on thinking it over, I could see had been played on me.

"I don't see what you're complaining about," she said that night. "And I don't see why you expect me to be so surprised. After all, you knew that Mr. Lacey was impressed by your scheme, he'd told you that."

"I know, but—"

"He wouldn't have spoken to you as he did at his club the other night unless it was more or less settled. Did he say what it would mean in extra money?"

"No. He said a lot more work and a commensurate increase in salary. I suppose it must be another two hundred and fifty pounds. But the thing is, don't you see, I've been tricked. I don't believe Gimball recommended me, in the first place. Only a few days ago—" I stopped, because I didn't want to tell May about the kind of blackout I must have had when I forgot those letters.

"Yes, what happened then?"

"He picked on me over something. He's always picking on me."

"But he did recommend you. He said so."

"I don't believe it. He told me that afterwards. The thing is that Lacey has simply pinched my idea and put it forward as his own. My name won't even be mentioned. I'm being bought off by getting Gimball's job, that's all."

May looked down her long nose. "You don't *know* that's true. It's just what you think. Mr. Lacey didn't say your name wouldn't be mentioned."

"It's obvious as soon as you begin to think about it. Saying he'd streamlined my original ideas, all that sort of thing, and then telling me that *his* scheme had been put forward and approved. And then the way Gimball talked—there's just no doubt about it."

"Even if it's true," May said almost timidly, "does it matter? I know it's wrong you shouldn't get the credit, but it does mean that you get Gimball's job. Isn't that the most important thing?"

It was, but somehow I couldn't admit it to May. "You don't understand."

"You certainly don't seem very pleased."

The irritation I felt was as violently physical as if it had been caused by a rash on my body. "It was my idea and it's been stolen so that my name won't appear." I found myself actually shouting. "Does that mean anything to you? You simply want to know how much extra money I get, that's all. Money, money, it's all you think about."

"John." May backed away from me across the room.

"Will there be enough to pay the deposit on a nice little car so that we're as good as the Joneses. Isn't that lovely? Nobody will ever guess then that I was Barney Colter's daughter and brought up in a Battersea slum." I picked up a small china horse and threw it at the fireplace. The horse knocked aside the paper frill, struck the fireplace and broke into several pieces.

May burst into tears. "How could you? I bought that for our last wedding anniversary."

"I'm sorry." May was fond of china ornaments of that kind and they meant a lot to her. I could see that I had been behaving badly and that breaking the little horse was an awful thing to do. "I'm truly sorry, May."

"It doesn't matter."

I crossed the room and put my arm round her thin shoulders. Beneath my hand I could feel the fragile bones. I led her over to the sofa. She sat down on it, but kept her face turned away from me. I kept repeating that I was sorry and stroked her shoulder. She said nothing.

"We'll order a car. As soon as I know how much the rise is we'll order one on the h.p. You can get eighteen months to pay."

"No."

"What would you like? A little Ford Popular would just about do us, or one of those Morris Minors. I want it as much as you do, really."

"You don't. You'd always be saying that I got it because of my family. You don't love me any more, you want a divorce."

"Is that it?" I pushed her back on the sofa, began to kiss her neck. There was something exciting about the fact that she was crying. She very rarely cried, and her tears gave me an ardent feeling towards her that I hadn't experienced for a long time. I put my hand on her knee.

"Don't," she whispered, while the tears rolled down her cheeks. "Don't, please. Not in here. Not with the light on."

"Let's go to bed then."

"Oh no, please. It's too early in the evening."

"Come *on*." I half-carried and half-dragged her across to the bedroom. There, with the light out, we coupled together. May didn't resist me at all, but she sobbed all the time. When I put my fingers on her face afterwards I found it wet with tears.

"You hate me," she said after it. "You hate me."

I have wondered since then if she was right. At the time, however, I wasn't conscious of anything more than a relaxed tenderness. "Don't be silly. Shall I tell you something else? We're going to have a holiday this year too. With this rise we can afford it. What would you say to going back to where we had our honeymoon?" She sobbed more loudly. I felt my irritation returning a little. "Don't you think that's a good idea?"

"John, you don't really hate me, do you?"

I laughed. "Haven't I just shown I don't?"

"I don't know," she cried. "Oh, John, wasn't it a lovely honeymoon we had. I did think it was wonderful. It was all I'd ever dreamed of."

How different can people be, I wondered? To me that honeymoon had been just about the biggest disillusionment of my life, to May it had been a wonderful experience. "Then let's repeat it," I said.

The sobs stopped. "I don't believe you really want to. You've been so strange lately."

"I'm sorry. A lot on my mind. A few things that went wrong, nothing important, but Gimball had me on the carpet."

"You should have told me."

"Perhaps I should, but it doesn't matter now. Wouldn't you like to go back, I don't mean to the same hotel, but, you know, go back and sort of have another honeymoon."

"As good as the last—oh, it couldn't be that."

"Perhaps better in some ways." I put my hand on her naked thigh and pressed it. She didn't move away, but I could feel the same little shiver of distaste run through her that I remembered from long ago. I took my hand away.

"I do love Brighton," she said. I realised then—this will hardly seem possible, but I swear that it's true—I realised then that I was suggesting we should spend our holiday in the place where Sheila was spending hers. Mention of the word *Brighton* brought it home to me. You can say of course that the intention to go to Brighton had been in my mind all the time, and I can't say whether or not that is true. I only know that with the actual mention of the town something clicked into place in my mind. *Brighton*, I thought, then *Sheila*, then *the first two weeks in June*.

"What are you thinking about?"

"Brighton's awfully crowded in the summer."

"You mean we should go somewhere else?"

"'It's finer, remember, in June and September,'" I quoted, from the railway advertisement. "Why not go in June?"

"But it's nearly June now." May always hated things to be sprung on her in a hurry.

"I think we should go in June. The weather experts say the early part of June is going to be the finest for ten years."

"But what would they say at the office? You've only just got your promotion, and you're going on holiday."

"Very good thing too. Gimball leaves in August and I shan't be able to take my holiday just before, or after, he goes. I'm pretty certain they'll be glad for me to take it as soon as possible. I don't see what you've got to do except put a few things in a suitcase."

"It's rather soon. The Edwards are going away in August

to a guest-house in Devon. It sounded awfully nice. I wondered if we—"

Edwards owned a local garage and both he and his wife were keen bridge players. I gathered up the sheet and squeezed it hard. It helped to keep my voice even. "In the first place I don't want to go away with the Edwards. You may like to listen to them talking about cars all day and then play bridge every evening, but I don't. In the second place, I told you I can't possibly go away in August. In the third place, I want to go to Brighton, and I thought you did too."

"I do, you know that."

"Then I'll ask about it at the office to-morrow. All right?"

Her "Yes" was pitched in a tone so low I could hardly hear it.

That night, while May breathed regularly and quietly by my side, I thought of the holiday at Brighton. I saw myself playing tennis with Sheila, diving into the sea with her and racing out to a raft, putting pennies in the slot machines on the pier, and at night clasping her tightly to me on the beach, murmuring words that were lost in the waves' soft suck and roar. Didn't I know all this was fantastic, something that could never come true? I did, but then again in a way I didn't. After all, most of us indulge in fantasies at some time or another, day-dreams we call them. This was no more than another day-dream, although at times I managed to make it seem profoundly real. Certainly, in spite of the questions I had asked Uncle Dan, I had no intention of doing harm to anybody.

XVI

Gimball was quite agreeable to my having the first two weeks of June for my holiday, and thought it was a good idea as I had known he would. I wrote to Brighton and booked a room at the Prince Regent Hotel, which is just off the front between the Palace and West Piers. I didn't tell Sheila, however, and in fact didn't see her before the holiday. This may seem strange, after I've said that it seemed to me I'd been given an almost open invitation to come down to Brighton when she was there. I think, to make things as clear as I can, I ought to try to explain it.

When you're indulging a fantasy like mine you try to make it as real as possible, that's one thing. That's why I'd taken Sheila out, tried to make love to her, played tennis as well as I could. Those were all part of the attempt to make the fantasy real. But there's another part of you that tries to do just the opposite, that flinches from putting the fantasy to the test because it's afraid of being told that the whole thing is a day-dream and you're just being stupid. You want to make the fantasy real yet you want to prevent it from being broken, and the reason I didn't try to see or speak to Sheila in the two weeks before we went away was because I wanted to preserve the dream. But then again this was something I never completely admitted, even to myself. Does all this explain anything? If not, it's because I can't really explain things even to myself.

During the two weeks before my holiday things didn't go well at the office. There was one satisfactory thing, and that was the note about my promotion which came through, initialled by Lacey. It confirmed that I was to take over as the manager of the reorganised Service and Complaints Department, and that my salary from August 31 would be increased to eight hundred and fifty pounds a year. This was fifty pounds more than I had said to May, and it helped to reconcile me to the fact that, as I was quite certain by now, Lacey had pinched my idea.

The unsatisfactory thing was my relationship with Gimball. He was supposed to be showing me how the wheels went round, although I knew this pretty well, and he was simply unable to do this without being as icily sarcastic as Gimball knew how. He was always saying things like: "This is the way I used to arrange the flow of correspondence, but I fear that it may appear antiquated to anybody with all your up-to-date ideas," or "This is what you will no doubt call the old fogey's filing system, which you will reorganise in a manner much more complicated, and so marvellously efficient that it is proof even against any blackouts that may be suffered by the department manager."

When he said this I really saw red. I slapped my hand on the desk. "You don't really think I'm capable of doing this job, do you?"

Gimball twinkled at me. His eyes were of a very bright, piercing blue. "I must confess to being a little worried by your, shall we call it forgetfulness."

"You said you put forward my scheme with your warmest recommendation. That isn't true, is it?"

Gimball fingered the silver ink-stand that had been given him after twenty-five years' service. "Those who ask silly questions—"

I knew that there was little point in going on, yet I couldn't stop. "You don't like the new scheme and you don't like me, that's the answer, isn't it?"

"I like efficiency. You can draw your own conclusions."

"You don't think merging Service and Complaints is going to lead to greater efficiency?"

Gimball shook his head. "It's one of those ideas that look good on paper. In practice I doubt very much if it will work, particularly with the reduction of staff Mr. Lacey envisages."

"So he's using my idea simply to cut down staff. Is that what you mean?"

Gimball shrugged his neat shoulders. "I said you could draw your own conclusions. No doubt I'm out of date."

I had to push right through to the end. "And you don't think much of me, you don't think I'm efficient?"

"You won't rest until you know, will you?" He stared at me, then went through the ritual of finding a key on his golden chain. To-day it was not used to unlock the wine cupboard, however, but a drawer of his desk. From this drawer he took a sheet of flimsy, which he handed to me.

I read:

Report on John Wilkins

You have been good enough to ask for my views on Wilkins's capacity to act as manager of the proposed merged Service and Complaints Department. As you know, he has been in this department for several years, and has risen to the position of my assistant. In the past he has shown undoubted administrative ability. He has done good work, and is ambitious. I do not think, however, that I could conscientiously recommend his promotion to a position of responsibility. In recent months he has shown a lack of stability. The standard of his work has declined and he has become careless over small points of detail. It may be felt that these are not vitally important, but my belief is that those who are careless in details will neglect larger matters also. As you know, I have little confidence in the proposed merger, but if a decision has been reached in favour of it I would advise that a departmental manager be appointed from outside the firm.

"I typed this myself," Gimball said. "You need not disturb yourself with the thought that anybody else has seen it."

I read and re-read it. "You gave this to Mr. Lacey?"

"Yes." Gimball permitted himself a tight little smile.

"And he appointed me in spite of it."

"Precisely. You can draw your own conclusions as I said before. I retain this sheet of paper just in case any queries should be raised in the future. One can never be too careful." The key was produced again, the flimsy locked away.

I thought about some of the phrases in Gimball's report all that afternoon. *I do not think that I could conscientiously recommend... What I can only call a lack of stability... the standard of his work has declined.* Those words should have meant that I couldn't possibly get the appointment. Instead Lacey had ignored Gimball, streamlined the scheme and taken the credit for it, and was buying me off. Thinking about what Gimball had put in the report, I had to admit that the standard of my work *had* declined. Somehow my ability to concentrate seemed to have gone. Yet even Gimball admitted that I had *administrative ability* and after all my basic idea had been accepted. I argued round and round with myself.

This was one of the evenings when May went to the Townswomen's and Housewives' Association. She would have left some cold meat, tomatoes and salad out for me, and there was no reason to hurry back for it. I walked out of Palings at half past five on that fine May evening and wandered down Oxford Street with the argument still going on in my head. When I found myself near to the little club called the Five O'Clock Shadow it seemed natural to go in. Without much believing it, I told myself that Uncle Dan might be there.

The club was just two rooms on a first floor, and Uncle Dan was not there. The proprietor's name was Tony. He was a big man with a blue growth on his chin which was said to have been the origin of the club's name. It may have been so, I don't know.

There were five people in the place, apart from Tony, when I went in. A scrawny-necked man was sitting in one corner talking earnestly to a young woman wearing jersey and trousers, and three prosperous-looking men wearing powerfully-striped suits stood at the bar discussing the afternoon's racing.

I asked Tony if he'd seen Uncle Dan. "Dan Hunton, thin man with a shock of grey hair, often holds his head on one side?"

"Talks nineteen to the dozen, calls Vat 69 the Pope's telephone number? Hasn't been in for a week or two." I sat down with a drink. Tony put his meaty arms on the bar and joined in the conversation of the three men standing there.

A fleshy-nosed man wearing a blue suit with a purple stripe, and with a trilby hat stuck on the back of his head, said, "Can't understand how Morrie's Folly came unstuck. If ever there was a bleedin' certainty, that was it."

"Wasn't tryin'." This was from a little man who had a

tiny unlighted cigar in his mouth. "In a race at Hurst Park a couple of weeks' time, wasn't tryin' to-day."

"What do you mean, wasn't tryin'?" said the fleshy-nosed man indignantly. "Didn't Mickey Day who trains the bleeder tell me to get right on it and do myself a bit of good. Didn't Jack 'Unter say it couldn't lose?"

The little man rolled the cigar round quickly. "All right then, cock, just tell me why it lost."

"I can tell you that," said the third man, who wore a grey suit with a black and red check pattern. "He lost because two others came in in front of him. Drink up and drown your sorrows. Same again, please, Tony."

I heard the tap tap of heels on the stairs. A woman came into the room. She was tall and dark, she wore a bright red frock, and she had beautiful dark hair. To my astonishment she walked directly over to me, put her hands on her hips and spoke.

"See what the cat brought in." I looked behind me in bewilderment. "Yes, it's you I mean, you, Johnny Wilkins."

I stood up. "Have we met before? I'm afraid I don't remember."

"Come on now, don't give me that." She threw back her head in a roar of what seemed to be perfectly genuine laughter. "It's not all that long ago that you stood me up in here."

"I don't think—"

"Oh, come on. It was a—let me see—a Wednesday, and you had big plans for the evening, dinner and a show and I don't know what else. And then you said just pardon me while I make a phone call, I shan't be two minutes, and that was the last of our wandering boy that night. Aren't you going to buy a lady a drink? Gin and tonic, in case you've forgotten that too."

I went up to the bar and got a gin and tonic. The fleshy-nosed man looked at me with what seemed to be distinct unfriendliness. Back at the table I said to the woman, "You know my name, but I don't know yours. Or if I do I seem to have forgotten it."

"You put on a good act. Chin chin." She raised her glass. "Hazel Denison. As if you didn't know."

"When I was in here before, did you kiss me?"

"What's that?"

"I'm not joking. I asked if—"

"I heard you the first time. I may be a model but I don't see that gives you the right to say that kind of thing."

I leaned across the table. Seen close to, her skin was revealed as full of tiny spots and craters, minute imperfections that had been covered with powder. "I'm sorry, I'm putting all this very badly, but when I was in here last I must have lost my memory for an hour or two. I honestly don't remember anything except that I was in here and then suddenly found myself at home with somebody's lipstick on my cheek."

"Kind of thing it's hard to explain, eh? Don't worry, I can see you're a married man, you've got the look. When you put it that way it's different and I wouldn't deny, Johnny, that you were a bit warm that night."

"Warm?"

"Oh, you know. Feeling your oats as you might say. And I wouldn't say but that in the heat of the moment some of my lipstick might have got on to your cheek. You certainly were trying to kiss me."

"In here?" I was horrified.

"Where else? Though as I said to you then, this is neither the time nor the place. Do you see my tongue hanging out?" An inch of pink tongue showed between blood-red lips.

"What? Oh, I see. Of course." I went up to the bar and ordered a whisky and a gin. The three men were still talking, but not about racing. The fleshy-nosed man glared at me, and spoke to the others. "I said to him, you just take those bones away, Randy O'Connell, and stuff them. They're loaded."

The little man rolled his cigar round his mouth. "That caused it."

"You bet your life it did. Just as well I had my knucks with me."

Back at the table I asked Hazel Denison, "What are bones?"

"Sevens and 'levens. Dice. Here's looking at you and hoping you won't disappear again."

"I hope not, too."

We sat at that table and talked and drank, I suppose for half an hour. Why did I do it? I just don't know. I knew I was spending money I couldn't really afford, I didn't much want to talk to this woman, I didn't find her particularly attractive. Yet there I was and there I stayed. "Do you like me?" I asked her.

"What do you think?" She looked archly at me.

"But do you really like me?" I waved my hand to express what I felt, and one of the glasses on the table toppled slowly to the floor, in slow motion as it seemed, and broke. I called out, "It's all right, I'll pay for it. What I mean is, do you like being with me or is it just—you know, having somebody to drink with?"

The smile seemed to cut right across her face. "I might as well ask, do you like me, Johnny?"

"What do you think, do I like you? Of course I do. I like your hair." I leaned over and stroked it.

She opened her handbag, looked quickly at her face in a

glass, and snapped the bag shut. "I've got a little place round the corner. What would you say to coming round for a cup of nice hot coffee."

Somebody was standing by the table. It was the fleshy-nosed man, his trilby hat still perched on the back of his head. "You don't remember me?"

"No."

"But I remember you, remember you when you were a nipper. Proper little squirt you were too. Big house in Kincaid Square."

"I'm afraid I don't—"

"You should." He rocked backwards and forwards slightly on his heels. "Remember you had a garden? Remember you had somebody to look after it? Barney Colter, who used to bring his little daughter along with him."

"Good God." I stared at him, seeing slowly, through the mists of time and drink, the face of the man who had dug and weeded our garden and had brought with him the shy little girl. Painfully, the memory came back, although I had never seen him since that time, and the vulgarly prosperous figure standing in front of me bore little relation to the shabby Barney Colter I remembered.

"Barney Colter as ever was. Thought you were too proud to talk to your father-in-law. He married my daughter, know that?" he said to Hazel Denison.

"Did he? He doesn't act that way. Do you want that cup of coffee, or are you going to talk over old times with your *father-in-law?*"

There was nothing I wanted less than to talk to Barney Colter. I said to him, "If you'll excuse me."

"A cup of coffee, it's the first time I've heard it called that." His face had gone very red. I remembered that he was an angry man. "I'm not good enough for you, eh?"

"It's not that."

He appealed to Hazel Denison. "Would you believe it, he's been married I don't know how many years to my daughter and I've never been asked round to see 'em, not good enough. What kind of a son-in-law do you call that?"

"We didn't ask you round because we were never quite sure when you were out of circulation. You've only just come out now, I believe."

It was a silly remark, as I realised the moment I'd made it, but I was not prepared for its consequences. Barney Colter roared like a bull and put his hand into his jacket pocket. I thought that he had a knife in there, and I ran forward and tried to pinion his arms. He shook himself free from me, drew something from his pocket and raised his right arm. I ducked, but not quickly enough. His hand, with the knuckle-duster on it, came down and struck me a blow on the shoulder, knocking me down. I pulled at his purple-striped trouser leg and brought him down with me. As he came down he upset the table at which I had been sitting.

There was pandemonium in the room. Hazel Denison screamed. The barman, Tony, was shouting something. I stumbled to my feet, hitting out blindly. I got one good punch in to Barney Colter's stomach and heard him grunt, but his friends had joined in. I was kicked and punched, dragged to the stairs and thrown down them. As I went down I thought, quite lucidly, that it was the first time I had ever fallen down a flight of stairs. I picked myself up at the bottom, to see a policeman looking in at me. "Been in a little trouble?" he asked.

"I slipped down the stairs." My shoulder and ribs hurt, but there seemed to be nothing broken.

He was a young policeman, and he looked at me with the

hint of a smile. "Sure you weren't pushed? Think I'll just go up and have a look." He came in and went with measured tread up the stairs. When he came down five minutes later his expression was a little grim. "They say they don't know anything about it. Sure you don't want to say anything more?"

"No. I fell down the stairs, that's all."

"Don't make a habit of it. You might get hurt." He nodded to me and went off. Stopping to look at myself in a glass I saw that I had a few superficial scratches. There were one or two on the cheek and a big bruise over my left eye. My coat sleeve was torn. I explained the damage to May by saying that I'd foolishly tried to jump off a bus while it was going round a corner at speed. She clucked a bit about the tear in my jacket, but seemed to accept what I said.

XVII

I'm afraid I may have given the impression that I was feeling pleased with myself about all this, thought I was no end of a fellow getting thrown down the stairs of drinking clubs, and so on. That would be quite a wrong idea to get about my state of mind. Part of the time I was thinking about Sheila and the Brighton holiday, part of it I was worrying about the office and the new job, and then there was that other part of me which was always thinking about the way I made up things and forgot things. Some people would say, I suppose, that all these thoughts were part of one big thing, that the fantasies and the forgetting came because I hadn't got a properly balanced life, or something like that. And then doesn't that make nonsense of what I really believe, that a man's got to take responsibility for his actions? I just don't know.

It was at one of the times when I was feeling worried that I found in my pocket a dirty bit of paper with Doctor Bowen Glenister's name written on it, and an address off the Edgware Road. On the spur of the moment I looked up his telephone number, rang up and made an appointment to see him. It was a woman's voice that answered.

At lunch time I took a bus down the Edgware Road, turned into a shabby side street and rang the bell of a shabby house. Outside it was a discoloured brass plate with Doctor Glenister's name on it. A woman wearing a dirty white coat opened the door and showed me into a room with three or four chairs round the wall and a few old magazines on a centre table. After five minutes she took me down a passage furred with dust, the carpet threadbare.

"Sit down, Mr. Wilkins," Doctor Glenister said. "Who sent you to me?" He was a dark man and very hairy. There was blue on his chin, hairs sprouted out of his wide nostrils and his ears and bristled upwards on his head. Patches of black hair lay on his cheekbones.

I sat down. The room was dark, oppressive. Out of the window I could see a yard filled with miscellaneous rubbish, empty petrol cans, bottles of different shapes and sizes, a broken bicycle. Inside a gas-fire hissed although it was a warm day, there were dusty books on shelves and on the mantelpiece behind the doctor were strange things in bottles. I found it difficult to speak. "My uncle," I said. "His name's Dan Hunton."

"Cigarette?" He pushed a packet over to me. I saw his wrist full of black hairs, the cuff unclean. "Hunton. A little man would he be, with a squint?"

"No, he's tall and thin with a lot of grey hair, holds his head rather to one side."

"I remember," he said unconvincingly. "Where would I have met him now?"

"At a little club in Soho, I believe, called the Five O'Clock Shadow."

"Business does take me there sometimes." His eyes, small, black and quickly-moving like the eyes of an animal, stared at me. "Why did you want to see me? Is it a girl?"

"No."

"I'm glad of it. I never do that thing, although I might know a name." He did not ask a question, yet there was a note of interrogation in his voice.

"It's nothing to do with a girl," I said, although that wasn't strictly true.

He looked upwards at the stained ceiling. I could see the fierce hairs going up his nose. "Then what is it? You don't want to play a guessing game with me, do you?"

In a faint, stifled voice I said, "I have blackouts."

"What's that?"

"Blackouts. Lose my memory, don't know where I've been for a few hours. I wondered if perhaps a course of treatment—" I knew I did not want any kind of treatment from him.

"You're sure that's what you want to see me about, black-outs? Married? Don't answer that, I can tell you are. Drink much?"

"Not really, but drink seems to have more effect on me than it used to have."

"Releases the emotional pressure. There's something you want, something you haven't got. You want me to supply it, right?"

"I don't know. I thought—I hoped—"

"Sex, isn't it? The bloody great stumbling block. You've got something you don't want and you want something you can't get? You've come here hoping I can do it for you, give you the things you're dreaming about. That's right, isn't it, eh?" He got up, a stubby man with powerful shoulders, and came round the desk towards me. His hairy hands moved like a crab's claws, waving.

"No, no." I rose too, and backed away from him.

"And I can do it, you devil. I can get you what you want,

do you hear? It costs money, but you've come to the right shop. Headaches, amnesia, lying awake at night, I can cure them all. Only don't give me all that stuff, don't try to pull any wool over my eyes, I can't take it and I won't have it, understand." All this Glenister said, and he said much more as he advanced towards me, his hands expanding and contracting. I backed, I gripped the door handle, turned it and ran, ran down the passage, out of the door, along the shabby street until I reached what seemed the sanity and safety of the Edgware Road. I tried to forget what I had seen and heard but the bristling hair and bright small eyes, the crab-like hands and the terrible things he said stayed in my mind.

XVIII

May and I went down to Brighton on Saturday the second of June. She made a great to-do, as she always did whenever we went away anywhere, about packing and getting ready, so that you would have thought we were going away for six months instead of a fortnight. However, we finally got there and settled into quite a comfortable room in the Prince Regent.

We got down in time for lunch, and after lunch I asked May if she would like to bathe. It was a fine day, although there was the kind of nip in the air that you get in early June.

She shivered. "Oh no, I couldn't. It's too cold."

"It's not really cold. Be lovely in the water."

"Really I couldn't, John, not on our very first day."

"What difference does that make?" We were leaning over the promenade railing, watching the people on the beach.

"I don't know, it just does. I mean, you have to get used to the sea air, don't you?"

"I don't see why." I began to feel annoyed. May was wearing a salmon-pink frock that didn't suit her at all.

"You go in. Don't worry about me."

"It's no fun going in alone. Is there anything you want to do?"

"I don't mind, really. What would you like to do?"

"I was asking what *you* wanted to do." I kicked my foot hard against the railing. "Surely there must be something."

"We could go on the pier," May said hopefully. "Would you like that?"

"I'm asking you. If you want to go on the pier, let's go." I began to walk with long strides in the direction of the Palace Pier.

Almost trotting beside me, May said tearfully, "There's no need to snap my head off, just because I don't want to go in the water."

I did not answer. I was wondering whether Sheila and her father had come down yet. If so, they might well go for a walk on the pier. But their hotel was nearer to the West Pier than to the Palace. I turned. "Let's go on to the West Pier."

"But why?" May looked at me in astonishment. "You always used to say that the Palace Pier was much better, because it's larger and has more amusements."

"The West Pier is more select." I knew that argument would appeal to May, and in fact she said nothing more. We went on the West Pier, walked up it, sat in the sun watching the concert party for half an hour, walked down the other side of the pier, and went back to tea at the hotel. I did not see Sheila. After tea we walked around the town a little, sat on the promenade, and it was really a matter of waiting for dinner. At half past six we went back to the hotel again. May said she must get ready for dinner, and I said I thought I would take another quick walk.

Out on the front I turned to the right and began to walk along briskly past the Mikado and the Grand Hotel. Where was I going? I swear that I was surprised when I came to Little North Street. The name stopped me, and I looked at the hotel that stood twenty yards along the street. I read the name *Langland*. Sheila had said her father was on the first floor, and I glanced up at the long windows that afforded a glancing view of the sea. I turned down the street, walked along to the hotel, and pushed open the swing-doors. There was a lounge to the left, but nobody was in it. I moved over to the reception desk and glanced surreptitiously at the Visitors' book, looking for Sheila's name.

A slick-haired young man hurried up. "Can I help you?"

"Perhaps you can. Has Miss Morton arrived yet?"

"Yes, but I'm not sure if she's in." He looked at the keys on the board. "She's out, I'm afraid. Would you like to leave a message?"

"No thank you, it doesn't matter."

"Shall I tell her you called. It's Mr.—"

"It doesn't matter at all, thank you very much." I had to control a slight feeling of panic, as I began to move away.

"No trouble at all, sir. Can I tell her you will call back?"

"Don't bother." I was half-way out of the swing-doors by this time. Turning as I went out, I saw his curious stare.

When I got back to the Prince Regent, May and I argued because she said I couldn't possibly come down to dinner in a sports jacket. I finally gave way and put on a suit. May wore a light-blue frock cut very low in front, which on her somehow seemed immodest, although had Sheila been wearing it I might have thought of it differently. We sat for the most part in silence through our brown soup, boiled chicken and peach melba. Every now and then May made some comment about one of the couples at the other tables or said that the service was slow or that she would have thought they would have put more than one little pat of butter on the table for each of us.

I agreed with everything she said, and thought I was

keeping my end up. It came as a surprise when she said, while we were having coffee in the lounge, "What is it, John, what's the matter?"

"I don't know what you mean."

"It's no use our coming on holiday if you're going to be like this. We'd better have stayed at home." May's voice was low, for she had a horror of scenes, but I could tell that she was near to tears.

There was an image in my mind, vivid, of my visit to the Langland Hotel. Instead of walking away I stood my ground, chatting easily with the slick-haired young man, asking him to tell Sheila that a very old friend had called. As I turned to leave the swing-doors moved, and who came through them but Sheila herself, flushed and smiling. The flush deepened when she spoke to me. "John," she said, and came forward with outstretched hands…

"I'm sorry." My voice seemed to come from far away.

"Something's wrong. I wish you'd tell me what it is."

"Nothing at all." I set my coffee-cup back upon its saucer with a tinkle. "A little tired, that's all. Must be the sea air. How about going to a cinema? They've got that thing you wanted to see on at the Regent, the one with Gregory Peck."

"That would be lovely."

We went to the Regent. The only thing I can remember about the Gregory Peck film is that it was set in Burma and there were a lot of air-raids. I sat through it all, with May by my side, thinking about Sheila, and letting my imagination go on from the point where she was so pleased to see me in the hotel to games of tennis, swimming, long walks together into the country.

Like a small mouse May's hand crept into mine. I drew my hand away.

We walked back to the hotel afterwards without speaking. At the door I said, "You go on. I shall have a turn along the front. I've got a headache."

She left me. I walked along the front almost as far as Black Rock, and then back. The pubs were shut or I would have had a drink. I went into a pin-table saloon and wasted a dozen pennies. When I went up to our room May lay with eyes closed, her long-nosed face as white as marble.

XIX

Sunday was very much like Saturday, with one or two differences. At breakfast I noticed that May was still eating her toast and marmalade in the same way. Later in the morning we bathed, but the water was rather cold and May came out after five minutes. She couldn't swim, and really didn't like bathing at all. We went on the Palace Pier instead of the West Pier, and played on a number of the side-shows like the Kentucky Derby, which we both enjoyed. In the afternoon we walked up to Black Rock, and had a round on the eighteen hole putting course on the way back. There was cold supper because it was Sunday, and after it we sat in the hotel lounge and watched television. I didn't go anywhere near the Langland Hotel.

I don't want to conceal anything, or to excuse myself. I was behaving badly to May, ruining her holiday, and I knew it. The only thing I can say, and it seems weak and foolish, is that I was in the grip of something stronger than myself, that I did the things I had to do. Yet I always wanted to be a good husband to May, I never wanted to hurt her.

On Monday morning I got up with the firm intention of being nice to May. I knew that she loved shopping in my company, and in the morning I trailed round Brighton with her while she tried on a lot of hats, finally buying a

green one that had been reduced to fifteen shillings in a
sale. She brightened up a lot, and even agreed to go and
have a drink in the Ship. When we got back to the Prince
Regent the desk clerk said that a gentleman had called, and
had said he would come back later.

"What sort of gentleman? What did he look like?" I was
uncomfortably reminded of my own call at the Langland.

"This sort of gentleman," a voice said, and I turned round.

"Why, Uncle Dan!"

"Uncle Dan it is, come down to see the lovebirds, and
welcomed I see with all the enthusiasm a bank clerk gives to a
bad fiver." And it is true that May was looking at Uncle Dan's
black and white check sports jacket rather as though it had
a bad smell. Personally I was extremely pleased to see him.

"Uncle Dan, however, is irrepressible. Having come down
with the spirit of good fellowship and hospitality in his heart
he is determined not to let it be quenched merely because
somebody is under the impression that he has crawled out
from the woodwork. In short, come out to lunch."

"But we've got lunch here," May protested.

"That's right," I echoed rather weakly. "Have lunch with
us."

"God forbid that your old uncle should be called a sponger.
I know a little place just round the corner which serves the
most unusual food in Brighton. I suggest that we wend our
way thither pronto, pausing on the way only to imbibe a
drop of corpse reviver." He added hurriedly, forestalling the
protest that I saw on May's lips, "I refer of course to sherry,
which is the only possible pre-prandial drink for a lady. I
happen to know a little bar where—"

I laughed. I found Uncle Dan in this mood quite delight-
ful. "Come on, May."

May came on, but I could see it was not very willingly. She sat sipping her sherry, almost in silence, while Uncle Dan and I had two or three shots at the Pope's telephone number. Then the lunch turned out to be in a Chinese restaurant, and she ate almost nothing but rice. I didn't feel too easy myself about shovelling all that food down on top of whisky, but Uncle Dan was an entertainment in himself. He knew a little Chinese, which he used with the waiters, and he dabbed about with chopsticks while we used a fork and spoon.

"A few lychee," Uncle Dan said, when we had polished off the last of the pancake rolls and the chicken and pineapple, "a few cumquats, some chow chow? A little ginger? Very good for the digestion, breaks up any amount of wind. Pity politicians don't use it. No? Just some fragrant tea, then, to waft away all our troubles."

"I don't want anything, thank you," May said. "I have a rather bad headache. I shall go back to the hotel and lie down."

It damped even Uncle Dan. He said quietly, "I'll get the bill."

"Please don't move, either of you." May stood hand to forehead, a martyr to sherry and Chinese food. "I know my way back perfectly."

We argued back and forth a while about that, and at last it was decided that I should go back with May to the hotel and then return for a cup of tea with Uncle Dan.

Almost in silence we walked back to the Prince Regent. Just before we got there I said, "You certainly made a mess of that lunch. You set yourself out to be as sour as possible. Anyone would think Uncle Dan had committed a crime by asking us to lunch."

"I hate him." We turned into the hotel lobby. She repeated in a low voice, "I hate him. Why did he have to come down here to spoil our holiday?"

"It's hardly that much of a holiday to spoil."

"And whose fault is that?" she asked, still in that low voice. "But I don't feel well enough to argue, I must lie down. You go back and talk to him."

"If there's anything I can do—"

"There's nothing anybody can do," she said, as she turned away and walked towards the stairs. "I mean, I'm just going to lie down."

There was a glass of brandy waiting for me when I got back to the restaurant. Uncle Dan sat with another cupped in his hands, his long legs stretched out in front of him, a foxy smile on his face. His spate of talk seemed to have spent itself and we sat in silence, sipping our brandy.

"Good stuff this," he said. "Not many Chinese restaurants where you can get it. Very unusual."

"Oh. Yes, it's good."

He drew from his pocket a carton of small, evil-looking cigars. "Try one of these, something special. No? I will, then." He set light to the small tube. "Terrible woman, May. Not surprised you want to murder her."

"Don't be ridiculous."

"I know, I know, McKenna case and all that. But come down to it, it's yourself you're really thinking about, and I don't wonder."

"Look here, there's something I must have out with you." I went to sip my brandy again, found that the glass was empty, and with a token protest from Uncle Dan, ordered another. "That man you put me on to—Doctor Glenister."

"Glenister?" Uncle Dan put his head on one side and looked foxily at me. "Did I mention his name?"

"You certainly did. Let me tell you, the proper place for that man is in a criminal asylum."

"Oh, come now, he's not as bad as that. Matter of fact, I don't know him well at all. Met him in the Five O'Clock Shadow a couple of times, that's all. Sorry if he was no help."

"No help." A shudder passed through me which I was unable to control. "I met Barney Colter in that club of yours. He picked a quarrel with me. I got thrown down the stairs. You'll probably hear about it next time you go in, so you may as well know now."

Uncle Dan had his long nose stuck in the brandy glass. He lifted it out, stared at me, stuck it back again, raised the glass and tossed off the brandy at a gulp. "Troubled waters," he said obscurely. "Haven't seen Barney Colter in a couple of years. What did you fight about?"

I told him what had happened. It seemed absurd as I told it.

"Give you a bit of advice, Johnny boy." Uncle Dan stared at his socks, dark blue with red clocks on them. "Cut it out. These little clubs and girls with lipstick and all that. Sorry I ever took you along to the old Five O'Clock Shadow. Doesn't suit you, that kind of life. You just stay home, sit tight."

"That isn't what you said last time. And only a few minutes ago you said May was a terrible woman."

"So she is, boy. I still think you've got to put up with her. You're the respectable type and that's all there is to it. But let's talk about it over an honest glass of beer. I can see they want to get rid of us here."

He paid the bill, except for the two brandies, and we went out into the June sunshine. I looked at Uncle Dan and felt a sudden revulsion from him, his foxy look and narrow grey head and pointed shoes. "Do you mind if we don't have that beer just now?" I said. "I'm pretty full."

"'Course not, my boy. Feel all right? Let's get a couple of deck-chairs."

"I want to think things out," I said vaguely. "I'll just go for a walk alone, an hour or so. We'll meet later on."

It took a lot to disconcert Uncle Dan, and he wasn't put out now. "Right you are, me boy. I shall just go down on the beach, get a deck-chair, put a newspaper over my face and have a nap. No offence, I trust."

"No, it was a wonderful lunch. Just that I want to be alone. Let's meet at, say, half past six, at—where do you think?"

"The Lord Providence in West Street is a cosy little pub. Don't know what May will think of it, though."

"I'll see you there, anyway. What time are you going back?"

"Last train's good enough for me. And if I happen to meet some nice little filly—well, Dan's your uncle." He gave me a prodigious wink, raised his hand and went down the steps to the beach.

XX

Now that I was alone I felt extremely light-hearted, almost irresponsible. I knew beyond doubt what I meant to do. I walked along the front, turned down Little North Street, pushed upon the swing-doors of the Langland and strode inside. There was nobody in the hall. I beat a little tattoo on the bell, and the slick-haired young man I had seen before came in.

I said boldly, "Miss Morton?"

"Yes, sir. She's expecting you, no doubt. Room 23, on the first floor."

I nodded and walked up the stairs, feeling as if there were springs in my heels. I heard a murmur of voices from Room 23. A party perhaps? I tapped lightly on the door and opened it.

There were four people in the room, but the first thing I was conscious of was the old man in bed. He lay propped high by pillows, a grey-faced man with streaks of red mixed with the grey, his thin hands moving upon the sheets in front of him, his breathing uneasy. A yellow bed-jacket round his shoulders made the grey of his face particularly noticeable. Had I come into the wrong room? Then I looked at the other people there and saw Sheila, but a Sheila so pale, worn, harassed, that I did not immediately recognise her. I saw also an old man, grave, elegant, goatishly bearded, with a black bag, and a young one with familiar face, fair and chunky with crew-cut hair. It took me a moment or two to realise that the old man must be a doctor and that the young one was an old acquaintance, Sheila's cousin, Bill Lonergan.

I say *a moment or two*, and although the time before Sheila spoke could only have been measured in seconds, the scene was fixed in my mind, Sheila staring at me haggard and wide-eyed, Bill Lonergan with his thick brows creased in a frown as though I represented some problem, the old man apathetic, the doctor gravely inquiring.

Then Sheila spoke. Her voice was not friendly. "John Wilkins. What are you doing here?"

"Isn't this—?" the doctor began.

The answer was sharp, though obscure. "It certainly isn't."

Bill Lonergan came forward, smiling, brows relaxed, hand extended to grip mine firmly. "If it's not Johnny Wilkins. You remember me, don't you? Good to see you again."

I said apologetically, "They told me in the hall to come straight up."

"They thought you were somebody else," Sheila said. "My father is ill, as you can see for yourself. Doctor Burrows says he must be spared any excitement."

The doctor nodded his neat head and spoke precisely, in a rather high goatish voice. "That is so, yes, excitement should be avoided as much as ever possible."

"I'm sorry." I turned to go, but now the man in the bed spoke complainingly.

"Wilkins, did somebody say Wilkins? Is that Geoffrey Wilkins's son?"

"My father was Geoffrey Wilkins."

"How very interesting. Please come to the bedside. Sheila, where are my spectacles?"

"But, Father—"

"Now now, it will not excite me to talk to this young man for five minutes, will it, Doctor Burrows?" The doctor moved his head non-committally. "You have dragged me down to this atrocious place, a journey which there can be no doubt has caused the heart condition from which I am suffering. It is hard if an old man cannot say a few words to somebody in what may be the last hours of his life. Where are my spectacles?"

"Here." Sheila gave them to him, sat down in a chair and began to cry quietly. I approached the bed.

"Sit down." His voice had a kind of whining impatience. "So you're young John who used to be the apple of your father's eye. I haven't seen you since you were, let me see, five years old. We were great friends, your father and I."

I sat in a chair by the bedside, uncomfortably conscious of Sheila's sobs behind me. I remembered now that I had sometimes heard my father mention Morton, Morton the timber merchant, when I was small. Then his name had dropped out of conversation, and by the time I was seven or eight I never heard it.

"Great friends." A little saliva appeared at the corner of his mouth and he wiped it away. "I want my teeth, where are my teeth?"

Sheila produced teeth from a cup and handed them to him. The old man fitted them in, giving a push of the thumb that produced a final click. "Better." Indeed, his voice did sound clearer and his face appeared buttressed by the teeth, as though a support had been added to an uncertain building. "Remember you well, little Jim."

"John."

"Your father now, he was a stubborn man. Headstrong,

you might almost say foolish. A clever man, I grant you that, but his own worst enemy. Couldn't recognise a chance when he saw one. Know the pond?"

"The pond?" It seemed to me that the old man's mind was wandering.

"The big pond on the Common, island in the middle."

Doctor Burrows gave a deprecating cough. "I don't think there's anything further I can do usefully at the moment. I shall be in again to-morrow morning."

The sick man's attention was distracted from me immediately. "Am I going to die, Doctor?" he whined.

The doctor tittered. "We are all going to die, Mr. Morton, all in our time. But you look after yourself, do what this young lady tells you, ten more minutes' talk at the most, don't try to get out of bed or any of that nonsense, avoid excitement, remember the ticker mustn't be strained. Now a word with you, my dear young lady."

Sheila and Bill Lonergan followed him out of the room. The sick man moved uneasily. "Pillow's not comfortable." I changed its position, and as I did so my fingers touched his shoulders, thin as knives. "They think I'm dying, that doctor thinks I'm dying, and so does Sheila. Why else is young Bill here, come to pay his last respects to his old uncle, I've got nobody else. But I'm not dead yet."

"That's right," I said, for the sake of something to say.

His watery eyes looked at me uncertainly. "You're young Wilkins, hasn't Sheila mentioned you?"

"Perhaps. I don't know."

"She's been a good girl to her old father. I've been nothing but a trouble to her for the last five years. I shall leave her comfortably, tell you that." The watery eyes fixed me for a moment. "Not like your father."

I was surprised. "What's that?"

There was a faint whistling sound in his breathing. "The pond on the Common. Remember one evening we walked round it together. Your dad had you with him, little fellow, trotted about and then threw stones in. I was hard up for money, wanted your dad to come into the business, put in some money, take a share of the profits. Good share of them. He wouldn't do it."

"He made a mistake." I said it for something to say. Why had my father refused, I wondered? Probably from inherent laziness, for he could not at that time have had any money difficulties.

"Didn't recognise a chance when he saw one. Ended up with nothing, for all his big house in Kincaid Square. And me—I'm comfortable, I've told you that." The whistle in his throat became worse, he stretched out a hand that trembled. "Pills in that bottle. Give me two."

They were tiny pink pills. I gave him two which he took with a sip of water. I went to the door. Sheila, Bill Lonergan and another man were talking in the corridor. I called Sheila.

She came running, and went over to the bedside. "Daddy, are you all right?"

He groaned slightly, and smiled at her with what seemed to me an assumed feebleness.

"I gave him two of those pills."

"You've been making him talk too much," she said angrily, and then spoke to him quietly. "Daddy, Doctor Burrows says you need complete rest. He's sending in a nurse for to-night, but of course I'll be here too and she can call me if there's anything you want."

He groaned again. "Nothing but a bother. Better dead." He was ill, no doubt, but I gathered the impression that he did not feel as ill as he sounded.

"You're not to say that," she said passionately. "And you're not to talk any more. Say good-bye, John."

"Good-bye, Mr. Morton." I took the thin, dry, unresponsive hand. He murmured something unintelligible.

Sheila walked across the room with me. "I shouldn't have said that about making him talk, it wasn't your fault. How did you happen to come along here?"

"I'm staying in Brighton for a few days and remembered you were going to be here." She seemed to accept this without question. We reached the door and I opened it. Outside Bill Lonergan was standing talking to the other man I had already noticed.

"You've met each other," Sheila said. "John Wilkins, Leslie Jackson. But I don't suppose you know that Leslie and I became engaged last week."

The man with Bill Lonergan was the big blond I had met at the tennis club, the man who had played in the doubles. And Sheila was engaged to him. I couldn't believe it, just couldn't take it in, though I noticed now the glitter of diamonds on the third finger of her left hand. I stared from one to the other of them, waiting for them to tell me what kind of a joke they were playing.

The silence must have been awkward. Sheila said, "That was why you were let in straight away, you see. They were expecting Leslie. He's come down from London."

"I see." My tongue felt thick in my mouth as I spoke. "I must congratulate you both."

Jackson ignored my congratulations and spoke to Sheila. "Is your father worse?"

"I don't think so, he's just been talking too much. He's very ill though."

"Is it heart trouble?" I asked.

"Yes, he had a heart attack on Saturday night, and nearly died then. Doctor Burrows says if he has another—" She did not complete the sentence. "Good-bye, John."

I took her hand, and did not let it go. That must have looked strange. Bill Lonergan said, "Come on out and have a drink, Johnny. What about you, Sheila, you must be worn out."

She withdrew her hand from mine, shook her head. "I can't go out until the nurse comes. Then I shall go for a walk. On my own. I want to get away from everybody and everything." In her voice there was for the first time the sound of strain. Jackson put his large hand on her white arm. She dabbed at her eyes with a handkerchief. "I must sit with daddy now."

She went into the room, Jackson beside her, and closed the door. She did not give me a backward glance.

XXI

"God, how I hate sickrooms." Bill Lonergan shivered a little. "Let's have a pint to take the taste away."

We walked along the front, went into a small pub called the Lock and Key, where he ordered beer for himself and whisky for me. I remembered that he had always been a great beer drinker.

"It's rough on Sheila, poor kid. The old boy's had it, you know, that's why I'm down here."

"What do you mean?" I just couldn't seem to take in anything.

"He won't last more than a couple of days, the doc thinks. So Sheila got in touch with me up in Brum. I work up there for Welding and Laycock, constructional engineers, you've heard of them. She told me my presence was required down here pronto."

"*Your* presence?"

"Sure, the old man hasn't got any near relatives except Sheila, I'm the nearest. We haven't told him why I'm here, said I had to come down south on a job, but it's my bet he guessed. He knows he's going, had a bad heart for years. It's rough on Sheila, bringing him down here, must be feeling bad about it."

"Yes."

"You known her long? She used to come and watch the school cricket."

"She told me that, but I don't remember her." I ordered another drink and passed my hand across my forehead.

"You're looking a bit under the weather yourself. Down here for a holiday?" His square face, pale, with freckles on the nose, expressed friendly concern.

"Yes."

"Wife with you? You're married, that's right, isn't it?"

"That's right. My wife is with me."

"I haven't got hitched yet." He laughed as if he had made a joke, and perhaps he had. "How did it happen that you walked in on Sheila? Keen on her?"

"I—" There was a choking feeling in my throat. I took a sip of whisky, and felt better.

"You don't have to tell me. Just the way you looked when she said she was engaged to Jackson was enough. As if you'd been hit on the head, and not gently either." His laughter was buoyant, zestful. "Don't like his type, do you?"

I gulped some whisky. "He's not good enough for her."

Bill Lonergan swilled beer round in his glass thoughtfully. Drops spilled on the table top where we sat, a small puddle formed. "Sheila's a sweet girl, sweet as they come. Take that from me, I've known her since she was a kid. Trouble with her is she can't say no. Don't get me wrong there, I don't mean she's been with a lot of men or anything like that, she's not that kind. I just mean she hates to say no. You say to her come out on the river, Sheila, she won't like to say no if she doesn't want to. She'll say I can't come this week-end, I've got to look after father. All right, you say, what about next week-end? That's no good, I've got a date to play tennis. The week-end after that, then? And she smiles and says that would be lovely. You think that means she really wants to go on the river, you'd be wrong. She just hates to say no, disappoint people. I know, I've had some."

"So have I." I remembered the theatre and afterwards, the touch of my lips on her cheek and her low voice asking me to take her home. I began to laugh.

"You really were sweet on Sheila, I can tell that. So was I. Don't mind telling you we were as good as engaged at one time. At least that's what I thought." He rubbed his nose, grinned. "Now I think it was just that she couldn't say no. I'm not really the marrying kind anyway. But you're married. Did Sheila know that, now?"

"Yes, she did." Now, again, I found myself saying things which were untrue, yet which even now I can hardly seriously consider as lies, because after all one tells lies for a purpose, and there was no purpose in the tales which I told. "Or rather, found it out after we'd been out together a few times. If it hadn't been for that—" I found a full glass of golden whisky in front of me, and took a drink from it.

"Yes."

"It was a great shock to Sheila when she found out I was married. Before that she'd been—I don't mind saying she'd been pretty keen about me. Couldn't keep her away as a matter of fact, always after me to take her out. Shouldn't have done it, I know, but my wife's a bitch."

"Not so loud."

"What's that?" I stared at Bill Lonergan, noticing that on his forehead and freckled nose there were beads of sweat. There were only half a dozen people in the bar, but one or two of them were looking at us.

"I think I ought to go back to the hotel."

"One for the road."

"I don't think so."

"Yes." Silver came from my pocket, shone on the bar counter, several pieces from which the barman picked two. "A bitch. No good, you know what I mean. Now, Sheila was different."

"Shut up." Bill Lonergan's face was fiery red.

"When she found out I was married she was upset, but before that there was no stopping her."

"I said shut up. I'm going back now. Are you coming?"

Why should I talk to Bill Lonergan, I asked myself, when we had never even liked each other at school. What did he mean by telling me to shut up? "I'm staying to finish my drink."

"Be seeing you." He raised his hand, pushed open the door and was gone.

I looked at my watch and saw that the time was twenty minutes to seven. With a vague consciousness that the people in this pub were showing some hostility to me, and suddenly realising that I must have been here some time, I drank the last of my whisky in one gulp, and left the pub.

XXII

That is the last I can remember of this Monday evening. At twenty minutes to seven I left the Lock and Key. I remember nothing more, nothing until I woke in my bedroom at the hotel next morning.

Part Two

AFTER

I

That monday night was a velvety one, moonless. At a quarter past twelve a young garage engineer from Croydon named Sydney Pethers was walking along the promenade with his girl-friend Thelma Wayne. They had had the day off, and had come down to Brighton on Syd's motor-bike. They had eaten a fish tea at Sam Isaac's, gone to see an ice show and then on to a dance. Now Syd was trying to persuade Thelma to go down on the beach for a breath of air.

"I know your breath of air, Syd," she said. "Quite enough air for me up here, thank you. Besides, we ought to be getting home."

"Come on, Thel, what's the hurry, won't take more than an hour to get back this time of night. Not afraid of the dark, are you?"

"'Course not."

"Well then." He whispered to her and she giggled.

"Just five minutes then, Syd, but we must go home soon, honest, we must. I don't know what my mum will say."

They went down the steps. There they stood in utter darkness for perhaps five minutes, locked together, while Thelma giggled and Syd urgently whispered.

"But it's so uncomfortable down there," she said.

"You can have my jacket."

"Just for a minute then, Syd." They stumbled across the shingle towards the sea, his arm around her.

"Here, this'll do."

"A bit farther, Syd, I've got a funny feeling. As if we were being watched."

"You and your feelings. Come on then." They walked another dozen steps and then she tripped over. "Hey, what's up, Thel?"

"Syd." Her voice was high. "There's somebody here. I fell over someone, Syd."

"Take it easy. Someone asleep, probably. Get my lighter." The wheel turned, the light glowed. Syd Pethers sucked in his breath, the light went out. "Christ!"

"What is it, Syd, what is it?"

"You get up and come along with me, Thel, like a good girl. There's been an accident."

"What do you mean, accident?" She moved to get up and her hand slipped on something wet, something sticky. Thelma Wayne began to scream.

II

Some weeks after the gruesome discovery made by Syd Pethers and Thelma Wayne on Brighton beach, Mrs. Wilkins and Uncle Dan had an interview with Mr. Likeness, of Likeness, Bale and Moody, solicitors. Mr. Likeness, whose family name a generation ago had been Leibowitz, was a smiling man with a face like a sagging yellow balloon, and a few strands of hair plastered down on a shining skull.

Mr. Likeness rose when his visitors came in, and offered them chairs. A girl brought in cups of tea. While they drank and he made polite conversation, the solicitor looked at his clients to see if there was any likelihood of an emotional scene. Mr. Likeness disliked emotional scenes very much. Mrs. Wilkins sat solidly in her chair, her square face was set like a wood carving, the hand holding the teacup was firm. Her companion was jittery—he had a nervous tic affecting one eye—but not, Mr. Likeness thought, likely to make trouble. Mr. Likeness shuffled the papers on his desk, produced something quite irrelevant to the case in hand, pretended to examine it closely, and began.

"Just let me put you in the picture. I wanted to let you know that everything is going as smoothly as can be expected. We're past the Magistrates' Court stage now, which is purely a formality, as I've told you, and the case is fixed to come on at Lewes in a month's time. Now we've got to settle the matter of counsel. Have you any ideas or preferences about that?"

Mrs. Wilkins and Uncle Dan looked at each other. "We've talked about it," Uncle Dan said in a voice that would have seemed to those who knew him remarkably low and hesitant. "We wanted Sir John Banbury."

"Banbury." Mr. Likeness made a note. "Any other ideas?"

"Or Miles, H. F. Miles, who got an acquittal in that Wolverhampton case recently. But our first choice would be Banbury."

Mrs. Wilkins spoke. "I am not a rich woman, but I am prepared to spend every penny I have to help John. Money is not important, Mr. Likeness."

A formidable old woman, Mr. Likeness thought. "Banbury and Miles are good, of course. I'm not sure that we can get them."

"Why not?" Mrs. Wilkins fixed him with a basilisk stare before which many men might have quailed. Mr. Likeness did not lose his pleasant smile.

"Banbury is pretty well tied up already, but I will find out about him. Miles is on the Midland circuit, and we should have to pay him an extra fee. I doubt if it's worth it. Tell me, have you talked with your son about this?"

"With John? No, has he talked to you about it?" Mrs. Wilkins looked surprised and almost offended that her son should discuss his own defence with anybody except her.

"Yes. He is anxious that we should approach Magnus Newton."

"I've never heard of him." It sounded decisive.

"He is not so well known as Banbury, perhaps, but that may not be a bad thing in some ways. Your son seems to have been impressed particularly by his conduct of a case involving a man named McKenna."

"Hit his wife on the head with a rolling-pin," Uncle Dan said, with a bark of uneasy laughter.

"That's right. I should like at least to approach Newton, together with the other two. I am sure you could have every confidence in him."

"Very well," Mrs. Wilkins said, with the air of one making a considerable concession. "Now, what about this man who has been coming to see John every day?"

"Doctor Andreadis, the psychiatrist, you mean?"

"I suppose so. John said he had been talking to him a lot. What is the idea of that?"

"Doctor Andreadis is an eminent member of his profession," Mr. Likeness said with his gentle, deprecating smile. "Your son talks to him easily. It is often useful for us to have such an indication of our client's state of mind."

"You mean you think he did it? You think my boy is a murderer."

"Nothing of the kind."

"You think he's guilty, and you want this doctor to say he's mad, is that it?"

"My dear Mrs. Wilkins—"

"If that is what you think, say so. My brother here recommended your name, but I have no doubt that another solicitor would be prepared to take the case."

Uncle Dan made feebly reproachful gestures. Mr. Likeness did not lose his smile, but the words that came out of his sagging yellow face were sharp ones.

"It's your privilege to approach another firm of solicitors to act for you. If you want to damage your son's defence I can think of no better course than to change solicitors at this point."

"Melie, Melie," Uncle Dan said.

Mrs. Wilkins's square face showed no emotion, but her chest moved up and down. "What else are you doing?" she asked.

Mr. Likeness knew that he had won. He looked from one to the other of them, and wondered how much to tell them. "Through Doctor Andreadis we are obtaining an insight into the workings of your son's mind, and an account of his activities for some time before the murder. I cannot anticipate the use that counsel will make of this, but it is immensely useful information. Then there is the question of his movements on that Monday night, which he can't remember. If we could establish all his movements between the time he left Lonergan and the time he returned to his hotel, that would help us a great deal."

"He was due to meet me at six-thirty in a pub," Uncle Dan said. "Never turned up. I went to quite a few pubs in Brighton myself that night, before I caught the eleven o'clock train. Never a sign of Johnny. Have you had any better luck?"

"Investigations are proceeding," Mr. Likeness said evasively.

"What I want to know is this—what progress have you made towards finding the real murderer?" Mrs. Wilkins asked. "Obviously the police won't try to find him."

Mr. Likeness paused for thought before his reply. Relatives who are insistent about the innocence of their accused son or father or brother, mother or daughter or sister, are the most troublesome clients a solicitor can have. At the same time it is unwise even to hint at the possibility of guilt. Mr. Likeness temporised. "We have first-class people down in Brighton. Their job is to find evidence which shows that your son is innocent. You can rely on it that they won't miss anything that can help him."

"That's all very well—" Mrs. Wilkins began. Mr. Likeness held up a creased yellow hand.

"If you want to pursue private inquiries of your own there is nothing to stop you."

"You'll try for Sir John Banbury?"

"I'll get in touch with him immediately. Don't pin too many hopes on him, though. Newton is a very good man."

When they had gone Mr. Likeness picked his nose thoughtfully while staring at the old hunting prints on his walls. Then he went along to see his tall, thin, dyspeptic partner, Moody.

"It's all right," Likeness said. "I'm pretty sure we can get Newton. He'll do a good job."

"Did you have any trouble?"

"They wanted Banbury or Miles."

"Banbury." Mr. Moody turned down the corners of his thin mouth. "Wouldn't touch a sex case like this with a barge pole."

"No. Besides, Wilkins wants Newton, and why shouldn't he get what he wants, poor devil?"

"I suppose there's no doubt he did it."

"Shouldn't think so." Mr. Likeness was looking at the cricket scores in the stop press news of his partner's paper. "But you never know. I'm going up to Lords for a couple of hours. It looks rather like an exciting finish up there."

III

A day or two later Mr. Likeness had a conference with Magnus Newton, Q.C., who had agreed to take the case. Newton was a rising silk who welcomed a case that, whatever its outcome, was certain to bring him a lot of publicity. He was short, puffy and self-important, and in cross-examination sometimes produced the impression that he was a little slow to grasp obvious points. Yet witnesses who tried to take advantage of this apparent obtuseness almost invariably found themselves pulled up by a disconcertingly pointed and unpleasant question. His chief fault as a cross-examiner was that of occasionally ignoring an obvious line of questioning while pursuing some fanciful idea of his own. Was Newton in fact a man who combined patches of brilliance with dull moments, or were his occasional errors the result of too great a subtlety of mind? Mr. Likeness, who had watched him in action several times, had never quite made up his mind.

Now Magnus Newton stretched out his little legs and listened to the solicitor talking about the long statement which they had received from Doctor Max Andreadis.

"I sent Andreadis to see him as a matter of course. But Wilkins took to him at once, seemed to want to talk, and soon Andreadis had the idea of getting somebody to take it all down. This is the result of a dozen or more long sessions."

Newton nodded, his lower lip stuck out. "It means we've got to keep him out of the box. If he goes in and says the kind of thing he's said to Andreadis, any jury would find him guilty in ten minutes."

"Do you think so?" Slumped in his chair, chin on chest, Newton asked the question with every appearance of serious interest.

With a touch of impatience which he quickly checked, Mr. Likeness went on more moderately, "He's admitted motive, said he can't account for his movements, and worst of all given such a picture of his own personality that..." Mr. Likeness, who generally controlled his dramatic gestures, spread out his hands. "But if you don't put him in the box..." He left that sentence unfinished too.

"Ha," said Magnus Newton. Ash dropped from his cigarette on to his waistcoat. He made no attempt to brush it off.

"You wouldn't," Mr. Likeness said hesitantly, "like to see Wilkins yourself, I suppose?"

"I would not."

Mr. Likeness suppressed a sigh. It never does happen that counsel want to see their clients in such cases, even where it might conceivably be useful to do so.

"What's he like?" Newton asked.

"There's an intelligence report somewhere."

"No, I mean this fellow Andre—what's his name?—Andreadis."

"Andreadis." Mr. Likeness, whose smile had not been much in evidence during this conference, produced it now. "As a matter of fact I asked him to come here to-day, thought you might like to talk to him. He may be here now."

Newton grunted, and picked up the telephone. "When a Doctor Andre-ad-is arrives—oh, he's here. Ask him to come in." To Likeness he said, "Pity his name's not Andrews, go down better with a jury if you want to call him."

"In this case that may not matter." Newton understood what was meant when he saw Doctor Max Andreadis, who was an exceptionally handsome man in his forties, dressed in impeccably discreet English clothes, and with only the faintest trace of a foreign accent.

"Doctor Andreadis," Newton said. "First I must congratulate you on obtaining this very remarkable statement from Wilkins. You must have established a great imaginative sympathy with him. I don't think I can ever recall seeing a statement of exactly this kind before, one so complete and informative. It is almost a life history."

"Thank you." Andreadis gave him a brilliant smile. "Wilkins was completely co-operative. It was a relief to him to talk."

"At the same time the very completeness of this statement presents those of us responsible for his defence with a problem, on which we should welcome your expert guidance." He certainly knew how to lay it on thick, Mr. Likeness reflected. "What kind of a witness do you think this young man would make?"

"It is hard to say. He is of average intelligence according to his I.Q. A little slow, and yet there is an impression of honesty. Or at least of a great endeavour to be honest. He says quite frankly, I cannot think that I committed this crime, I feel great revulsion from it, but I had a mental blackout and I do not know."

"How do you think he would stand up to cross-examination?"

"I don't think I can offer a useful opinion. I can say only that at times he is easily confused."

"Our problem, you see, is that if we put him into the witness box and he says some of the things he said to you, he will damage his own case. Yet if he does not go into the box that will also be damaging, in a different way." Andreadis bowed his head courteously as if to say that the problem was theirs and not his. "What about insanity?" Newton barked suddenly.

"Insanity?"

"You've been talking to him for days, man. Is he sane or not?"

"That is not an easy question." Andreadis spoke carefully. "Wilkins is a maladjusted personality. Profoundly maladjusted. He suffers from a conviction of inferiority, a feeling that he is not capable of doing his job satisfactorily, of satisfying his wife sexually, of living a complete and integrated life. He finds compensation for his maladjustment in creating fantasies. But he knows that the fantasies are not reality, he takes refuge—unconsciously, of course—in fits of amnesia. There are some psychotic symptoms, but it is not easy to say—"

"Doctor," Magnus Newton said softly. He had risen, and was standing with his puffy red face thrust forward in his favourite attitude for cross-examination.

"Yes?"

"How often have you given evidence in a case involving a capital offence?"

"How often?" Andreadis cast a startled glance towards Mr. Likeness, but the solicitor was staring at the floor. "Why, never, as it happens. But my years of experience—"

"Years of experience are not important here, I'm afraid. If you had ever given evidence in such a case you would know that this kind of psychological analysis does not impress juries, and can be torn to pieces by any good cross-examiner. You have heard of the MacNaughton rules?"

"Naturally."

"You know what they are—the distinction they draw between a man's knowledge of right and wrong?"

There was a slight flush on Doctor Andreadis's handsome cheek. "The MacNaughton rules are very much out of date."

"Possibly, but they are part of the law of this country. Tell me this, Doctor Andreadis. Is there any chance that we can plead that Wilkins was guilty but insane *under the MacNaughton rules?*"

There was silence in the room for more than a minute. Mr. Likeness watched two flies crawling up the window-pane and made a mental bet with himself that the smaller would reach the top first. He clucked with annoyance as the larger fly flew off before his bet could be resolved. Magnus Newton, face red as a turkey's gills, looked at his shining black shoes.

"No," Doctor Andreadis said. "I think there is no chance that you could successfully plead insanity under the Mac-Naughton rules."

"Ha. I'm obliged to you." Newton stood with head sunk on chest for a moment. "You'd better go and see this feller, Likeness. Here's what I want to know…"

IV

To those outside the legal profession the problem of a counsel's attitude towards the guilt or innocence of his client is a fascinating one. Supposing that counsel for the defence in a murder trial becomes convinced of his client's guilt, should he give up the brief? The fact is, however, that such things are not matters of concern even for those barristers who most pride themselves upon their moral susceptibilities. Quite early in his career the aspiring lawyer learns that the guilt of his client is a matter that must be left to judge and jury; he learns how desirable it is, and indeed not merely desirable but absolutely essential, that upon this question he should have no opinion. Thus, although Magnus Newton would have agreed readily enough that there was a strong case against John Wilkins, he never discussed the matter in terms of the young man's possible guilt. Magnus Newton was conscious of himself as an actor with a part to play—or, to put it less fancifully, as a man with a job to do—and he assessed the various people involved simply in relation to his own position.

Mr. Likeness, as we have seen, had no such inhibition, and he was pleasantly surprised during this interview with John Wilkins. He had seen the young man once before, when Wilkins had seemed merely a dazed, hangdog figure, the kind of person who would not merely become flustered under questioning, but would also produce an impression of shiftiness in ordinary conversation. Now he had apparently recovered his spirits a little and Mr. Likeness, making a reassessment, saw him as a well-set-up young fellow with a shy smile, a ready tongue, and a friendly manner. Was the tongue a little too ready, so that its owner gave an impression of over-eagerness? Was the manner so friendly that it was on the verge of puppyish fawning? Perhaps—but John Wilkins was the kind of young man that any woman on the jury could think of easily, and without displeasure, as her son.

"I'm delighted to tell you Mr. Newton's agreed to take the case," the solicitor said. "You couldn't be in better hands. But if he's to help you, you've got to help him, you understand that? You've got to try to remember what happened on Monday night after you left this Lannigan."

"Lonergan, Bill Lonergan."

"Lonergan. You must try to remember."

"I've tried, don't you think I've tried." The young man's lower lip trembled. He looked slightly repulsive, and slightly pathetic. "I never can remember after I have these blackouts."

"You've been extremely frank in talking to Doctor Andreadis. Some of what you said is to your benefit in relation to this trial and some—I'm speaking quite frankly myself—some of it isn't. But the most important thing you can possibly do is to remember what you were doing between half past six and the time you got back to your hotel on that Monday night."

"Mr. Likeness." The young man's slightly damp hand was touching his, the dog-brown eyes looked at him pleadingly. "I said it to Doctor Andreadis, and it's true, I don't want to avoid responsibility if I did it. It's a thing I could never have done if I'd been myself, and if I did it, well, it can only have been that something else took possession of me, something that must be stamped out. If I did it I ought to be punished."

The solicitor withdrew his hand from the alien touch. "How far back do these blackouts go?"

Wilkins had noticed the withdrawal of the hand, he seemed to shrink backwards into himself. "Three or four years."

"They had been growing more frequent."

"I suppose so." He said it without much interest. "And it was because of them that you went to see Doctor Glenister. You know we are calling him for the defence."

Wilkins shuddered. "He's a horrible man."

"But his evidence may be useful. Now I want to talk about your marriage. That's a delicate subject, but you've been so frank with Doctor Andreadis that I know you won't mind being frank with me. It wasn't a happy marriage."

Wilkins looked boyishly rebellious. "I don't know. I made a good home for May, the kind she wanted, and I'd just got this rise—"

"Yes. But we aren't talking about that side of it. The two of you were—you were not fitted for each other's emotional needs."

Still rebelliously, Wilkins said, "I don't know that May ever had any emotional needs."

If only, Mr. Likeness thought, one could deal with reasonable, sensible people. But the trouble is that people who are tried for crimes of violence are never really reasonable or sensible. "We shall probably call your wife as a witness. Her evidence about the time you got back to the hotel may be immensely important."

"All right." Wilkins seemed to have lost interest.

"But when we put her in the box she will be exposed to

cross-examination. She has made a statement to the police, and although they cannot call her as a witness, in cross-examination they may elicit certain facts—"

"I hate May." Wilkins spoke with eagerness now, even with passion. "I told Doctor Andreadis. I hate her. The way she ate toast and marmalade, the way she was so house-proud, a dozen different things."

Mr. Likeness sighed, and continued probing. He got nothing more out of the young man.

V

"Where are you off to?" Uncle Dan asked, when Mrs. Wilkins came down wearing her best black coat, and with a tightly-fitting black hat skewered firmly in place with a hatpin.

"I am going out."

"That I can see, my old duck. But whither bound, dressed in such finery?"

"I am going to see May," Mrs. Wilkins said, and left him gasping, for in all the time that John and May had been married, she had never called on them at the flat. "I wrote and told her I was coming."

At Windover Close May opened the door and showed her into the lounge. Looking round, Mrs. Wilkins had to admit that the room was very nicely kept, not a speck of dust anywhere, and the tables well polished. Two cups were ready on a tray, together with a plate containing four biscuits, and the electric kettle was just on the boil. Mrs. Wilkins sipped her tea, which was thin straw-coloured stuff, not the dark brew she liked. "I hope I haven't kept you from an engagement," she said formally.

"It's my evening for the Townswomen's Association, but I couldn't have gone."

"Why not?"

"They don't want to have the wife of a murderer at their

meetings." May's thin mouth was very pinched, her long nose looked very long and her close-set eyes very small, as she said this.

Her mother-in-law put down her cup with a clatter. "How can you say such a thing? You've got no heart."

"Do you expect me not to notice the way people look at me, the things they say? It's true, you know yourself it's true."

"You're no wife to him."

"You don't think so? Let me tell you something. I might have been a much better wife to him if it hadn't been for you." In a sarcastic whine she said, "Have some more steak and kidney pie, you don't get it at home. Draw your chair up, it's a real coal-fire, dear. I know May only has the electric. You've always tried to fight me since the day we were married, now perhaps you're satisfied."

Impregnable in righteousness, Mrs. Wilkins said, "I have never interfered."

May got up, took a cigarette from a box with a slightly shaking hand. "What's the good, I didn't mean to quarrel. What did you come to say?"

"You haven't been to see John in prison."

"No."

"Are you going to give evidence for him, May?" Mrs. Wilkins asked this question with no change in her granitic countenance, but with something in her tone that showed it had cost her some effort.

"I suppose so. If they ask me. I shall tell the truth."

"You must do what you can to help him. He's your husband, May."

"Not for long."

Mrs. Wilkins was startled, and showed it. "What's that?"

"I said not for long. You're so worried about your precious son, he's all you think about. How do you think I feel?"

"I should think any wife would want to stand by the man she married."

"Oh, would you? When he's been going around after some other woman, some creature who was engaged to another man already but wanted to have him too. You think I don't know what they're saying about me, all the filthy jokes and lies about being a woman who can't keep her man?" Her voice was as insistent as a cutting saw. "I'll tell you exactly what I'm going to do as soon as this case is over. I'm going to get a divorce, I'm going to change my name, I'm going to leave London and get a job in a town where nobody knows me and points at me and says 'There's May Wilkins, you know, the one whose husband murdered a girl on Brighton beach.' And if you don't think I mean it, you just watch me and see. Do you know what your precious son's done to me, your son who's so fond of the steak and kidney pies that mother makes? He's ruined my life."

She stopped, breathing hard as if she had been running. Mrs. Wilkins took a handkerchief out of her big crocodile-skin bag, blew her nose, put back the handkerchief, got up, opened the door, and left the flat without speaking another word. She walked home across the Common and as she walked her lips moved.

Uncle Dan met her at the door. "I'll make a cup of tea."

"She gave me one." Mrs. Wilkins went into the sitting-room and took off the formidable hat and the black coat. "I think we ought to do what you said a day or two ago. I think we ought to see a private detective."

VI

Uncle Dan had seen the name in a lift, and had made a note of the details. "George H. Spaulding Detective Agency. Investigations undertaken with utmost discretion. Divorce and other work. Reasonable charges. Apply 22 Rodd Street, W.C.2."

Rodd Street was a narrow lane off the Strand, and the agency occupied two rooms on the second floor. In the first of them a girl sat typing. Uncle Dan gave his name and was led into the second room, where a military-looking figure sat smoking a pipe at a desk crowded with a variety of slightly dusty objects, which included a thermometer embedded in an elephant's tooth, a packet of peppermints and a packet of cheese biscuits, an empty cigar-box, three or four large legal-looking volumes, a mouth organ and a piece of lead piping.

"Mr. Spaulding?"

"Captain Spaulding, sir, at your service." The detective gripped Uncle Dan's hand firmly. He wore a tweed jacket slightly frayed at the cuffs, well-pressed grey trousers, a Guards tie. Above the pipe was a clipped moustache, above that a pair of keen blue eyes, thin hair neatly brushed. The whole appearance was both military and sporting, marred only by a rather bad squint. "What can I do for you?" Captain Spaulding asked.

Uncle Dan wriggled uncomfortably in the chair, crossed one long leg over another, put his head on one side. "It's a delicate matter."

"Can I help then, break the ice." Captain Spaulding knocked out his pipe sharply, one, two, three. "Divorce?"

"Eh? No, I'm not married."

"Breach of promise, spot of blackmail? Involved with a young lady? Happens to all of us."

"Nothing like that. This is a case of murder."

"Murder." Captain Spaulding's eyes squinted fearfully. "No good coming here about anything like that. You're mixed up in a murder, you'd better go to the police."

"I'm not mixed up in a murder," Uncle Dan said, exasperated. "This is in connection with John Wilkins, who is to be tried for murder at Lewes next week. I'm his uncle, and I want to know if you can undertake some investigations."

"Oh. Go on." Captain Spaulding picked up his pipe again and refilled it.

"We feel sure—that is, his mother and I—that John didn't do it. He had a blackout on the night the murder took place, and can't remember what he did between six-thirty and the time when he got back to his hotel. The prosecution have got a witness to say they saw him on the promenade at twenty to twelve, and the hall porter says he came in at ten minutes to the hour. Also, at some time in the evening he cut his thumb and got blood on his clothes. They say the blood came from the girl who was murdered. We think it would help if we could find out where and when he cut his thumb."

"Probably would. Any idea where he might have been?"

"I should try the pubs. The solicitors have had a chap on it already and he's found out that at nine o'clock John was in a pub called the Toll Gate, but that's not of much importance. They've turned up nothing else."

"Got a photograph?" Uncle Dan produced one. "Well-set-up young chap. Married, isn't he?"

"Yes."

Captain Spaulding put the photograph into an envelope. "Anything else?"

"Just this." Uncle Dan spoke hesitantly. "If you happen to come across anything that gives you an idea of who did it—"

"Bear it in mind. Probably a sex maniac, though, didn't even know the girl. Four a day and up to three expenses, all right?"

"That's seven pounds a day." Uncle Dan was startled.

"Give you a statement of expenses, might come to a bit less. Not much, though. Got to stand a few rounds on this kind of job."

"You'll work on it yourself?"

"My dear chap." Captain Spaulding pulled at his military moustache. "Who do you think's going to run the office, handle other business? Put my very best man on it, keen as a ferret, report every day. Time's a bit short, scent's pretty cold, but Lambie will track it down if anyone can. Now there's some other information I want. Let's get down to it."

They got down to it.

VII

Legal histrionics are out of date nowadays. The coldly merciless prosecutor, the wrathful defence counsel who bullies the truth out of witnesses, these belong to the past. Counsel for the defence may be relied on to give a lying witness an uncomfortable time, but he will be at pains to avoid any suggestion of bullying. It is generally agreed that, in these equalitarian days, the spectacle of a witness battered into submission by bulldozer methods is likely to arouse the jury's sympathy for that witness. As for the coldly merciless prosecutor—well, nobody could look at James Hayley, who was conducting the prosecution, without recognising that he was the kind of warm, sympathetic (for some tastes perhaps almost over-ripely sympathetic) personality who has achieved in recent years so much success in television and radio programmes.

Red-faced, stout and jolly, speaking with an assumed rustic accent that masked what might have been slightly too cultured tones, Hayley could make a rape sound like a chummy evening out, robbery with violence a boyish prank gone wrong. We are all human, he seemed to say, we can all understand the temptations to which a young man is exposed in the company of a pretty woman, but at the same time we must have laws, people really can't be allowed to go around doing this kind of thing… Such anodyne eloquence was extremely effective with juries.

Now Hayley was on his feet opening, with his usual jovial mateyness, the case against John Wilkins, giving them the usual warnings of what they should and should not consider, and going on to outline cheerfully and simply the events of that fateful Monday the fourth of June, as they concerned Sheila Morton.

"Before we come to Monday, though, let's trace the whole course of this unhappy seaside holiday which Miss Morton had only undertaken from the desire to give her invalid father a change. Miss Morton had arranged that it should be a quiet holiday, so that she could give undivided attention to her father. They came down on Friday, and engaged in what you might call a round of pleasure, although not a very hectic one. On Friday night they went to see a musical show, on Saturday morning they were on the pier, and in the afternoon they went on a charabanc tour. Not very hectic, I think you'll agree—the kind of thing that you and I would do in the ordinary course of things—but it was too much for Mr. Morton. On Saturday evening he had a severe heart attack. Doctor Burrows, of Brighton, who attended him, told her that it was touch and go, and Mr. Morton's condition remained grave for some days. Now, I am happy to say, he is restored to his former state of health." Hayley cast a beaming smile round, pleased to irradiate the grim proceedings with this single item of good news.

"In these unhappy circumstances Sheila Morton acted with what you may feel to have been her customary promptness and efficiency. On Sunday she sent a telegram to her cousin, Mr. Lonergan, who works as an engineer in Birmingham, and asked him to come down if possible. She also telephoned to Mr. Leslie Jackson, to whom she had recently become engaged. Her father was very ill, and not expected to live. Mr. Lonergan came down to Brighton on Monday morning, and Mr. Jackson in the evening. A night nurse had been engaged to take some of the strain off Miss Morton."

The attention of the prisoner wandered away from Hayley's account of his visit to the Langland Hotel, to consideration of the court in which his whole future life was being decided. Above the head of red-robed Mr. Justice Morland, incongruous among all this mahogany panelling and brown paint, was an electric lamp in a large pink silk shade. Why pink, John Wilkins wondered, why not a shade in keeping with this austere courtroom? His eyes closed wearily, but he brought himself back to reality with a start, and listened to what Hayley was saying.

"Just after ten o'clock, with the night nurse safely installed, Miss Morton went out for a walk alone. As a result of what she said to Mr. Jackson before setting off, he was somewhat surprised when she had not returned at a quarter to eleven, and went out to look for her. He walked up to the West Pier and beyond, and returned at eleven fifteen without having seen her. Mr. Lonergan had gone out to the cinema, and was not staying in the hotel, so Mr. Jackson had no help in his search.

"What happened to Sheila Morton on her walk? We can find nobody who saw her after she left the hotel. We know only that at twelve fifteen a young man named Sydney Pethers and his friend Thelma Wayne found her body on the beach near the Palace Pier. Her head and face had been savagely beaten by several blows from some blunt instrument. Her clothes were torn, and there were scratches on the inside of her legs which indicated an attempted sexual assault, although she had not been violated. I have to tell you now that we have not found the instrument with which the crime was committed. It is at least possible that the instrument was a large stone, of which there are many on Brighton beach. I have to tell you also that, because of the peculiar conditions surrounding the crime, the medical experts cannot place the time of death more precisely than to say that it took place between ten-thirty and midnight."

Outside the sun shone fiercely, but it filtered through into Lewes courtroom only as a thin supplement to electricity. Filtered through to get a glimpse of an English attempt to obtain what is called justice: which is achieved by dressing up men in wigs and robes, then setting them talking to persuade eleven sheep (three tough housewife ewes in this lot actually) that the pale-faced sheep in the dock gave way to unnatural instincts and for an hour or two became a wolf. Was it so? Out then, wicked wolf (his apparent sheepishness now, his persistence in saying that he has never thought or acted unsheepishly, do not deceive us), out from the society of sheep for ever. Mr. Justice Sheep pronounces sentence upon you, you are to be confined within walls, poor wolf-sheep, dangerous sport of the flock, for ever...

Such at least might have been the heretical view of anybody present who lacked respect for the solemnity and majesty of English legal processes. Fortunately such a person is purely imaginary, and so far as is known nobody in open court, or even in the public gallery, had such thoughts in mind while Mr. Hayley's opening speech wound on its way and Mr. Justice Morland made strange designs in his black-covered notebook and Magnus Newton tapped his mouth to conceal a yawn and Mr. Likeness, sitting in front of him, studied some papers at the same time that he picked his nose.

"On that Tuesday afternoon Detective-Inspector Kenning interviewed Wilkins at his hotel, and he will tell you that Wilkins seemed very upset, even distraught. He had visited the Langland Hotel that morning, and so already knew of Miss Morton's death. He seemed anxious, Inspector Kenning says, that his wife should know nothing of his acquaintance with Miss Morton—and I think we are sufficiently men and women of the world to agree that such a wish is quite natural—but he was anxious about something else too. This second cause of anxiety became apparent when the inspector asked Wilkins if he could help at all. 'How can I help?' Wilkins answered. 'I don't know where I was that night.' There was a sports jacket on the back of a chair in the room where they were talking, and the inspector noticed some dark stains on the sleeve. He pointed these out to Wilkins, who said, 'I cut my thumb last night. Some of the blood must have got on to the jacket.' He showed the inspector a small cut on his right thumb. When he was arrested later that day Wilkins made another remark which you may think significant. He said, 'I loved Sheila, I would never have hurt her if I'd been in my right mind.'"

And here Hayley stopped and looked at the jury with a look in which mateyness had for a moment been replaced by a man of the world's lifted, questioning eyebrow. Ten minutes later he was coming to the end of an opening speech in which he had drawn the threads of the case together with inconspicuous skill.

"Let me recapitulate the circumstances on which the Crown case is based, that we believe justify us in asking you to bring in a verdict that John Wilkins, in a fit of passion, killed Sheila Morton in this beastly and brutal way. There is, first, the evidence bearing on his pursuit of Sheila Morton and her rejection of him—for it was a decisive rejection that took place at the tennis club, as you will hear. But even after this rejection he did not give up hope, and when he learned that Sheila and her father were coming to Brighton he persuaded his wife to come down here for their own very early holiday. On Monday evening came the final twist when he learned that this girl, for whom he nursed such a hopeless passion, was engaged to become the wife of another man. Witnesses will tell you of his evident shock when he learned the news of her engagement. You will hear of the conversation he had afterwards with Mr. Lonergan, when he made remarks and suggestions which implied, quite falsely, that he had been intimate with Sheila Morton.

"Members of the jury, John Wilkins had ample motive for the crime. And he was the only person with such a motive. I do not know whether the defence will suggest that this murder may have been committed by that passing tramp who is so much favoured by fiction writers. If so, I should like you to remember this. Sheila Morton was a friendly girl, but she was a good girl, in the real sense of that phrase. She was a virgin. Is it likely that she would have gone to the beach with a man whom she did not know? I submit to you that it is not only unlikely, it is impossible.

"Second, there is no doubt that John Wilkins had opportunity. We have not traced all his movements from six-thirty until he returned to the hotel, but we do know that at nine o'clock he was in a public house called the Toll Gate. We know also that a witness saw him on the promenade at twenty minutes to twelve and was impressed by his ghastly appearance. At ten minutes to twelve the hall porter at his hotel saw him come in, and was also impressed by his strange appearance and manner.

"Third, there is the matter of positive proof. It was to be expected that the murderer should have blood on his hands and person. There were bloodstains on Wilkins's jacket and on his trousers. This blood is of the same group as Sheila Morton's, that is, Group O. Since this is also Wilkins's own blood group, however, no deduction can be made from this. Wilkins claims that the marks came from his cut thumb, although he cannot say where or when he cut it. You will hear expert evidence to the effect that the thumb cannot have bled freely enough to cause all the marks on jacket and trousers. You will hear expert evidence also of the benzidine test carried out on his jacket, trousers and shoes, which revealed the presence of blood in minute quantities on all of them. And you will remember those words he uttered on arrest. 'I loved Sheila, I'd never have hurt her if I'd been in my right mind.' I believe that when you have heard all the evidence, you will agree that John Wilkins killed Sheila Morton, killed her in a fit of violent passion when she resisted his sexual assault. Each man, the poet tells us, kills the thing he loves. That is generally a piece of what we call poetic licence, but in this it is the simple truth. We shall try to show that John Wilkins loved Sheila Morton and, in a fit of frustrated passion, killed her."

VIII

Fairly formal police and medical evidence occupied the rest of the morning. When, at one o'clock, Mr. Justice Morland punctually called a halt, Mr. Likeness took his friend Robin Pinkney to a pub named the Two Brewers. Pinkney was down on a small fraud case which was being held in the court opposite. "How's it going?" he asked.

"Too soon to say yet." Mr. Likeness crunched a roll. "It's not really a very strong case, you know. Depends a lot on what Newton makes of the medical experts. This chap Ritchie, you know the chap from that new lab they've got out at Maidstone, he's a tough nut. I've come across him before. It's all very circumstantial, though."

"Still, a jury can convict on circumstantial evidence."

"Course they can." Mr. Likeness shovelled steak pie into his mouth. "Didn't see you at the club last weekend." They belonged to the same golf club.

"Too much to do. Some of us have to work for our living."

"Went round in eighty-seven. Funny thing happened to me at the twelfth. You know it's a dog leg…" Mr. Likeness began to arrange fork, spoon and salt cellar in a demonstration.

Magnus Newton lunched with his junior, Charles Hudnutt, who was a ruggedly handsome former rowing Blue. "Do you think the jury really likes that smarmy tone Hayley puts on?" Hudnutt asked. "You know, that we're all boys together and it might have been you or me except that we love the little woman, and we all know he had a rough time with his wife but you'll have to find him guilty just the same… that tone," he finished, slightly out of breath.

"I dare say. Never can tell what they will like. Morland didn't like it much. Very fair, Morland, very reliable."

"I suppose it's because I know Hayley's really such an old ram," Hudnutt said. "I used to know a cousin of his rather well once, Jerry Pottingley. Got smashed up in his sports car a couple of years ago. Jerry told me…" He lowered his voice.

"Really," Magnus Newton said. Hudnutt went on talking and Newton, eyes slightly protruding, red face puffed out, punctuated his discourse with "Really… really… really…"

· ● ● ● ● ·

Mr. Justice Morland's lunch consisted of two pieces of Ryvita without butter, a green salad without dressing, and an apple. While he ate it he read Aristotle's *Ethics*. Lacking his robes he looked a rather timid and weaselly little man.

· ● ● ● ● ·

John Wilkins found it almost impossible to eat, and difficult to think. He felt a kind of sick excitement. He got up and began to walk about the small whitewashed cell. On the door were messages written by former occupants: *I swear before God I am innocent and it will be a cruel injustice if they find me guilty.* Underneath another hand had scrawled *You lying bastard.* John Wilkins sighed.

It was remarkable how old Mr. Morton's health had improved since Sheila's death. He had come down to Lewes for the trial, he had followed the morning's proceedings with avidity, and now his knife carved away quite vigorously at his roast chicken. Bill Lonergan ate with much less enthusiasm.

"Fascinating, these details of court procedure," Mr. Morton said. "No doubt about it, there's a drama in the English courts you don't get anywhere else in the world. It's all the ceremonial, I think."

"Yes." Bill Lonergan pushed away his plate.

"You take that young man, Geoffrey Wilkins's son, he doesn't look like a murderer. And did you see the way the jury stared at him? They liked him. And why not?" Mr. Morton attacked his apple pie. "If you met him in the street you wouldn't worry about letting your daughter go around with him, would you? Eh?"

"You seem very sure he's guilty."

"I certainly am." Mr. Morton's false teeth clicked as he removed a pastry obstruction. "That's not to say he'll be found guilty, mind you. Many a murderer walking about scot-free. For drama there's nothing like a murder trial."

Bill Lonergan put down his fork and spoon. "Didn't you feel anything for Sheila at all?"

The old man looked at him in surprise. "Haven't I said I want to see her murderer punished?"

"If you'll excuse me." Lonergan got up. "Something to do in my room."

Almost alone among the people principally concerned, Uncle

Dan and old Mrs. Wilkins discussed the trial throughout the whole of lunch. Mrs. Wilkins expressed dissatisfaction with the lackadaisical attitude of Mr. Likeness and the casual cross-questioning of Magnus Newton. "And that man of yours has done nothing, nothing at all. How is he occupying his time, that is what I should like to know."

Uncle Dan's long head was on one side, his expression was gloomy. "You've seen the reports."

"The reports. They say nothing."

"Lambie's their best man."

"Best man." She snorted, a strangely masculine sound. "He seems to spend most of his time in pubs. An excuse for a drinking bout, if you ask me."

Uncle Dan's face had taken on new lines in recent weeks, his voice was weary. "Do you want me to call him off?"

"No." She looked down at her plate. "No, don't call him off."

IX

John Wilkins was not a particularly imaginative man, but the effect on him of seeing a number of people he had known coming into the witness box, holding up their hands, swearing to tell the truth about him, and then telling—what could you call it? Not lies exactly, but equally it was not the truth, unimportant incidents appeared extraordinarily magnified, and those that would have provided the key to a situation seemed to be ignored. As he stood in the dock, gripping occasionally the small spiky brass knobs that surrounded him, watching Hayley drawing on the witnesses to tell their misleading stories, the little judge taking an occasional note, he wanted to call out, "Stop all this nonsensical question and answer game, just listen to *me* for a few minutes, I can tell you what really happened." At other times he mentally threw up his hands in a gesture of despair, feeling that he was like a man who had got on to an express train going the wrong way, and that any little protest he might make must be hopelessly feeble.

He felt like this particularly as the prosecution painstakingly traced his movements on that Monday afternoon, each witness adding an outline, a brush stroke, a few blobs of colour to the picture that was being built up, the picture of John Wilkins as a man driven to violent, atrocious action by his frustrated passion for Sheila Morton. Here was that slick-haired young hotel receptionist telling them of his two calls at the Langland, of his embarrassment on the first occasion and his self-confidence on the second. And here was blond Leslie Jackson, telling first of his behaviour at the tennis club, of the way in which he had pursued Sheila and pestered her. Surely that was not, could not be, true?

"What was your attitude towards the prisoner's pursuit of Miss Morton?" asked Hayley's junior, suavely elegant Maurice Mallin-Fry.

"I didn't think much about it," Jackson said. "Sheila and I weren't formally engaged then, so I hadn't much right to say anything."

"You did not regard Wilkins as a serious rival?"

Jackson's mouth twisted in a laugh gone sour. "I didn't. He was too silly for that. It was just like having a dog round you all the time. Sheila thought so too. She said—"

Charlie Hudnutt was on his feet, but the judge had already intervened. "You must not tell us what Miss Morton thought or said to you. Confine yourself to your own observation."

"Yes, just answer the questions," Maurice Mallin-Fry said cheerfully, and went on to ask Jackson about the visit to the hotel. Was that true, John Wilkins wondered, had he been like a pestering dog? He listened with the same sense of unreality to the things Jackson was saying about his behaviour at the hotel.

"Did anything about him strike you particularly?"

"Yes. He had obviously had quite a lot to drink."

"Would you say he was drunk?"

"Oh no. But his manner was much more free and easy than usual, and his voice was louder. Generally he was rather—restrained, you might call it."

"And what was his reaction when Miss Morton told him of your engagement?"

"He looked like a sheep hit by a pole-axe," Jackson said contemptuously. Mallin-Fry frowned a little.

"Was he shocked by the news?"

"He certainly was. Dazed, as though he couldn't take it in."

"And then he went out to have a drink with Mr. Lonergan. Before that, was anything said in the prisoner's presence?"

"Yes. Sheila was invited to go out for a drink, and said she couldn't go until the nurse came. Then she wanted to go for a walk on her own, because she wanted to get away from everybody and everything."

"The prisoner was there when this was said?"

"Yes."

"Did anything special happen when they said good-bye?"

"Yes. Wilkins took hold of her hand and didn't let go. She almost had to drag it away from him."

Hard, breezy Charlie Hudnutt cross-examined. He was a bit caustic about the exact length of time that John Wilkins had held Sheila Morton's hand, suggested that pole-axed sheep don't usually commit murder, and established that in spite of his dazed condition the prisoner had offered congratulations to the happy couple.

Followed Mr. Morton, wearing a polka dot tie and looking remarkably spry and jaunty, but really with little to say except to confirm the strangeness of the prisoner's manner on that visit to the hotel. Followed Bill Lonergan, his crew-cut hair sticking up like pins, his gaze directed every which way, at the judge, at counsel examining him, at the pink silk lampshade, anywhere but at the figure in the dock. And what Bill Lonergan had to say, John Wilkins vaguely realised, was damaging to him. He had said things in that pub which he should not have said, would not have said but for the shock of hearing about Sheila's engagement.

When they went to have a drink, had Wilkins seemed upset, Mallin-Fry was asking? Yes, he had. In the pub he had drunk whisky. Was he drunk? No, quite coherent, but excited. Had he said anything specific about Sheila Morton? Bill Lonergan's tongue came out and touched his lips.

"Why, yes. He said Jackson was not good enough for her. He said—he said it was a shock to Sheila when she found out that he was married. He said she had been pretty keen on him, and he'd had a job to keep her away."

"Can you remember the exact words, Mr. Lonergan?"

The sweat stood out on Bill Lonergan's forehead. "Something like this. He said, 'I shouldn't have done it, I suppose'—"

"That is, shouldn't have gone about with Miss Morton without telling her he was married."

"Yes. 'Shouldn't have done it, but my wife's a bitch. When Sheila found out I was married she was upset, but before that there was no stopping her.'" He hesitated. "He implied that Sheila had been his mistress. I told him to shut up."

There was little room for cross-examination, but Charlie Hudnutt did his best. "You were engaged to Sheila Morton yourself at one time, Mr. Lonergan?"

Bill Lonergan looked surprised. "In a way. We were both pretty young, and it wasn't a formal engagement."

"Did you break it off, or did she?"

"Mutual consent, I should say. It wasn't that serious."

"When the prisoner began to talk about her you were angry because of your feeling for Miss Morton?"

"I suppose I was. I knew it wasn't true. Sheila wasn't that kind of a girl."

Charlie Hudnutt switched abruptly. He asked if Wilkins

had shown the slightest intention of committing an act of violence, whether he had been violent in his youth, whether he had seemed angry with Sheila. To all these questions Bill Lonergan returned, for what they were worth, negative answers.

X

"A half pint of mild and bitter, please," said little Mr. Lambie. He stared sadly at the drink when it came, sipped it, and then began the task of finding out from another publican whether he had seen John Wilkins on the night of Monday, June the fourth.

Edward Lambie did not look much like the ferret of Captain Spaulding's description. He looked, rather, like a clerk in an insurance company, one who has missed promotion and knows that life holds nothing for him now but a steady descent to the grave. His features were insignificant and almost shapeless, but somehow melancholy. His clothes were respectable, a bowler hat, fawn raincoat, pin-stripe suit, but without being worn out they gave an impression of shabbiness. Mr. Lambie had never had much luck in his life—not much luck of any kind, good or bad. When he left the grammar school where, naturally, he was known as Baa Lamb, he became a clerk in a small engineering firm.

At the death of his parents he left this job and used the few hundred pounds they had left him to start a sports shop. The sports shop was on its last legs when the war came and saved Mr. Lambie from the need to worry about what he was going to do next. He volunteered at once, served for seven years with no particular distinction. When the war was over Mr. Lambie, who had during the sports shop period collected a wife and child, drifted into a variety of jobs, most of which he kept for only a few weeks. He had been employed by Captain Spaulding now for two years, a length of office which might be attributed equally perhaps to the fact that he was prepared to work for low wages, and to a dreary pertinacity in him that did sometimes produce surprisingly good results. Not that, in general, the results could be either good or bad, since it was usually just a matter of obtaining divorce evidence—evidence which sometimes, as Mr. Lambie said to his wife, made you wonder what the world was coming to.

Mr. Lambie had had an unproductive couple of days in which he had drunk a great deal of beer, which in a quiet way he rather liked, and asked a lot of questions. Now he had come back to the Toll Gate, his starting-point.

"You're absolutely sure, aren't you, Mr. Holloway, that Mr. Wilkins never said anything about where he was going?"

Mr. Holloway, red-faced and beefy, drew a pint. "Absolutely sure."

"And he left here about a quarter past nine, that's right?"

"That's right."

"He didn't say anything like 'I'm going to have another one round the corner' or 'I've just remembered an appointment,' did he?" Lambie asked hopelessly.

"Now, look, I want to be helpful. I'm not a man who says 'Clear off, I've told it all to the police.' Not me. I like to help everybody. But I've told it all to you before. I'll say it just once more and that's the end of it, understand? He came in here about a quarter to nine, maybe just after. He was well-loaded, but no more than that, or if he was he didn't show it. He had two whiskies, he talked a bit to me and a

couple of other people in the bar, and about a quarter past
nine he went out."

"You don't remember anything about the conversation?"

"I said that's an end of it." The big man moved away up to
the other end of the bar. Mr. Lambie contemplated his beer.
A hand touched his shoulder. He turned, and confronted a
villainous-looking old man, with a cunning eye, grey hair
dyed a patchy brown, and brown moustaches stained nicotine
yellow in the middle.

"Forgive me butting in, sir. Couldn't help overhearing.
You're making inquiries about this fellow on trial now at
Lewes."

"That's right." There was something obscurely military
about the old man's appearance, something that reminded
Mr. Lambie of an ancient, immensely decayed Captain
Spaulding.

"Might be able to help you. Happened to be in here
when that chappie was having his drink." The old man
smiled, showing a mouth full of rotten teeth, and expelled
his whisky-tobacco breath at Lambie. "Major Mortimer,
R.A.S.C., retired."

"My name's Lambie." He suddenly became aware that
his companion's glass was empty and that he was drumming
with his fingers on the bar. "What's that you're drinking?"

"Large whisky and splash." The major downed half his
drink at a gulp, and wiped his moustache. "Yes, I had the
privilege of speaking to our mutual friend, shall we call him,
and gave him a little advice."

"You haven't been to the police?"

"I have not, sir. What's the point? This isn't a hostelry
I often favour, and they haven't sought me out. But you,
now—you want to know where this feller went when he left
here. I might be able to tell you."

"Yes?" Mr. Lambie found it difficult not to move back from the rotten teeth and the whisky breath.

"There's no taste in nothing. What's it worth to you? Is it worth a tenner?"

"Good gracious, no." Mr. Lambie was scandalised. "I had thought—"

"Yes?"

"I had thought of buying you another drink."

Major Mortimer laughed heartily. "You're a good chap. Come on now, what's it worth? Can't be worth less than five smackers, surely?"

"If you like to tell me what you know, I can say what it's worth."

"Oh, no, no. Can't catch an old bird with that kind of chaff. Softly softly, catchee monkee, eh?" Mr. Lambie watched in fascination as Major Mortimer's withered Adam's apple moved up and down, signifying his consumption of more whisky. He was in a difficult position. On one hand Captain Spaulding grudged spending money on this kind of thing, on the other he was reluctant to let pass the first apparent clue to John Wilkins's movements. Something told him to go on bargaining. He did so, a pound note changed hands, and Major Mortimer told his story.

"He was in here, this feller, and a bit the worse for wear, you might say. Talking about his wife, how she was no good to him, that kind of stuff. Something about this other kid, Sheila, seems she'd done him down in some way. Between the two of them the poor chap was out on his feet. Only one remedy for that kind of thing, I remember when we were out at Poona in twenty-seven there was a lot of unrest among the men, one thing and another. Only one thing for it. Arranged trips to the local red light district, nothing damn' well voluntary about it either, proper parade you understand, C.O.'s orders. Marched 'em down, went in by numbers, had no trouble with 'em afterwards."

"I don't quite see what that's got to do with Wilkins."

"Same problem, old man. Wanted a woman, to quieten him down. Told him so, and told him where to go too."

"You mean—"

"Little pub in Kemp Town, place called the Diving Bell, you get all sorts in there. Take it from me, old chap. I *know*." There was something really horrifying about the leer which Major Mortimer now gave Mr. Lambie.

"And you suggested he should go up to this place? You don't know if he went."

"Don't precisely know, old chap. But from my knowledge of human nature, which is pretty considerable—he did."

It was five minutes to ten when Mr. Lambie came out of the Toll Gate. He wondered whether he had wasted the pound. It was in any case too late, he said to himself thankfully, to trail up to Kemp Town to-night on what was very likely a wild goose chase. He walked back to his boarding-house, kissed the photograph of his wife as he did every night, and went to bed.

XI

The most important witness for the prosecution, Magnus Newton had said to Charlie Hudnutt in discussing the case, was the scientist Ritchie. But before the important Mr. Ritchie there was another witness who was by no means unimportant. His name was Fanum, and he was a thin, nervous man in his sixties with pince-nez perched uncertainly on his nose. He had been to visit a friend in Hove, he told Hayley, and had been walking back along the promenade. At twenty minutes to twelve he had heard, from the direction of the beach, a terrible laugh. What had it been like? It was like nothing, Mr. Fanum said, that he had ever heard, a wild howl like that of a wolf or the keening of a dog, which was yet in some extraordinary way a laugh.

He seemed prepared to elaborate on this, but Hayley managed to prevent him from doing so. Mr. Fanum had then seen a man walk up the stone steps from the beach. His face was of a ghastly pallor, and he had staggered as though ill or drunk. The man had gone on in the direction of John Wilkins's hotel.

"You saw this man under a street lamp?" Hayley asked.

"That is so, sir."

"The light was quite a bright one."

"Quite bright. The lighting along there is very good."

"You later picked out the prisoner as the man you saw, at an identification parade?"

"That is so."

"And you have no doubt of the identification?"

Very firmly Mr. Fanum answered, "None at all, sir."

Puffing a little, Magnus Newton rose to cross-examine. "You are an—um—retired architect, Mr. Fanum. And you had been visiting your friend Mr.—um—Royston, I think you said. What had you been doing in his company?"

"We had supper, then a game of billiards."

"Supper and a game of billiards, yes. Anything to drink?"

"Just a bottle of beer, you know. I never take more than a bottle of beer."

"I am glad to hear it, Mr. Fanum." Mr. Newton and Mr. Fanum smiled and bobbed at each other. Mr. Fanum's pince-nez dropped off and he stooped to pick them up, a little flustered. "And you say you left Mr. Royston's house at half past eleven. How can you be so sure of the time?"

Mr. Fanum looked offended. "I looked at my watch. My watch is never wrong."

"*Never* wrong, Mr. Fanum? Has it never been so much as five minutes fast or slow?"

"Not in twenty-five years," said Fanum triumphantly.

"So that you are absolutely sure the time was exactly twenty minutes to twelve when you saw this man."

Mr. Fanum wagged a finger. "Not *exactly*, sir. I should allow a margin of—let me see—two minutes on either side."

"But the time could not possibly have been half past eleven when you saw him."

"No, certainly not." Mr. Fanum appeared scandalised by the suggestion. More smiling and bobbing.

"Then you heard this remarkable sound. Could you, again, say what it was like?"

Mr. Fanum leaned forward eagerly on the ledge of the box. "It was like the laugh of a hyena when it has its prey at its mercy."

There was a faint murmur in court, that might have been laughter. "I am obliged," Newton said. "When were you last in Africa?"

"In Africa." Mr. Fanum gave a brief giggle, sharply cut off. "I have never been outside England in my life."

"Really?" Newton rocked backwards and forwards, considering. "Then how do you know what a hyena sounds like when crouched above its prey?"

"I—well—" Mr. Fanum took off his pince-nez and rubbed them, quite at a loss. Hayley rose to his rescue.

"My lord, I don't see the force of this line of questioning. Mr. Fanum heard some sound which drew his attention to the beach. Surely its exact nature is not important—we are prepared to agree that it cannot be established."

"I don't wish to appear obstinate, my lord, but I think it is," Newton persisted. "Mr. Fanum heard this remarkable sound, then a minute or two later he saw a man whom he has identified as the prisoner come up from the beach. The connection between the two things is obviously of interest."

The judge coughed. "Yes, I think so. Continue your questioning."

"Now, Mr. Fanum, perhaps we can get some more exact idea of this sound. You are sure it was a laugh?"

"Yes, I think so," said Mr. Fanum, very unsurely.

"It could not possibly have been, for instance, a girl screaming for help?"

"Certainly not, nothing like that."

"I am obliged. Was it a laugh like this?" Newton vented a deep ho-ho-ho of false enjoyment.

"Oh no, not at all like that. That wouldn't have frightened me."

"The laugh frightened you, did it, Mr. Fanum?"

"It made my blood run cold," Mr. Fanum said with an air of triumphant originality, and giggled again.

He's really turning this one inside out, Mr. Likeness thought, and doing it beautifully too, so that the old fool thinks he's doing well and the jury can see that he *is* an old fool. His hand wandered to his nose and he began to pick it, which was a thing he very rarely did in court.

"Supposing that you had not heard this strange sound, are you quite sure you would have noticed the figure coming up from the beach?"

"Oh yes. No doubt about it."

"Why?" Mr. Fanum goggled at him. "Why would you have noticed him? What was there so remarkable in his appearance?"

"He staggered a little. His face was very pale. He was muttering to himself—"

"You have not mentioned that before," Newton said sharply.

"I—why, no. It's just come to me."

"Do you mean that he was muttering words you could hear? Or just that you saw his lips moving?"

"I didn't hear any words." Mr. Fanum jammed his pince-nez down on his nose defiantly.

"Then you say that his face was pale. Do you know that the light under which you saw him was fluorescent, and that under such a light everybody—you and I and everyone else in this courtroom—would take on a most unpleasing pallor?"

"I—well, I didn't notice."

"So that this person under the lamp could have looked

no paler than you looked yourself." Newton rocked again on his heels. "What suit was this man wearing?"

"He was wearing a sports jacket and trousers."

"Of what colour?"

Mr. Fanum spread out his hands in agitation. "I couldn't exactly say."

"Ah. Was there any blood on them?"

"I couldn't say. The light was not good enough—"

"The light was not good enough. But it was good enough for you to recognise the prisoner, a man whom you had never seen before. How far were you from him?"

"About five or six feet."

"And how long did you see his face? Would you say— since you're so exact about time, Mr. Fanum—would you say five seconds?"

"Well, I don't know."

"In any case, it was no more than the time it took him to walk past you. In that time you identified him." Newton thrust his head forward. "Mr. Fanum, did you see photographs of the prisoner in the papers before you made your identification?"

"I may have done, I really don't know." Mr. Fanum looked as if he were going to cry.

"Mr. Fanum, I suggest to you that you were walking along and you heard this very unnerving laugh—which you can't exactly identify except to say that it *was* unnerving—and then you saw somebody coming up from the beach. If you had not heard the laugh, you would not have given the man a second glance. Isn't that so?"

Mr. Fanum looked at him with dazed incomprehension. "It was a murderer's laugh. That laugh had in it the colour of murder."

"That laugh had in it the colour of murder," Newton repeated, savouring the meaningless phrase, making sure the jury took it in too. "So naturally the next person you saw must be a murderer. And John Wilkins, who happened to be wearing a sports jacket like thousands of other people in Brighton—do you agree now that you can't swear to the identification?"

"I still think I saw him." Mr. Fanum pushed his pince-nez lop-sided on his nose and looked at the prisoner. "And I tell you this—that laugh had the colour of murder in it."

Why, Hayley wondered as he rose to re-examine, without much hope that he could eradicate the impression of ineffable foolishness suggested by Mr. Fanum, why are witnesses with a perfectly straightforward story to tell so stupid?

XII

"Your chap did pretty well this afternoon," said Robin Pinkney.

"I hope so." Mr. Likeness, that perpetual small smile on his crumpled yellow face, sighted carefully down his cue at the only red left on the table, and cut it sharply into the top pocket. "He certainly made Fanum look an absolute fool. Was that a good thing to do? I expect it was."

Pinkney looked at him curiously. "It's not like you to have doubts."

The yellow was an easy ball. Mr. Likeness screwed back beautifully to obtain perfect position on the green. "You're right there, Rob. It's going well, and Newton's pretty good. I've got a feeling, though—"

"What sort of a feeling?"

"I don't know." He played a delicate stroke which put the cue ball just behind the pink, a difficult snooker. "The fact is, he's an uncomfortable young man to have around, this young Wilkins."

"You mean you feel sorry for him?" Pinkney tried to get out of the snooker, failed and swore.

"Not exactly. In fact, he's pretty unattractive. But there's a kind of innocence about him—"

"He didn't do it, you mean?"

"I don't know what I do mean," said Mr. Likeness pettishly, and took brown, blue, pink and black on this visit to the table.

"There's nothing innocent about *you* when it comes to playing snooker," Robin Pinkney said. "That's ten bob I owe you, and quite enough. Let's go along to the bar."

● ● ● ● ●

Magnus Newton also was obscurely disturbed, and tried to say something of what he felt to Charlie Hudnutt. That briskly cynical young man, however, persisted in considering his senior's expressions of doubt as mock-modesty after his success that afternoon. After dinner Newton left him, and rang up his wife at their home in Hampton Court. He learned that their only child, ten-year-old Viola, who had a severe attack of mumps, was no better. Newton adored the child, and wondered if worry about her condition was the cause of his own disquiet.

Rather to his surprise he found himself, on his return to the hotel lounge, seeking out the company of Doctor Andreadis. The doctor had been told that, unless some unforeseen move was made by the prosecution, he would not be called as a witness. Nevertheless he had appeared that afternoon, a handsome and debonair figure looking (thought Newton, who was a devotee of both theatre and cinema) rather less like a doctor than like Anton Walbrook playing the part of a doctor in some Hollywood drama. Now Andreadis greeted him with a grave but brilliant smile. Newton dropped into a chair beside him.

"Good of you to come down, Doctor. Staying for the whole trial?"

"I think so. The case interests me. This young man—there

is something interesting in his personality." The doctor waved an elegant hand.

"Yes?" Newton found himself waiting with a certain tense-ness for what Andreadis was going to say.

"I don't know exactly how to express it. He is almost, it would seem, a predestined victim. I mean that whether or not he killed this girl, he is the kind of man who is made the scapegoat for such a killing."

At most times Newton would have dismissed such talk as nonsense. On this particular night, however, something must have made him susceptible to it, for he merely nodded thoughtfully.

"Take that statement he made to me. It is an attempt to tell the truth, of that I am convinced. Yet if you put him in the witness box—"

"*When* we put him in the witness box."

"It is decided, then. When you put him in the witness box he will again tell the truth, according to his lights. And you say that will be fatal to him."

Newton began to pace the floor as if he were in his chambers, and became aware that people were looking at him. "Damn it," he said irritably, "can't talk here. Will you come up to my room, if you've got five minutes."

In the impersonal hotel room Newton poured himself a drink of whisky and Andreadis a glass of tonic water. "I owe you an apology. Last time we met I was pretty sharp about the MacNaughton rules and so on. I'm sorry."

"It was nothing."

"Don't know why I feel as I do about this case. Everything went well to-day, wouldn't you say that?"

"I admired your skill."

"Yet I've got a feeling—I don't know." Newton charged

about the room, head down, like a little red-faced bullock. "My young daughter's ill with mumps, face puffed out like a balloon, very painful. Do you think that's what's worrying me?"

"It is possible." Andreadis leaned back in his chair, relaxed. "But no, I do not think that is what is worrying you."

"Neither do I. Look here, Doctor, this man has talked to you as he won't talk to me. What do you think about him?"

"I have told you that he suffers from a feeling of inferiority. That is the basis of his actions."

"Yes, yes. But there's something wrong, Doctor. Do you understand what I mean?"

Swinging one leg lightly over the other, Andreadis said, "Perhaps. But I shall not guess. You must tell me yourself."

"Wilkins killed the wrong woman. Understand me? If he was going to kill somebody, I don't believe it would have been Sheila Morton. He loved her. But this bitch of a wife he'd got, why, there can't be any doubt that she hated him and he hated her. Do you know why Wilkins wanted me to defend him? Because I defended that negro McKenna who killed his wife."

"I thought something like that was in your mind," Andreadis said, with that expert's assumption of foreknowledge that is always infuriating to a layman.

"Now this is my problem, or one of my problems. Fanum says he saw Wilkins at twenty to twelve. The hall porter says he got back at ten to twelve. But May Wilkins says he came back and was in the hotel bedroom at twenty-five to twelve. If the jury accept that it rules out Fanum completely."

"Then I don't see the problem."

"I don't really want to call her. That's why I went all out to discredit Fanum to-day, make him look as big a fool as possible. Did I succeed? I don't know."

"Why don't you want to call her?"

"Don't know what she might say when Hayley gets at her in the box. I tell you, I believe they hate each other." Newton flew off at a tangent. "Do you believe he really can't remember about that evening?"

"Oh yes. He is a builder of fantasies, that young man. He is not capable of conscious deceit."

"He's *got* to remember. This amnesia stuff is no good for a jury. You agree with what I say, don't you? He killed the wrong woman."

Andreadis looked at Newton for a moment as if about to say something, then checked himself. "It is an interesting speculation. But psychologically there is no certainty in these matters."

"Psychology's a dead loss as far as the criminal courts are concerned. Look here, will you go and see him again, try and make him talk? I'd feel a lot happier if you would."

Andreadis agreed. "But you still don't look very happy."

"No. Damn it," Newton said irritably, "I wish my daughter were better."

XIII

It was lunch-time on the following day when Mr. Lambie went into the Diving Bell. Inside, the pub was flashy but seedy. The red Rexine bar-stools were shabby, there were beer stains on the little tables.

He had hoped to eat a hot lunch here, but compromised on pork pie, a faded salad, and half a pint of bitter. He perched himself awkwardly on one of the Rexine stools and said to the blousy barmaid, "Not very busy to-day."

"Too early." She polished a glass, and looked at him speculatively. He timidly invited her to have a drink, and almost before the words were out of his mouth she had poured a measure of gin, added water, and sipped. "Thanks. Good luck. One and ninepence."

Mr. Lambie reluctantly pushed a shining half-crown across the counter. "I wondered if—"

"Wednesday's my free afternoon, but I have some free time most evenings."

It was a warm day, but he shivered slightly. "As a matter of fact I really wanted to know whether a friend of mine had been in recently." He produced a photograph of John Wilkins and she looked at it with a frown of concentration on her fat face.

"Can't say I remember him, but it seems a bit familiar

somehow. I'll ask Mr. Harrison, that's the manager, he's just upstairs."

"Don't do that," Mr. Lambie said hurriedly. He had learned from long experience that it is much easier to obtain information from subordinates. "The fact is, my friend met a young lady in here a few weeks ago and left a certain article with her, by accident you might say. Do I make myself clear?"

"As mud," she said cheerfully. She served two men with beer and came back to him.

It was not Mr. Lambie's purpose to make himself very clear. "This article had a—as you might say, a sentimental value. It was a cigarette case which had been presented to him by his firm, and he's very anxious to get it back." He stuffed a piece of pie into his mouth. "Now, the fact is he'd had—ah—one over the eight that evening, and he quite honestly can't remember much about the lady in question."

"Men," the barmaid said. "Why didn't he come down himself? Couldn't face it, I suppose."

"He's up in the north at present. But the fact is, again, that his wife has been asking about the case." Mr. Lambie tittered slightly, drew out his wallet, and produced from it a ten-shilling note which he held between thumb and index finger. "I wondered if you might be able to tell me the lady's name."

"Could have been one of half a dozen. Didn't he tell you anything about her, tall or short, dark or fair? You don't know much, do you? Sure *you* aren't your old friend, are you?" Mr. Lambie drank the last of his beer with an affectation of confusion. "You quiet ones are always the worst. This is strictly against the rules, you know, this kind of thing. If the guvnor caught me I don't know what he'd say." She leaned forward and took the note from his fingers. "Has that one got a brother? You'll get what you came for, don't worry. Got a bit of paper?"

She began to write on a sheet torn by Mr. Lambie out of his reporters' notebook. "Here you are, three friends of mine, two blondes and one brunette. Mind you, these are ladies."

"And they all come in here during the evening?" he asked, a shade too eagerly.

"Most evenings, yes. What is it you're after, I should like to know. Still, I suppose it's no skin off my nose. *Has* it got a brother now?"

Reluctantly, and with the feeling that there must have been some better and cheaper means of achieving his end, Mr. Lambie handed her another ten-shilling note.

He spent an appalling afternoon, calling on Miss Millie Tyre, Miss Olivia Lawrence and Miss Betty Prenton. Miss Tyre called herself a masseuse, and was in her forties. The photograph meant nothing to her, but she offered to give Mr. Lambie a full body massage, stimulating and invigorating, for two guineas. Miss Olivia Lawrence called herself a model, and received him in a room that had a camera and a backcloth in it. She recognised the photograph immediately as that of John Wilkins, on trial for murder, and asked if he was a nark.

"I am a private investigator," Mr. Lambie said bravely. "There is reason to believe that this young man visited the Diving Bell on the evening that the crime was committed."

"You're a nark. Get out."

"It won't hurt you to say if you saw him. I'm not asking anything more than that."

"Anything connected with narks hurts me. I hate a nark." She put two fingers to her lips and blew. A man almost as insignificant as Mr. Lambie appeared in the doorway. There was one difference between them. This man carried a knife.

"Nark," said Miss Lawrence. "Calls himself private. Wants to know about that girl done in on Brighton beach."

The man jerked his thumb. "Get."

"You're being most unreasonable." Mr. Lambie's voice was an indignant bleat. "I would pay for information—"

"She's a model, gets five guineas an hour. You pay that? Then get."

Mr. Lambie got. A few minutes later, drinking a refreshing cup of tea in a café, he asked himself, as he had done often before, whether it was really worthwhile. If he spent money he would be blamed by Captain Spaulding, if he didn't he would get no information. He had to deal with beastly people living sordid lives. And, worst of all, the whole thing was probably a mare's nest, depending as it did upon the word of one drunken sot who might very likely have been lying.

It says something for that pertinacity which was Mr. Lambie's only, but considerable, virtue as an investigator that when he had had another cup of tea and eaten a Bath bun he telephoned Miss Betty Prenton.

Miss Prenton lived on the second floor of a small block of flats, and apparently did not call herself either masseuse or model. She received him wearing a dressing-gown, and smoking a cigarette in a long holder. The room into which she showed him contained a bed, a gas-fire which was full on, making the room stiflingly hot, and a number of photographs. The curtains were drawn.

Her manner was brisk, business-like, and somehow ascetic. "My fee is three pounds. Put it on the mantelpiece, please, and then take off your clothes."

"No no." Mr. Lambie gripped his jacket as though it afforded some kind of protection. "I'm not here for—for that. I just want a little information."

"Don't be shy. Just put the money on the mantelpiece and come here." Miss Prenton began to take off the dressing-gown and revealed that she was wearing nothing underneath it.

"*Please*," Mr. Lambie said. He closed his eyes and opened them again to the unexpected sound of laughter.

"If you could see your face. Don't worry, little man, just turn round. I'll get dressed." When he turned round again he saw that she had put on a blouse and a grey coat and skirt. She regarded him with an amused and slightly pitying look. "You certainly do meet all kinds. What do you want?"

Mr. Lambie had but one approach. He drew the photograph from his pocket. At sight of it she exclaimed sharply. "Do you know this man?" he asked.

"I know that picture. He's the chap on trial now at Lewes for doing a girl in. What are you showing it to me for?"

"I'm trying to trace his movements on the night of the murder. I believe he was in the Diving Bell."

"You do, do you?" She stubbed out the cigarette from her holder and stood looking down at him, a big woman with platinum hair and a hard, intelligent face. "And what's that to me?"

"If you met him there," Mr. Lambie said falteringly. "If you know anything about him—if he came home with you—there might be a reward in it for you."

"What sort of a reward, a fiver?"

With a sinking heart—what would Captain Spaulding say?—he said, "It might be as much as that."

"And what's the use of that to me?" She strode across the room, pulled back the curtains. "I make thirty quid a week here most weeks. And I like what I'm doing, you understand that? I get thirty quid a week for doing what I like, what I'd be doing for free anyway, can you beat that? And you offer me a fiver."

"But you can't *like* it." Mr. Lambie was scandalised. "I mean you're in a sense, well, an outcast from society, you can't like that."

"——— society," she said, and snapped her fingers. "Do you think I want to talk to the silly bitches who haven't got an idea in their heads beyond marriage and children and housekeeping? Wasn't it Bernard Shaw who said that marriage is licensed prostitution without payment?" Mr. Lambie shook his head feebly to indicate that he did not know. "To me, sex is a career like any other, and if you can keep away from gangs and ponces it's a good one. I'm thirty-three now. When I'm forty I shall retire. I shall have made my pile, and how many women, or men either, can say that at the age of forty? Let's have a cup of coffee, shall we?"

Mr. Lambie contemplated her broad back. "After you retire won't it be difficult to—settle down?"

"You've got a point there. These are the good years now. After forty I'll have to find something to occupy my time. Learn embroidery, buy a little business, something like that. One thing I shan't do, though, get married. If you ask me, marriage is against nature. Staying with the same man all your life, it's just not common sense. Take sugar?"

"Two lumps, please. About John Wilkins," Mr. Lambie said, as he sipped his coffee in a gentlemanly way.

"To hell with John Wilkins. What's your interest in him?" She sat with her well-shaped legs stuck out in front of her, contemplating them gloomily, while he told her. "It's all wrong, the way life's organised. Why should I have to look after John Wilkins?"

"You saw him that night? He came here?" He could not prevent eagerness from entering his voice.

"Yes. Picked him up in the Diving Bell. I felt sorry for him. It's a mistake to feel sorry for people. Where does it get you?"

"And he stayed here—how long?"

"He left just after eleven. I had a client coming. He wanted a shoulder to lean on, that was all, and I gave him mine. Nothing else happened, any more than it did with you, little man. Never again, though, never again."

"Did he make that gash on his thumb here?"

She hooted with laughter. "I gave him baked beans on toast. Like a gentleman he opened the tin for me, cut his thumb on it."

"Did the blood from it go on his jacket?"

"Oh, hell, I can't remember," she said wearily. "I think so, but I just can't remember."

"It's important."

"You don't have to tell me. I read the newspaper reports. I just can't remember, that's all."

Mr. Lambie felt a rare indignation rising slowly in him, an indignation that was obscurely connected with the shocking things this woman had been saying. "It's your duty to give evidence." She said nothing. "Do you want to see an innocent man put in prison for the rest of his life?"

She turned on him fiercely. "How do you know he's innocent? He had time to do her in after he left me. And what about me? He's been fool enough to marry a woman he hates and then to go yearning after a silly little fool who was just a —— at heart." She used a phrase that made Mr. Lambie flinch. "Oh, he told me all about them both while he was crying on the bed. But what's this going to do to me if I give evidence? First, nobody's going to believe me. Second, the police will love me, won't they, for trying to make a muck of their case, they just love that kind of thing from someone like me. Third, it's the end of my business here. Do you think respectable people are going to come along to see someone who's been mixed up in a murder case?"

Mr. Lambie got up and faced her. He did not flinch, although he felt as much trepidation as if he had been in a cage with a lioness. "It is your duty."

"Can't."

"And I believe you know it."

She looked at a wrist-watch. "You'll have to go, I've got a client coming. And if it's of any interest to you, for once I'm not in the mood."

"I'm sorry. You'll come along with me to-morrow morning."

"I'll *what?*" It was as though the lioness had put a paw through the bars of her cage.

"To the defence solicitor."

"You mean you expect me to—" The claws were almost on him. Mr. Lambie did not flinch.

"Yes. It's your duty."

"I'll be damned. You've got a nerve. I almost admire you. Now clear out."

"You'll come with me to-morrow?"

"How the hell do I know?" she suddenly shouted at him. "I told you I've got somebody coming. Do you want to run me ragged so that I don't know what I'm doing? Ring up."

"I'll ring later on to-night."

"Not to-night, to-morrow morning. You want me to ruin myself, you might give me the night to think it over. To-morrow morning."

"At ten o'clock."

"Have a heart. Remember some of us have to work at night. Eleven." He picked up his hat and raincoat and was at the door when she stopped him. "Hey. What's your name?"

He told her. She put out a hand and touched his face. He felt that the claws were about to rake his cheek, but she merely patted it and turned away. "Lambie, that's a good name. I like you, little Lambie."

What did it all amount to, Mr. Lambie wondered afterwards, writing the report in his boarding-house bedroom? He couldn't be sure. That night he looked at the photograph of his wife for a few seconds before he kissed it. He also said a prayer before getting into bed.

XIV

"If I can break the hall porter as well," Magnus Newton said to Charlie Hudnutt, "then perhaps we need not call the wife." But Charlie Hudnutt didn't agree with him, thought that his fears about May Wilkins were exaggerated. After all, he had said reasonably enough, if she'd wanted to do her husband dirt she need never have said anything at all about the time he got in. Newton could say what he liked about having discredited Fanum, but you could never be quite sure how much a jury was accepting and rejecting of a witness's cross-examination. If they called May, that should at least put the finishing touch to Fanum. Granted it didn't mean that Wilkins was in the clear, or anything like that, but wasn't it foolish to ignore a witness who could at least cast some doubt on the evidence given by Fanum and the porter. But of course, Charlie Hudnutt added hastily, feeling that he had let exuberance carry him a little far, of course it was up to Newton. Magnus Newton grunted and said that he was aware of it.

The hall porter was a square, solid man in his sixties named Shaddock, and his story was simple enough. He had been on duty in the hall when Wilkins came in, swaying and obviously drunk. Shaddock was a little worried as to whether Wilkins would press the right button in the self-operating lift, and had asked if he would like to be taken up. Wilkins said he could manage on his own. Shaddock had then glanced up at the clock, and seen that the time was ten minutes to twelve.

There seemed little room for casting doubt on the story, let alone breaking it, but Newton was armed with one possibly useful piece of information furnished by Mr. Likeness, who had gone to the length of visiting the Prince Regent hotel in person. The cross-examination began quietly.

"You were on duty this Monday evening and you were sitting—now, just where were you sitting in the hall?"

"In my cubby hole, sir. That's just round to the left as you go in." Shaddock's heavy, moustached face might have been devised for concealing emotion of any kind.

"Round to the left, yes. Then Wilkins came in and you thought he was drunk. Why?"

"He was swaying, sir, and his eyes were glassy-like."

"Then you asked if he would like to be taken up, and he said no. Was his speech slurred?"

Shaddock considered. "Wouldn't say it was, sir. Only spoke a few words, though."

"And in fact he got up to his room without trouble."

"That's so, sir. Course, he only had to press the right button."

"Quite so. Now, had you moved from your cubby hole during this time?"

"No, sir, I hadn't moved."

"You saw the clock, and noted the time."

"That's right, sir."

"But the clock is round to your right. It is concealed from view by the hall doors. How could you possibly see it?"

Shaddock ruminated, chewing his moustache. "There's a mirror in front of me. Clock's reflected in that."

"So that what you saw was merely the reflection of the clock, with the hands the wrong way round?"

"That's right, sir."

"And what time did it show?"

Shaddock ruminated again, unperturbed. "Why, sir, you might say it showed the time as ten past twelve, that's the way it might look to someone who didn't know it. But I knew it was ten to the hour, see?"

"Mr. Shaddock," Newton said softly, "does it occur to you that this is a very unreliable way of telling the time? To look at a clock-face in reverse—do you really think that is satisfactory?"

Shaddock considered. "Yes, sir," he said at last. "Seeing that I've done it so often."

"Supposing another witness said that Wilkins had come into the hotel at twenty-five minutes to twelve, what would you say then—remembering that you did not see the clock, but merely its reflection in a mirror?"

This was Shaddock's longest ruminative period. At the end of it he said, "I should say they were mistaken, sir."

Try as he would—and he cast round and made three or four different approaches—Newton could get no farther. Shaddock insisted that the clock was perfectly accurate, checked every day by the wireless, and that he had looked at the mirror reflection so often that he could not possibly be mistaken. At the end of the cross-examination Newton had decided (or almost decided) that he must call May Wilkins as a witness.

XV

The evidence of Ritchie—that is, of Kenneth George Norman Ritchie, head of the South-Eastern Forensic Science Laboratory at Maidstone—was regarded by both prosecution and defence as the most important single feature of the case. If the jury took Ritchie's evidence at its face value, they were almost certain to convict. If Newton managed to cast some doubt on it, that would be a great stroke in the prisoner's favour. One of the problems facing the prosecution was, as it always is when expert scientific evidence is involved, that of making Ritchie's statements about the blood on John Wilkins's clothing intelligible to the jury.

There were two small dark patches on the left sleeve of Wilkins's jacket and two on the left leg of his trousers. These were visible, and had been proved to be blood by standard tests. But in the laboratories Ritchie had performed a further test, known as the benzidine test, on Wilkins's clothing, and this had revealed the presence of minute traces of blood upon other parts of the jacket, both legs of the trousers, and the shoes. Smoothly, Hayley led Ritchie through his preliminary evidence. Not, indeed, that this back-room boy needed much leading. Ritchie was a tall man with rather longish fair hair that occasionally fell over his forehead, a fine aggressive nose, and an immensely self-confident manner. Yes, he agreed, there were two dark patches on the jacket and two on the trousers that had responded to the usual blood tests.

"You can positively say that these are bloodstains."

"Quite positively."

"And that they are recent?"

"They had been made very recently when I examined them."

"It has been suggested that the stains came from the prisoner's own thumb, which he had cut. Would you say that was possible?"

"They were certainly of his blood group. I should say, however, having regard to the comparatively small cut and the nature and position of the stains, that it is most unlikely."

Jacket and trousers were now taken out of the brown-paper parcels in which important evidence is traditionally kept, and handed round to the jury, who saw for themselves the stains that might help to keep a man in prison for years.

"You then made an examination for further bloodstains by means of the benzidine test. Will you explain just what the benzidine test is?"

Ritchie pushed back his lock of hair and looked first at the judge, a midget in scarlet, then at the jury stolidly awaiting light on their darkness, finally at red-faced country-man Hayley expectantly awaiting his performance. This was Ritchie's moment, and he gave every indication of enjoying it.

"The benzidine test is a simple and effective colour test for the presence of blood. It depends on the fact that there is a substance in the blood-colouring matter which in the presence of hydrogen peroxide causes a rapid oxidation of these various bases to coloured salts."

"And how is the test carried out?"

"We take a section of the material to be tested, press a

piece of white filter paper slightly moistened with water on to it, and add a drop of the benzidine reagent. The presence of blood is indicated by the immediate production of a blue colour which radiates out into the filter paper."

"Thank you," said Hayley. Had the jury really understood the explanation, he wondered, looking at their anxious faces. Was it, even, desirable that they should completely understand it? "And when you applied the test what did you find?"

"I obtained many positive reactions on the front of the jacket, at various places down the fronts of the trousers and on the uppers of the shoes."

"That is, on very extensive areas of these articles. And by positive reactions you mean blood reactions—showing the presence of blood?"

"I do."

"Were these such traces as you would expect to find in the case of a crime committed in the open air?"

Ritchie had a long, strokable chin, and now he stroked it. "In the open air, yes. Or in any case where blood was spattered about and diffused in the atmosphere. In these cases it is quite normal for minute particles to be found in clothing by the benzidine test, although they are invisible to the naked eye."

Hayley easily leapt his most difficult hurdle. "These particles—I am not talking now about the four distinct bloodstains—are invisible to the naked eye?"

"They are."

"You can identify them quite positively, however, by the benzidine test?"

Ritchie radiated certainty. "Quite positively."

"Mr. Ritchie, how often have you carried out the benzidine test?"

"That's difficult to say." Ritchie stroked his chin, tossed back his lock of hair. "If I said five thousand times that would be a conservative estimate."

"And you have always found it an accurate test for blood?"

"In my experience it is an accurate test for blood."

Watching the jury through half-closed eyes, Magnus Newton thought that they were impressed, even deeply impressed. This is an age of specialists, and it is difficult for an ordinary man not to be impressed by their certainties, their appearance of absolute omniscience in their own field. Ritchie's evidence was damning because of the impression it gave that Wilkins's clothing was really covered with blood, jacket, trousers and shoes, an invisible shower of gore. Such is the suggestive power of the expert.

Yet this power is accompanied by a strange fallibility. The common man is ruled by the expert, certainly. He obeys the persuasive power of the propagandist in his eating, drinking, sanitary and even sexual habits, in the clothes he wears and the entertainments he attends, in his attitude towards his fellow-men and towards God. But at the heart of obedience there is the desire for revolt. There are few things the common man—represented here by these eleven very common-looking jurymen and women—desires more than to see the expert utterly discomfited. The rules that govern the conduct of modern counsel in relation to witnesses do not apply to experts. When an expert is in the box counsel may be as ruthless and destructive as he likes. The jury are on his side, they applaud the expert's occasional collapse as they are delighted when a top-hatted man slips on a banana skin. Victory over Ritchie would by no means assure John Wilkins's acquittal, but defeat by him—defeat in the sense that his arrogant certainty was left untouched—meant almost the certainty of conviction. When Newton rose to cross-examine he knew that he had reached one of the crucial points of the case.

"Mr. Ritchie, you are an accredited scientific expert, are you not?"

"The description is yours, sir. I am a scientist."

"And you have carried out the benzidine test, say five thousand times, and you regard it as an accurate test for blood."

"That is so."

"Blood produces a"—Newton, common man, searched for the right words—"a positive reaction, is that so?"

"That is correct."

"But there are other substances which produce a positive reaction to the benzidine test, are there not? Sputum produces a positive reaction."

"A reaction, yes. But not like blood."

"Pus produces a positive reaction. Some plant juices produce a positive reaction. Some metals produce a positive reaction. Do you agree?"

"Yes. But not so rapidly as blood."

Newton put thumbs in button-holes, stuck head back, chest out, gave a short barking laugh. "Urine produces a positive reaction, did you know that? So do a number of bacteria. Why, even milk produces a positive reaction. These stains, these deadly stains invisible to the naked eye, that you have discovered—why, they may be drops of milk."

"No, sir." Ritchie was polite but firm. "All these substances can produce a positive reaction, but a laboratory expert can distinguish them from the reaction of blood."

Newton glanced at the jury. They were with him, he saw, they wanted him to win. "How are they distinguishable?"

"Their reaction is less rapid than that of blood."

A false question. What was the exact time difference? Newton, whose information had been mugged up for him, did not know. Rocking backwards and forwards he decided to move to his second line of attack.

"Mr. Ritchie, we have been talking about positive reactions, but that is rather misleading, don't you think? I mean, the benzidine test is really a negative test. Do you agree?"

"It is generally regarded so, but I have found it produced very positive results."

"Mr. Newton." The judge intervened, as Newton had known that he must. "This is becoming a little too much for me, and perhaps for the jury too. Can you explain simply what you mean by a negative test?"

"I will try, my lord." Newton folded his arms and enunciated slowly and clearly. "I mean that all the text-book authorities agree that the benzidine test is valuable in a negative sense. Stains which *do not* produce a reaction can be ruled out, as not being blood. But there is not a single medical authority"—Newton tapped lightly a pile of books beneath his hand—"who would accept a positive reaction on a benzidine test as proof of blood."

The judge considered. "What have you to say to that, Mr. Ritchie?"

Ritchie smiled, perhaps a little too confidently. "I don't want to become involved in an argument with the text-books, my lord. But in my experience, which has been a very wide one, it is always possible to recognise a positive blood reaction on a benzidine test."

Mr. Justice Morland hesitated, looked at the jury, and then merely nodded. Newton opened the first of the books on the table. "I am afraid we shall have to refer to the text-books. Is Taylor's Medical Jurisprudence known to you?"

"Of course."

"It is regarded as the standard work in this field, is it not?"

"Certainly it is a standard work."

"Here is what Taylor says. 'The value of the test lies in the fact that if it is negative, the stain is not due to blood. If the test is positive the stained area is marked out for further tests which definitely prove the presence of hæmoglobin.' Do you agree with that?"

"So far as it goes, yes. These are general remarks, you understand. I am offering you the result of direct laboratory investigation."

"Which improves on Taylor?" Newton asked sweetly. "Have you published the result of your—ah—revolutionary investigations in any journal?"

"No. I am a practical scientist, not a theoretician."

"'*If the test is positive the stained area is marked out for further tests.*' Did you carry out further tests?"

"No. In these particular conditions it was not possible."

"Very well. We will move on to Gault…"

An hour later Newton paused and surveyed the heavily-battered but still impenitent expert before him, who was certainly much removed in manner from the confident Kenneth George Norman Ritchie who had entered the box. Then he closed the books and said gently, "We have established, it seems, your disagreement with all six of these text-books. Now, Mr. Ritchie, I should like to consider your evidence in its most favourable light—favourable to the prosecution—and see the very most that it can mean. You say that these invisible stains are blood. Can you tell me how old they are?"

"Not with any certainty, no."

Newton permitted himself a slight raising of the hands in surprise. "Let us see, then. You mean they might be a year old?"

"That is unlikely. But I suppose it is possible."

"Certainly they might be six months old?"

"Yes."

"Or one month old—one as easily as the other?"

"Yes."

"You could not possibly say that they were made on June the fourth rather than, say, May the fourth?"

"No," said this new, subdued Ritchie.

"Nor could you say whose blood made the stains? It might have been Wilkins's own blood?"

"It might have been."

"You cannot possibly connect these stains in any way with this crime?"

Ritchie was stung again into a moment of aggressiveness. He said, with his large nose pushed forward, "It was no part of my examination to connect these bloodstains with any crime."

Gently, menacingly, Newton tapped the books beneath his hand. "Do you persist in calling them bloodstains after what I have read from these books? Are you prepared to swear upon oath that none of them was caused by pus or milk or urine or any other of the twenty different possible causes?"

Ritchie was obstinate. "I can only repeat that in my experience what I have told you about the benzidine test is accurate."

Mr. Justice Morland had been for some time moving uncomfortably on his chair, in a manner which is said to be a sure sign of irritation in a judge. Now he spoke.

"I am not quite sure what you are telling us, Mr. Ritchie. Am I to understand that, in spite of all the authorities Mr. Newton has cited, you still assert that the benzidine test is a positive one for blood?"

Ritchie said carefully, "In my experience, my lord, it produces positive results."

The judge tapped his desk. "But you are not prepared to contradict all the text-books outright, are you?" There was no reply. "Are you, Mr. Ritchie?"

In a voice now defiant Ritchie said, "I can only speak according to my experience, my lord."

"But then, if these stains are blood, you cannot say whose blood it was or when it came there, can you? It may have come there one or six months ago, as Mr. Newton said?"

"That is so, my lord."

"Very well. That makes things clearer for me, and I hope for the jury. Go on, Mr. Newton."

With his effect established, Newton moved on to the doubtful ground of the four visible bloodstains. He emphasised again that they were of Wilkins's own blood group—although they were also of Sheila Morton's—and induced Ritchie to agree that Wilkins's thumb might, just might, have bled sufficiently to produce them. The jury, he saw, were not deeply interested. He sat down. Hayley, leaving ill alone, did not re-examine. Kenneth George Norman Ritchie left the witness box head up, nose pointing firmly forward and upward, an expert defeated but not dismayed.

XVI

"This is Mr. Lambie," said Uncle Dan, "who is an agent of the George H. Spaulding Detective Agency. And this is Miss Prenton."

They sat in a room at Mr. Likeness's hotel and he looked from one to the other of them with a distaste which never showed itself for a moment on his yellow, smiling face—the wretched little man carrying his fawn raincoat, whose thick head of hair was a reproach to the few strands plastered on Mr. Likeness's skull, the brassy, heavy blonde who so obviously belonged to a certain profession, and of course his two clients, grey-haired, twitching Dan Hunton and old Mrs. Wilkins, sitting there like a lump of clumsily-carved granite. He asked wearily, "How does the George H. Spaulding Detective Agency come into this?"

"I engaged them," Mrs. Wilkins said. Just for a moment Mr. Likeness was as surprised as if a Henry Moore statue had spoken. "To find the proofs of my son's innocence."

"Yes." Mr. Likeness smiled. "And he has done so?"

"What I've done," little Mr. Lambie said in the colourless dreary voice that went so well with his raincoat, "what I've done is, I've found this lady who, with whom I mean, Mr. Wilkins spent the evening."

Mr. Likeness looked at Betty Prenton again, the brassy hair, the tight frock, the spiked heels. Unexpectedly, she laughed. "Don't worry. I won't look like this when I'm in court. If you want me there, that is. Let me tell you, I'm not here because I want to be. It's my social conscience working, or something like that."

While she told him about it, speaking in an even voice but with an occasional touch of mock bravado, Mr. Likeness made notes of the times involved and wondered whether it was in some way a put-up job. The woman would have the intelligence for it, he thought, but this little Lambie would never put her up to it. Mrs. Wilkins would no doubt do anything to save her son, but this kind of thing would simply never occur to her. Hunton? Yes, he might do it, he was sly enough and half-smart enough, but he would be likely to find a more respectable witness. On the whole, Mr. Likeness thought the story was probably true—although, to do him justice, he was much less concerned with that abstract and useless question than with the possible effect of the story upon a jury.

"Let me see if I've got it right. You met Wilkins in this pub, the Diving Bell, he asked if he could go home with you, you agreed. You didn't have intercourse, but made him baked beans on toast—" He stopped. Betty Prenton had laughed. "What's the matter?"

"Nothing, just the way you put it. Right so far."

"He cut his thumb opening the baked bean tin, you think some blood went on his jacket but you can't be sure, he left just after eleven o'clock because you had a client coming. Correct?" She nodded. "Why didn't you come forward with this before?"

"What you ought to ask is, why am I here now? I don't

know why, I must need my brains testing, as I told little Lambie here. I felt sorry for the kid, but it's no skin off my nose if they do find him guilty. Call it public spirit."

Lord, thought Mr. Likeness, who seemed to find that everything depressed him to-day, a public-spirited prostitute. He allowed a faint tinge of irony to enter his voice.

"Now that you have come forward you're prepared to go into the witness box?"

"If I wasn't prepared to, I wouldn't be here."

"All right."

Mr. Likeness put away his notebook. Mrs. Wilkins, monumental on her chair, moved and spoke.

"By no means all right, sir. You can't leave it like that. We want to know what steps you intend to take to use this important evidence which has been obtained for you. Obtained, I may say, when the agents employed by *you* found out nothing at all."

"I shall have to see Mr. Newton."

"*I* should like to see Mr. Newton. I have not spoken one word to him since the beginning of the trial."

"You must realise that he is very busy."

"Too busy to see a mother who is fighting for her son's life?"

Patiently Mr. Likeness said, "We are all fighting for your son's life. Miss Prenton, if you will tell me where we can find you."

"I like that." She stood with hands on hips glaring at him. "Is that all you've got to say? Not so much as a thank you to Lambie and me for coming here?"

"Thank you, Miss Prenton, thank you." Mr. Likeness's habitual smile turned almost into a grimace. My God, he thought, what a bore this woman's going to be.

He said that, or something very like it, to Newton and Charlie Hudnutt later that evening.

"A prostitute," Newton said doubtfully. "What's she like? How will she stand up to Hayley?"

"Very tough, self-opinionated, full of remarks about public spirit. Comes out of George Bernard Shaw or someone, you might say." He probed with a toothpick.

"She might stand up then, might be rather good. What's her record, police convictions and so on?"

"Says she's never been in any real trouble. She'll stand up to questions, don't worry about that. She's not too sure about the blood from his clothes going on the trousers, but that can't be helped. Trouble is, what will the jury think of it, and of him for going with her."

"You said he only wanted sympathy, that nothing happened."

"That's what she says." Mr. Likeness's seamed yellow face showed an almost endless understanding of human deceit and folly. He dislodged a recalcitrant fragment of meat and chewed it with satisfaction. "That's what she says."

"It could be true." Newton repeated the words with some sharpness when Charlie Hudnutt laughed. The fact was, though Newton hardly admitted it even to himself, that he was becoming emotionally involved with this case in a quite ridiculous way. Such emotional participation is dangerous, a thing to be avoided, as he well knew.

"Tell me the old old story," sang Charlie Hudnutt. Newton felt his irritation increasing.

"I don't think there's any doubt that we must use this woman. She's the only proof we have of Wilkins's movements during the important times that evening. And the point about his thumb is absolutely vital, even though she's not certain about the blood."

"And we shall have to use the wife," Charlie Hudnutt said. "If he didn't leave this tart until after eleven and got back at twenty-five to twelve, there wasn't much time for bashing the girl about on the beach. Oh yes, we shall have to call the wife."

"All right, all right." Newton spoke more testily than he should have done, feeling Mr. Likeness's yellow, considering gaze upon him, aware of Charlie Hudnutt's look of slight surprise.

XVII

The evening was hot, thunder in the air. Mr. Morton sat in the hotel lounge, fanning himself occasionally with a handkerchief. "My word, that was a good dinner. A really beautiful piece of lamb. Roast lamb and mint sauce, green peas and new potatoes, there's nothing to beat it."

Bill Lonergan, who had the evening paper before his face, grunted.

"Newton did very well this afternoon, I thought. Didn't you think so, eh?"

"Very well."

"To-morrow the defence opens. Be interesting to see how young Wilkins stands up in the box, eh? Would you like a glass of brandy, Bill, my boy?"

"No, thank you."

"I don't believe he will stand up to it, you know, shouldn't be surprised if he breaks down in court. I don't know if Hayley's quite the man for the job. Marshall Hall, now, was different. He'd have torn a young scoundrel like this limb from limb. Before your time, of course. I think I shall have a glass of brandy. Are you sure you won't join me?"

"You shouldn't drink, you know that."

"Brandy is medicinal. Besides, I'm feeling so much better."

Indeed he did look better, almost well, this dapper little gentleman in his tweed suit.

"I shall go back in the morning, uncle." The freckles stood out clearly on Bill Lonergan's nose and forehead.

"Go back?" Mr. Morton put down the glass from which he had been delicately sipping, and stared. "Bless my soul. Not see the end of the trial, not see Geoffrey Wilkins's son in the box."

"I've got to go back, had a letter from my firm. Besides I've given my evidence. Nothing to stay for."

"You could easily stay another couple of days." Mr. Morton's voice assumed the whine with which he had once addressed Sheila. "You don't want to miss the defence. I wouldn't mind betting Newton's got one or two things up his sleeve."

Bill Lonergan turned on his uncle furiously. "Don't you realise I hate every minute of this damned business, this cat and mouse game. It makes me shudder." He stopped. "I'm sorry, Uncle. I've really got to go to-morrow. There's a train at 8.30, I shall catch that. I'd better do some packing."

His uncle watched him go, finished his brandy and ordered another. Then he quavered across on his stick-legs to a table at which two other men were sitting. They knew him, but he was upon them before they could get up. "Another good day in court," he said. "That man Newton, now, he tore the so-called expert to ribbons. Let me tell you…" A frail eager-eyed grasshopper, he sat down unsteadily in a chair.

"Do you remember a woman named Betty Prenton? Or you might just have called her Betty?" Doctor Andreadis asked.

John Wilkins shook his head. It was still light outside,

but only a little light pervaded the cell. Wilkins sat on the bed with hands upon knees, apparently apathetic. When the psychiatrist had repeated Betty Prenton's story he said, "I don't remember."

"She says you were upset, talked about your wife and how you hated her. Do you remember that?"

"I said that to everybody, and it was true. I still hate her."

Wilkins looked at him directly, and in his eyes Andreadis could see no expression. The psychiatrist had for a moment the strange illusion that he was speaking to a dummy. To break the silence he said, "You could remember what happened on that Monday night. If you wanted to remember, you could remember."

"What time did I leave her?"

"Just after eleven."

"Then I still had time to do it."

"Your wife says you came in at twenty-five minutes to twelve."

"But there was the man who saw me coming up the steps from the beach at twenty to twelve."

"Listen to me, John." Andreadis took hold of the prisoner by his shoulders. "You heard Newton's cross-examination of that man in the box. He isn't sure of the identification. What this woman says will help you. She says you were with her up to eleven o'clock. She explains the cut on your thumb. You have a very good chance of acquittal, do you understand? But it depends on *you*. Tell your story simply. Say exactly what happened as you remember it. Don't try to conceal anything. You hated your wife—say so, if you're asked. Tell the truth, that's all you have to do."

"Tell the truth," Wilkins said without expression. "But what is the truth?"

"You have nothing to be afraid of. There are no tricks. You can't be trapped into saying something you don't mean, unless you make foolish answers. Don't try to be clever or sarcastic. Don't get angry. Just tell the truth as you know it."

Wilkins looked up. Andreadis hoped that he would ask some intelligent question. "This Betty Prenton—what is she?"

"What is—oh, I see. She's a prostitute. Showed courage in coming forward."

Wilkins nodded, murmured something, and his head sank forward again. Andreadis could not be sure, but thought he heard the word, "Disgusting." When he left a quarter of an hour later it was with the knowledge that he had merely been scratching the surface of things. The prisoner had retreated from all those confidences about his past life into some Berchtesgaden of the mind.

"Have the other half," Betty Prenton said. "Come on."

"I really shouldn't."

"It's not every day you get the chance of tracking down a vital witness in a murder trial. Another half of bitter there."

"Not quite so loud." Mr. Lambie looked nervously round the bar. He sipped his bitter. "My word, Miss Prenton, it's hot."

"Certainly is." Betty Prenton was wearing a thin blouse through which outline of brassiere and firm shoulders could be seen. "You're a persevering little devil, aren't you? Tell me, do you really like being a nark? I can't imagine anything more like hell."

"You see life, you know. But I won't say it's what I'd choose. I haven't always done this kind of thing, you understand that.

Before the war I had my own shop, Lambie and Company, sports outfitters. But afterwards things were, well, difficult. If I could have kept the shop on—if I hadn't gone into the armed forces—it seemed to be my duty." He brooded quietly on an imaginary past.

"You're pretty hot on duty." She drank her gin and unobtrusively ordered another. "Married, aren't you?" From a stained leather wallet the little man produced a worn photograph showing a round dumpling of a woman. "Of course that was taken some years back, just after the war. Goodness gracious, what's this?"

"It's the third half."

"But my dear Miss Prenton—"

"Betty."

"My work here is over. I told Mrs. Wilkins and Mr. Hunton that I thought there was nothing further I could usefully do. I have to catch a train. I mustn't arrive home—er—a little bit tiddly."

"I'm not going to go home tiddly, Lambie. I'm going to get downright tight before I go home. Do you know why?" The little man shook his head. "Because I hate what I'm doing. I hate helping the bloody police in any way whatever. Do you know why I'm doing it?"

"Why, Miss Prenton—Betty—it's your duty."

Her forceful, intelligent face was red with drink. "Duty's got nothing to do with it. I don't believe you had much to do with it either."

"Then what—"

"Christ, but it's hot to-night. Tell you something, Lambie. I didn't like him. Wilkins, I mean. I'm not a mother by nature. I don't like young men who want a shoulder to cry on. And shall I tell you something else? I don't believe he did it, Lambie. He's not the type." Her face was now so close that by leaning forward slightly he could have kissed her. Instead he drew back an inch or two. "But once the cops have got their claws on someone they don't let go. They're going to find him guilty."

XVIII

As the trial progressed—or perhaps from the time that his defence opened—John Wilkins became the subject, or victim, of a curious delusion. This was, that the court and all the people in it were becoming smaller. The exact nature of the delusion varied. At some times it seemed to him that he was outside the court himself, a mere spectator of some fantastic quiz to which there was no final or definitive answer. At other times he was aware of his own participation in what was going on, but the whole thing seemed to be moving farther and farther away from him, as though he were the eye of a camera retreating from an observed scene.

With this delusion about distance there was blended some confusion in his mind about the witnesses who now appeared on the stand. This sprightly, frosty little Gimball now, doll-man with pearl stick-pin twinkling, was surely no friend of his. What was he doing, giving evidence for the defence? He sent down a little note, a scrawl you might call it, very hurried, asking that question. Back came an answer: *Establishing details of your blackouts.* What did that mean? He passed a hand over his forehead.

Now Newton was asking Gimball about the blackouts. Yes, the doll-man agreed, he had been compelled to speak to Wilkins about them. They had considerably affected his work, yes. At one point Gimball had even considered the possibility of transferring him to another department. To his knowledge there had been some three or four blackouts in all.

Blackouts acknowledged, then? But now Hayley rose to cross-examine.

"Mr. Gimball," he asked, "would you say that you liked John Wilkins?"

A tiny smile appeared at the corners of Gimball's mouth. "I don't dislike him."

"He had been in your department several years, you had got to know him?"

"That is so, yes."

"You reckon yourself a shrewd judge of character." Gimball hesitated. "Come now, you put down your views about Wilkins very emphatically in a certain report made when you were asked whether he was suitable for promotion. You stand by what you said in it, don't you?"

"Yes."

And now—oh, it was shameful, John Wilkins thought, really shameful to expose such matters—Hayley read the report, and repeated certain phrases. "'He has shown what I can only call a lack of stability. The standard of his work has declined and he appears to have become careless over small points of detail.' Nothing there about blackouts."

Gimball twinkled across from the box. "It seemed—ungenerous, shall I say—to mention them. The whole report may have been a little too kind. In his last weeks Wilkins's work was slovenly to a degree."

"Slovenly to a degree." Hayley looked mildly surprised. "Yet he was appointed manager of your department."

"It was the result of a merger. I was retiring."

"You were retiring, you put in as adverse a report as

possible on Wilkins, you said specifically that he was not fit to be appointed as your successor, yet he was appointed. Does that suggest anything to you?"

"I suppose you want me to say—"

"It suggests to me that he can hardly have been so inefficient as you suggest, that these so-called 'blackouts' did not affect his work. Do you agree?"

Gimball hesitated and then said, "No."

"Would you not agree, at least, that your superiors must have taken a much more friendly view of him than you did? How else can you explain his appointment?"

"He had originally put forward a merger scheme."

"Of which you disapproved?"

"Yes."

"But which your superiors accepted."

"Yes."

The judge interposed. "Mr. Hayley, I don't wish to stop this line of cross-examination if you really feel it to be vital, but I must say you are ranging very wide." Hayley bowed his head. "I have only two or three more questions, my lord. In spite of your report, then, Wilkins was appointed?"

"Yes."

"And you have no *direct* knowledge about these blackouts? For all you know, Wilkins may simply have spent his time away from the office in drinking clubs or at football matches?"

"If you put it like that, no direct evidence. But I feel sure—"

"Thank you." Hayley sat down.

And now, out of the nightmare of the past, crawled other figures. John Wilkins might have been inclined to cry out in court, saying, *No, no, these people do not know me, they are not my friends*, if he had not felt something in himself that was utterly remote from what was going on. There was a part of him that remained untouched by all the slime that those supposed to be defending him were drawing across his character. Untouched by Mrs. Hazel Denison, who smiled nervously at him before giving graphic details of his behaviour in the Five O'Clock Shadow, his failure to remember her at their second meeting, and the way in which he had been thrown out. Shameful, all that, but it did not touch the inner self that he hugged, the self that had loved Sheila.

Untouched, even, by the farcical interlude of Doctor Bowen Glenister, a minor disaster that led Charlie Hudnutt to scribble a caustically indignant note to Mr. Likeness, and that must be ascribed to faulty staff work.

Beady-eyed and hairy, like a great spider, Doctor Glenister took the stand and told of the prisoner's visit to him, of the blackouts, and the request for help.

"He specifically mentioned blackouts," Charlie Hudnutt said.

"Oh yes. There was no doubt of that."

"And asked for your help in dealing with them?"

"That is so." The doctor shot his rather dirty cuffs. "And how did your interview end?"

"He promised to come back, but never did so."

Charlie Hudnutt asked a few questions to confirm that the blackouts had been the sole reason for the visit, and sat down. Maurice Mallin-Fry's cross-examination began mildly enough.

"You say that Wilkins came to consult you about his blackouts. Was that the only reason for his visit?"

Glenister put his black nails to his mouth and nibbled. "But naturally."

"You are quite sure of that?"

"Yes."

"You are sure he did not ask you to procure a woman?"

Glenister raised his hands in horror, revealing soft, surprisingly pink palms. "An outrageous suggestion."

"That's absolutely untrue, is it? You wouldn't do anything of that sort?"

"I would not."

"You're a respectable doctor, aren't you?" Mallin-Fry's voice was taunting. Glenister glared at him like a trapped animal.

The judge moved in his chair. "Mr. Mallin-Fry, I trust you have some basis for the suggestions you are making."

"I am coming to it, my lord. Are you a qualified doctor?"

"Yes."

"Of what faculty?" There was no reply. "Of what faculty? Was it of the so-called St. Matthew's Medical School? Did they give degrees by post, after some elementary postal tuition? Was the man who conducted the school sentenced to two years' imprisonment for fraud?"

This question Glenister answered, "How should I know?"

"But you were a graduate of his school, that is your sole qualification as a doctor?"

"Yes. It gave good grounding in—"

"Never mind that. Just answer my questions. Were you charged in 1952 with helping to procure an abortion? Were you sentenced to six months' imprisonment?" No reply. "In 1954 were you charged again, this time for helping to run a brothel?"

Glenister put his nails to his mouth again. "It was a put-up job. The case against me was a frame-up."

"You were charged and found guilty. You received a sentence of twelve months' imprisonment. Is that right? Is it? Answer me?"

"Yes."

"So that if Wilkins had come to ask you about a woman you wouldn't have been so very shocked, would you? I suggest that he came to ask you to find a girl for him, isn't that the truth?"

Glenister's little black eyes stared unwaveringly, venomously, back at him. "No."

He comes here, John Wilkins thought wonderingly, he tells the truth, and it sounds like a lie. But the whole puppet-show was lies. How could he recognise himself in the caricature of a man that these witnesses were presenting? *This is not me*, he wanted to say, *I said some of these things, I did some of them, but these things are not me. You must understand my feelings when I said and did them, you must understand about Lacey and about May, you must understand that what I felt about Sheila was real in one way and in another way a game.*

They would say it was his fault, Mr. Likeness thought, as Doctor Glenister left the box, but they would be unfair. It is unusual for solicitors to check up on the antecedents of their own witnesses, although here there might perhaps have been a case for doing so. Gloomily watching Betty Prenton stride across court into the witness box, he thought, she had better be good.

XIX

Betty Prenton was good in her way, which was not the way of the jury, nor a way easily appreciated by anybody in that courtroom. She confronted them all, not so much with bravado as with something like contempt, and her answer to Magnus Newton's second question was given with positive relish.

"What is your occupation?"

"I am a prostitute."

Her plain skirt and simple blouse gave no idea of that occupation. The brassy hair, the watchful eyes, the hard mouth, the vulgar voice—all these, after all, were less stigmata of prostitution than the marks, say of any successful business woman. And it was as a business woman that she told the story of John Wilkins's visit to her, as she had told it in her flat that night to Mr. Lambie. It was a simple enough tale, told concisely and even with some humour. At the end of it Newton said, "One more thing, Miss Prenton. Would you tell the court briefly the circumstances that have led you to come forward with this evidence?"

"Yes." She leant her big arms on the witness box and half-faced the jury. "I read about the case, recognised Wilkins's photograph, said to hell with it, I don't want any trouble. Then this little man Lambie came to see me—"

"Lambie?" The judge had been writing busily, now stopped and raised a hand. "Is Mr.—um—Lambie to be called, Mr. Newton? I don't think his name has been mentioned before."

"My lord, I don't think that will be necessary. Mr. Lambie is a private inquiry agent who was employed by my client's mother, and his only importance in the case is that he persuaded the witness to come forward."

"Thank you, Mr. Newton." Mr. Justice Morland looked down distastefully at Betty Prenton. "You may continue."

"I only want to say that coming into court does no good at all to somebody in my profession. Much against my will, as you might say, here I am."

Magnus Newton sat down, mopping his head. Hayley, who had been engaged in frantic consultation with his junior since Betty Prenton took the stand, now got up. Prostitutes, like experts, are exceptions to the general rule that harsh cross-examination may have the reverse effect of that intended. An expert operates above the understanding of the common man, a prostitute outside it. In their very different ways both are felt to be a threat to society as jurymen constitute it, and it is a pleasure to see them discomfited. So it was that Hayley felt able to open his cross-examination by saying, with obvious irony, "Let me congratulate you upon your public spirit. Particularly, as you say, because you don't want to call the attention of the police to your occupation. How many times have you been arrested, by the way?"

"Five or six."

"You can't quite remember. And that was for—"

She shrugged her broad shoulders. "The usual thing. Picked up in one of these sweeps where they run girls into the van quick and ask questions afterwards. Forty shillings or a month."

"Ah yes." Hayley was feeling his way, probing for chinks

through which he might thrust the questions that would shake her self-assurance. "You were arrested last month, were you not?"

She was impatient. "It's always the same thing. The police have to do it, whether they like it or not. It's just a farce, and they know it as well as we do."

Hayley raised his eyebrows, looked at the jury, made no comment. The judge said sharply, "You were not asked for your opinions of police procedure. Please confine yourself to answering the questions."

"The police, then, are by no means ignorant of your occupation." Again she shrugged. "Are they?"

"Have it your way. All the same, I'm sticking my neck out by giving evidence here."

"Now, you picked this man up in the Diving Bell, you say, just before half past nine. He offered to buy you a drink, you accepted, and then—" Hayley laughed a countryman's laugh, the laugh of a rustic ignorant of big city vice. "I'm just not clear about that."

"He came home with me."

"Yes, but what I mean is, did you ask him to come home with you, or did he ask whether he could? I'm just not clear about it, you see."

For the first time Betty Prenton hesitated. "I'm not sure. When you get into conversation in a pub like that, why, it's often an understood thing. Anyway, I felt sorry for him, he looked so miserable."

"You felt sorry for him. But this was a business trans-action, you aren't denying that you expected to get money from this man?"

She put her hands on her hips. "It was a business trans-action, yes. And I still felt sorry for him. Does that seem to you impossible?"

"Just let me ask the questions," Hayley said easily. "Was any sum of money mentioned in the pub?"

"No."

"When you got home, then. And how much?"

"Three pounds."

"That is your usual fee? I am glad that you do not let sentiment interfere with business."

"He never paid it me." Her voice was harsh now.

"Really? That's very interesting. How did that come about?"

"He said he only wanted to talk, told me all about his wife and this girl Sheila. He cried. I felt sorry for him."

"And you said, No, no, put away your money, let me make you some baked beans on toast. Then he opened the baked beans for you and cut his thumb. And you are not sure whether blood got on to his clothing." Now, quite suddenly, Hayley's voice was openly mocking and derisory. Betty Prenton flinched from it for a moment, then blazed at him in fury.

"I've said already, I think some blood did get on his clothes."

"How could there be any doubt about such a thing? He opens the tin, cuts his thumb, calls out—did he call out?"

"Yes, he did. I was doing the toast. When I turned round his hand was all over blood."

"His hand was all over blood," Hayley repeated. "From a cut on the thumb? Come, come now, Miss Prenton."

"Were you there?" she asked. "Am I telling you, or are you telling me?"

The judge tapped on his desk. "You must not speak to counsel like that."

"But he can speak to me any way he likes, is that it?" she said bitterly. "His hand was all over blood, I tell you, and I think there was some on his clothes. It came out fast. Then he ran it under the cold tap for a minute and wrapped it in his handkerchief because it hadn't stopped bleeding. I think he still had the handkerchief on when he left. That's all I noticed about the blood. If I'd known I was going to be asked questions here about it I'd have written it all down at the time."

"You were too busy cooking the baked beans," Hayley suggested amiably.

"I was cooking the baked beans, is that so funny? I'm not ashamed of it. And I'm not ashamed of being a prostitute, let me tell you, it's quite as good an occupation as yours."

"You enjoy practising your occupation, do you?" Hayley asked silkily.

"Yes. I hope you enjoy yours as much—trapping people into saying things they didn't mean."

With the air of a man whose patience has come to an end, Hayley said, "And you are seriously asking the jury to believe that you, a prostitute, took this man home to get money from him, but changed your mind when you found he felt miserable—that you took no money from him, had no relations with him, and even cooked him a meal. Is that what you want the jury to believe?"

"Yes." Her voice was almost a shriek. "That's what happened. Shall I tell you what's wrong with you sharp lawyers? You've got no charity yourselves, so you don't think other people can have any. You sell your minds, but you're very shocked when other people sell their bodies."

Charlie Hudnutt leaned across to Magnus Newton. "She's rather fine, isn't she?" Newton nodded gloomily. Mr. Likeness was making a drawing of her. Now he added a stroke or two to make her expression that of a barking frizzy-haired poodle.

"You felt sorry for John Wilkins. But when another—what

did you call him?—another client arrived, you had no hesitation in turning him out." She did not answer. "Had you? You told him to go. That's true, isn't it?"

"Yes, it's true, but—"

"And then, although you felt so sorry for him, you didn't come forward when you saw that he had been arrested."

"I've already said I didn't want trouble with the police."

"But then this remarkably persuasive private investigator came along, and you saw the path of duty. Is that really what you are telling us?"

"If you want to put it that way I can't stop you. But it's not true."

Hayley spread out his hands. "What is untrue about it? Isn't it the truth that you love publicity, and saw the chance of a lifetime to get some when this Mr. Lambie came to see you?"

"No," she cried, and beat the top of the box with her fist.

"That you welcomed the chance to come and air your brazen views in court here about the life of prostitution which you lead—"

"No. No."

"And that really, if Wilkins came to see you at all, it was in the ordinary way of business for you, you took his money and had connection with him and he went away, and the rest is all the product of your fertile imagination?"

"Liar," she shouted at him. "You filthy liar. I didn't take his money."

"Control your language," the judge said.

"We could believe that to be the truth of it, I dare say, Miss Prenton. You're a business woman, as you've pointed out. A good business woman like yourself wouldn't allow a man to waste an hour and a half of your valuable time for nothing, would she? And then a public-spirited woman like yourself would have come forward immediately, wouldn't she, if your story had been true?"

She had recovered herself now. She said calmly, "You can be as sarcastic as you like. My story is true."

XX

May Wilkins's hair had been freshly waved. She wore a plain green frock and a triple row of pearls was strung round her neck. She answered Magnus Newton's opening questions with composure, telling of a happy married life, and saying that she knew of the blackouts. She had mentioned the question of going to a doctor, but her husband made up his own mind about those things.

"Did you notice any change in your husband's attitude towards you?" Newton asked. He had decided to solve the problem of putting May in the box, by admitting as much as was inevitable about the changed conditions of their married life. He was, so to speak, allowing her to show that Wilkins had been unfaithful in spirit for the sake of her evidence about the time. Indeed, Newton reckoned (although Charlie Hudnutt thought that his logic was too finespun) that if he could make it clear that May had come almost to hate her husband, it would make her evidence about the time of his return to the hotel more convincing.

"Yes, about three months ago." And she told of the incident when he struck her. "I had made a remark about his mother still regarding him as her baby. I was sorry for it afterwards. But I think the real reason was that this girl—"

"What you think is not evidence, I am afraid. Just answer

the questions. Now, did the prisoner ever speak to you about Miss Morton?"

"No."

"Did you know of her existence until he was arrested?"

"I did not."

"But you suspected that something of the sort was wrong. Why was that?"

"One day, it was about the second week in May, I think, John asked me what I thought of divorce."

"Can you remember his exact words?"

"Yes. He said he'd been reading something in the paper about a man who thought that when two people fell out of love with each other they ought to get divorced. I asked what he was trying to tell me, whether he'd been unfaithful. He was trying to pretend that it wasn't personal, hadn't anything to do with us, but of course I knew it had."

"And what was your reaction?"

May spoke emphatically. "I told him that even if he had been unfaithful, it wouldn't make any difference. I loved him. I should never give him up."

Newton left this dangerous ground, and led her on to the visit to Brighton. She told him how John had pressed her to go there, how she had mentioned a guest-house in Devon, but he had insisted on Brighton and on these particular two weeks, and she had given way at last, touched by his desire to return to the place where they had spent their honeymoon.

"But the holiday was not a success."

"No. John was very bad-tempered, and kept leaving me alone."

That's enough of concessions, Newton thought, and came to the evening of June the fourth. "You were worried about your husband?"

"Yes. I had not seen him since lunch. I thought he must be out with his uncle, Mr. Hunton."

"At what time did you go to bed?"

"Just before eleven o'clock. But I did not go to sleep."

"And what time did your husband come in?"

"At twenty-five minutes to twelve."

Newton repeated the vital time slowly. "You are quite sure of that?"

"Quite sure. I looked at my little bedside clock when he came in. And just before that I had heard the half-hour chime on a clock outside."

"Will you tell us what happened when he came in?"

"I asked him where he had been, what he had been doing, but he seemed to be dazed and unable to reply. His breath smelt of drink."

"Did you speak to him sharply?"

May pointed her long nose towards the jury. "I did, and why shouldn't I? I'd suffered enough from him on this holiday, if you could call it a holiday. Then he said he must wash his hands, and I noticed there was blood on them. He went to the basin and I asked what he had been doing. He said"—she faltered, and went on. "He said, 'Mind your own bloody business.' Then I noticed that he had cut his thumb."

This, Newton thought, was altogether too much of a good thing. He stopped her briskly. "And while he was washing his hands you noticed his jacket."

"Yes, I noticed the dark stains on his jacket and I said, 'Look, you've got some blood on your jacket.'"

"What was his reaction to that?"

"He snatched the jacket away from me and hung it over the back of a chair."

"Did he seem in any way alarmed that you had noticed the blood?"

"No."

"Did he make any attempt to clean it off? Then, or at a later time?"

"He did not."

"He did not seem in the least disturbed, either now or later on, either that he had blood on his jacket or that you had noticed it."

"No."

Newton sat down, feeling that he had got his vital piece of information about the time at a rather high price. And the price was not yet fully paid, as he gloomily realised while listening to Hayley cross-examining her with regard to that conversation on divorce, eliciting from her the statement that in no circumstances would she have considered divorcing her husband. What is she really up to, Newton wondered, looking at the slim, composed figure in the witness box, does she really hate him as much as he says he hates her? And not for the first time he found himself thinking that Wilkins would have had every reason to murder his wife.

Now Hayley was moving on to the question of time. "You know that the hall porter, Shaddock, says that your husband came in at ten minutes to twelve?"

"He is mistaken."

"When your husband came in, did you switch on the light?"

"No. I was sitting in bed, reading."

"Very well. And you took one quick glance at the clock, I expect—"

"I looked at the time, and it was twenty-five minutes to twelve. I am quite sure of it. And my little bedside clock keeps very good time."

Hayley made one last effort. "I suggest to you that what you heard was the clock outside striking *three* times not for the half hour but the three-quarters—and so you glanced only casually at the time on your clock."

"No." She was perfectly composed, and quite certain. We're over that hurdle, Newton thought. But five minutes later he was listening, appalled, to the evidence she was giving about the blood on John Wilkins's hands.

"You said there was blood on his hands. Could you be a little more precise? Was it on both his hands?"

Calmly May said, "There was quite a lot of blood on his right hand, and I am almost sure there was some on his left."

"On the back of his right hand, or on the palm?"

"On the back. I couldn't see the palm."

"And this was dried blood, his hand was not bleeding?"

"No. It was dried blood."

Mr. Justice Morland scratched away with his pen for some seconds. Hayley waited for him—a great deal of court time is occupied with this kind of waiting—and then resumed.

"Was there a handkerchief wrapped round his right thumb?"

"No, nothing at all. His thumb was not covered."

Leaning forward a little, looking first at the jury, then at the witness, Hayley asked, "Was there a bloodstained handkerchief in his pocket?"

"No. I took a dirty handkerchief from his pocket on the following morning. There was no blood on it."

So much for Betty Prenton's handkerchief wrapped round his thumb, Newton thought gloomily. Given a choice of believing wife or prostitute, which would the jury choose? There could be no doubt about the answer.

"Now about this cut on the thumb. Was it a bad cut?" Hayley asked.

"Not very bad. It wasn't bleeding."

"It—was—not—bleeding." Hayley measured out the

words. "Could the blood on the back of his hands have come from this cut?"

Newton was on his feet, an image of red-faced puffing anger. "My lord, I must protest on two points. First, what is the value of Mrs. Wilkins's opinion here? If the cut was not bleeding when she saw it, what opportunity would she have of knowing how much it bled? I claim that she should not answer the question. If she does answer it, her answer should refer to the right hand only, since she is not sure that there was blood on the left."

The judge listened to this contention with his head cocked like some exquisitely courteous little bird. Then he coughed slightly. "Would you find it possible to take another line of questioning that would meet Mr. Newton's objections, Mr. Hayley?"

"I will try, my lord. You have said it was not a very bad cut. Would you call it a pinprick?"

"Oh no, more than that."

"Was it a very bad, bloody gash that horrified you?"

Newton was on his feet again. "My lord, I really cannot see the force of this questioning. We already have medical evidence that this cut was—h'm—nearly two inches long, extending from the base almost to the top of the right thumb. What possible point can there be in asking Mrs. Wilkins about something already factually established?"

Now Hayley gave up, feeling perhaps that he had already made his point well enough. "You are quite sure, in any case, that there was no handkerchief round your husband's thumb, and that it was not bleeding when you saw it?"

Her demure composure unshaken, she said, "I am quite sure of that."

XXI

"Wilkins took the box wearing a dark-brown pin-stripe suit, with brown shirt and tie," wrote the *Daily Banner* reporter. "He answered the questions of his counsel, Mr. Magnus Newton, clearly and emphatically until he came to the events of the fatal evening…"

Clearly and emphatically: on the whole Newton was pleased with the effect Wilkins had created in the box so far, pleased with his obvious gawkish sincerity and his immediate answers. He had admitted his quarrels with May, admitted his affection for Sheila but insisted on its romantic nature, rebutted convincingly the prosecution's half-hearted suggestion that his blackouts were convenient inventions. Had he been a juryman himself, Newton knew that he would have believed the young man's evidence so far. But the real tests were yet to come, in the questions he was going to ask now and in cross-examination.

Newton looked at the jury, teetered back and forth, and put his next question very slowly. They would know his technique well enough by now to understand that he was emphasising its importance.

"You know that you left Mr. Lonergan at twenty minutes to seven. What is your next recollection?"

"Waking up next morning in my bedroom at the hotel."

"Waking-up-next-morning-in-your-bedroom-at-the-hotel," Newton intoned, like a communicant repeating the litany. "You positively do not recall any further incident of the evening?"

"No."

"At nine o'clock you were in a public house called the Toll Gate. You do not remember that?"

"No."

"Later you went home with a Miss Betty Prenton. Her evidence in the box meant nothing to you?"

"Nothing at all."

"Later still, your wife has told us of your return to the hotel, of blood on your hand and so on. Do you remember that?"

"I remember nothing."

The judge had been moving restlessly. "Mr. Newton, the witness has already said he remembers nothing of the evening after he left Mr. Lonergan. I fail to see the purpose of enumerating the incidents of the evening in this way."

"As your lordship pleases." Newton had been about to stop these questions anyway. Wilkins's replies were somewhat mechanical. He moved quickly to the end.

"I come now to your attitude when you were arrested. My learned friend mentioned in his opening speech that you said you would never have hurt Sheila Morton if you had been in your right mind. What did you mean by that?"

"Simply that I had had a blackout. I didn't know what I might have done."

"It was in no sense a confession, then?"

"No. How could I confess when I couldn't remember?"

"Now, this is my last question. Was there any intention in your mind, when you heard of her engagement, of hurting Sheila Morton?"

Now Wilkins lifted his head and spoke loud and clear. "Before God, I never meant to hurt Sheila Morton. I loved her."

Not so bad, Newton thought as he sat down, but we could have done without those last three words. Would Hayley exploit them at once, he wondered? But the prosecuting counsel, frowning with a countryman's uncertainty at all this psychological stuff, was off on another tack.

"These blackouts, as you call them, I should like to know a little more about them. Am I right in thinking that—how shall I put it?—a kind of shutter comes down on your mind for a few hours. You're absolutely blank about those hours, just can't say what's happened afterwards. Is that a fair statement?"

"Yes."

"And this has happened four or five times in the past year. That must have worried you a lot, no doubt."

"Yes, it did." The prisoner's voice was low.

"It would worry me, I know," Hayley said with the hint of a man-to-man smile to the jury, a smile which indicated the absurdity of the idea that anything of the kind could happen to a man so perfectly normal as himself. "Why, it was even affecting your work, wasn't it—mistakes creeping in here and there, very natural too."

"I had made some mistakes, yes."

"So, of course, you went to see your doctor." The prisoner did not reply. "What did your doctor say when you went to see him?"

"I didn't go to the doctor," Wilkins said. His hands tightly gripped the rail in front of him.

Hayley affected immense surprise. "Didn't go to the doctor. That's very strange. Here you are, suffering from these blackouts which affect your work and upset you, yet you don't go to see a doctor. Why not?"

Wilkins said something inaudible. The judge leaned forward, hand to ear. "I didn't catch that. Will you please speak up?"

Wilkins spoke up, his pale face flushed, his voice unnaturally loud. "Caused through drink. I knew they were caused through drink. I didn't want to see a doctor."

"But in the end you did see one, didn't you? You went to see Doctor Glenister. Why did you choose him?"

"He was recommended by my uncle."

"Yes. But why see this Doctor Glenister instead of your own doctor? What did you expect him to do for you?" Again there was no reply. "You were afraid of what your own doctor might tell you about your state of mind, isn't that so? You knew you had a disposition towards violence and you drank to get rid of it. Is that why you went to Doctor Glenister, and not to your own doctor?"

"No. No." Wilkins shouted the word twice, with a violence that quite startled the spectators in the galleries, and caused the jurymen and women to scrutinise him with particular care, as though he were an insect that revealed under the magnifying-glass a venom invisible to the naked eye.

Hayley persisted. "Then why didn't you go to see your own doctor? Why did you prefer this Doctor Glenister?"

"My uncle recommended him."

"But why hadn't you seen your own doctor long before that? Your wife was anxious that you should do so."

"She put you up to this." Now he was shouting again. "My wife put you up to it. She hates me."

Hayley waited, looking at jury, judge, prisoner, spectators. Then he said, "We will leave the point and move on to the last question of your examination. You answered, 'Before God, I never meant to hurt Sheila Morton. I loved her.' Now, what were your emotions when, on that Monday late afternoon, you heard of Sheila Morton's engagement? That must have been a shock to you, surely?"

"It was a shock." The brief flare of violence had died. The reporter from the *Daily Banner* noted: "Sudden changes of mood."

"What were your feelings towards her at that moment? Did you feel loving, angry, upset?"

"I was upset."

"Did you feel yourself betrayed?"

"No. I—she—I did feel she shouldn't have done it. But I loved her, I loved Sheila."

"Do you remember going out with Mr. Lonergan for a drink afterwards? Do you remember what you said to him?"

"Yes—I can't remember clearly." The prisoner's confusion now was very evident.

"I will remind you of what you said to him. 'It was a great shock to Sheila when she found out I was married. Before that she'd been pretty keen on me. Couldn't keep her away as a matter of fact, always after me to take her out.' Was that true?"

"We did go out."

"How often?"

"Once." The voice was faint.

"I will remind you of more. 'When Sheila found out I was married she was upset, but before that there was no stopping her.' Did you say those words?"

"I suppose so, something like them, yes."

"Then he said that you implied that Sheila Morton had been your mistress and he told you to shut up. Is that correct?"

"More or less."

"In fact, it was not true that you had been intimate with Sheila Morton, was it?"

"No." The voice was low now, almost inaudible.

"It did not even approach the truth—you had been out with her only once, she had no intention of going out with you again to your knowledge, and now she was engaged to be married. Those are the facts, aren't they?"

"I suppose so."

"But you couldn't bear to acknowledge those facts—you can hardly bring yourself to do so now. That is why you invented this—what shall I call it?—this fantasy, which you told to Lonergan." There was no answer. "Do you mean to say that fantasy was invented out of love for Sheila Morton?" There was still no answer. "Or was it an expression of a lust that had turned to hatred, a fantasy that later in the evening you felt compelled to turn to a hideous sort of reality?"

John Wilkins put his head in his hands and wept. When he raised his puffed, ugly face, the tears could clearly be seen on it. He was trying to say something, but whatever it was came through as an inarticulate gabble, from which there emerged clearly only one word, repeated over and over. The word was *Love*.

XXII

Mr. Justice Morland began his summing up almost con-versationally, like a red-robed lecturing midget talking to a class of students, not at all like the austere juridical figure of popular imagination—or rather, perhaps one should say, of the past, for the attitude of the bench has changed almost as much as that of counsel in the past thirty years, so that a judge now appears less as a great law-giver than simply as a man fitted by training and experience to lead other men through the mazes of legal terminology, reducing the complex to an everyman simplicity.

"Just after ten o'clock on that Monday night, Miss Morton went out for a walk. Her fiancé offered to accompany her, but she said she would prefer to be alone. Counsel for the defence has tentatively suggested, in his very able final speech, that she might have gone out to keep an appointment. You may think that is intrinsically improbable, bearing in mind the facts of her father's illness and her own recent engagement—and you may think also that there is nothing unlikely, after the strain under which she had been living for the past few hours, in her desire to be alone for a little and to take a breath of air.

"Now, at some time between ten-thirty and twelve o'clock midnight (these are the time limits suggested by the expert witnesses for the prosecution, and they were not questioned by the defence) Sheila Morton was brutally attacked and done to death on Brighton beach. Her head and face were beaten by several blows from a blunt instrument which has not been found, but may have been a large stone from the beach. Her clothing had been interfered with, but although there were signs that sexual assault had been attempted, she had not in fact been violated.

"Sheila Morton was a virgin. She was friendly in her manner, but not at all the kind of girl, you may think, to walk on a dark beach at night with a stranger. Bear in mind that she had just become engaged, and you may think that what was unlikely becomes incredible. You may think that when Sheila Morton went down from the lighted promenade to the unlighted beach it was in the company of somebody she knew and trusted. It is suggested by the prosecution that she met John Wilkins, accepted his invitation to walk by the sea, that there she resisted his attempts to make love to her, and that he killed her in a fit of passion. It is my duty to tell you that in this case there can be no question of any other verdict than that of wilful murder. The possibility that Wilkins is not competent to plead has not been raised by the defence, and no evidence has been offered in relation to it. This in spite of the fact that Wilkins can give no explanation of his movements between just after six-thirty that night and the next morning. Such brief periods of amnesia—or, as they are commonly called, blackouts—are not unknown after periods of heavy drinking, or under some mental stress, and although they might be used to suggest that the prisoner was not responsible for his actions, that suggestion has not been made by the defence. The defence is simply that he did not commit this crime.

"The prosecution has questioned the veracity of these

blackouts. In his final speech Mr. Hayley suggested that they might have been convenient excuses for Wilkins to absent himself from home. You will give what weight you think proper to that idea, but it is contradicted by the evidence of several defence witnesses, relating to periods when Wilkins could have had no obvious reason for lying about his actions.

"The prosecution case is based upon three main points—Wilkins's visit to the Langland Hotel on Monday which, it is suggested, provided the immediate motive for murder, the evidence of Mr. Fanum and the hall porter at the Prince Regent, Shaddock, relating to the late evening, and the blood-stains on his clothes. I will consider these factors in turn.

"You have heard the evidence of the receptionist at the Langland Hotel, of Miss Morton's father and of her fiancé, regarding Wilkins's behaviour when he learned of Miss Morton's engagement. He looked, Mr. Jackson said in an expressive phrase, 'like a sheep hit by a pole-axe.' Obviously it came as a great shock to him. Later on he had a conversation with Mr. Lonergan, after he had left the hotel, and you may think this conversation was of particular significance. In it Wilkins said that Sheila Morton had been 'pretty keen' on him, that he had had a job to keep her away from him. He implied that she had been his mistress. Lonergan, very properly, told him to shut up. What Wilkins said on this occasion was quite the reverse of the truth, but, members of the jury, what kind of state must the man have been in to say it? Was this merely, as defence counsel suggested, the kind of thing any man might say at such a time, no more than distasteful boasting? Or does it show the passionate frustration, leading to violent action, suggested by the prosecution? You must make up your minds about that."

Little Mr. Justice Morland sipped water as delicately as a

bird. Hayley listened to him impassively, arms folded, face becomingly serious. Magnus Newton nodded, blinked and puffed his cheeks. Their juniors looked suitably alert. John Wilkins stared across court at the judge with a face empty of expression. In the day's somnolent heat it was hard to believe, as the old man's voice droned on and on, seeming to get slower and slower, that anything serious was at stake.

"...the question of times," he was saying. "This is a point of the greatest importance, in which the evidence given by various witnesses is irreconcilable. Mr. Fanum, you will remember, said that he saw a man come up from the beach to the promenade at twenty minutes to twelve, and identified that man as Wilkins. In his cross-examination Mr. Newton made great play with a phrase the witness had used about a cry he heard on the beach, a cry which had in it, he said, 'the colour of murder.' It is a fanciful phrase, and you may think that Mr. Fanum is prone to such flights of fancy. He said the man's face was pale, and Mr. Newton pointed out that all faces look pale under sodium lighting of the kind installed at this point on the beach. He suggested that Mr. Fanum might have seen a photograph of the prisoner and was influenced by that in making his identification. You will have to decide how much significance to attach to Mr. Fanum's evidence. Is he merely fanciful, or was it really the prisoner he saw coming up from the beach?

"Linked with Mr. Fanum's evidence is that of the hall porter Shaddock, who testified that the prisoner came in at ten minutes to twelve. On the other hand Mrs. Wilkins, who looked at her bedside clock when the prisoner came into the bedroom, says it was then twenty-five minutes to twelve. Clearly they cannot both be correct. It is suggested by the defence that Shaddock was misled because he was reading the time only by a reflection of the clock in the hall. It is suggested by the prosecution that Mrs. Wilkins was deceived by a clock outside, which struck the three-quarters when she thought it struck the half-hour. You will make up your minds which of these witnesses was mistaken. I must point out, however, that if you believe Mrs. Wilkins, you will necessarily discount Mr. Fanum's evidence, since if Wilkins entered his bedroom at twenty-five minutes to twelve he cannot possibly have been seen on the promenade five minutes later. I must point out, too, that the usual distrust felt of evidence given by a wife in her husband's defence has little application here. Much of what Mrs. Wilkins had to say, under cross-examination, was so damaging to her husband, and it was evidence given with such remarkable composure, that she may be acquitted of any desire to shield him.

"And there is a further point related to this time question. If you find that Mrs. Wilkins's evidence was correct, and that both Mr. Fanum and Shaddock were mistaken, that does not by any means indicate that Wilkins was innocent of the crime.

"I come now to the evidence of the bloodstains. About these we must be very clear. There were two patches on Wilkins's sports jacket and two on his trousers, that were certainly blood. The prosecution say they got there when Wilkins murdered Sheila Morton. The defence attribute their presence to the fact that at some time during the evening Wilkins cut his thumb. Wilkins and Miss Morton were of the same blood group. You will have to decide whether these four small but distinct stains could possibly have been made when Wilkins cut his thumb. The cut was a quite considerable gash, nearly two inches long and fairly deep. Do you believe that this cut, however it was made (I will come to that later), could have caused the stains on jacket and trousers which you saw? Those four distinct patches? You may think that, only under the pressure of some extreme emotion, could the prisoner have failed to notice that blood was dripping on to his clothes.

"I must put into a different category the stains, invisible to the naked eye, which were identified as bloodstains by the scientific witness, Mr. Ritchie, through his use of what is known as the benzidine test. But are these marks bloodstains? You have heard Mr. Ritchie's evidence, and Mr. Newton's penetrating cross-examination. Mr. Ritchie says that in his experience the benzidine test always produces positive results, and he maintained this in face of a number of text-books. When, however, I asked him whether he could say whose blood it was, or when it came there, he admitted that he could offer no evidence on those matters. I think I am bound to direct you that it would not be safe, where experts disagree so violently, to rely on the results of the benzidine test. You will consider as evidence only the four stains positively iden-tified as blood."

Magnus Newton let his cheeks collapse slowly, with a sigh of satisfaction. He had been certain in his own mind that the benzidine test results would be thrown out, yet there was something comforting in hearing the actual words spoken. It was a point gained, and a considerable one.

"I come back, again, to the four undisputed bloodstains. In making up your minds about them you will have to remember the evidence of the wife. She told us that when Wilkins came in he said he must wash his hands, and she saw dried blood on them. There was quite a lot of blood, she said, on his right hand, and possibly some on his left. She noticed the dark stains on his jacket sleeve, mentioned those also, asked—very naturally—where he had been, and received the reply that she should mind her own business. She says that he snatched the jacket away from her, and hung it on the back of a chair. He did not, however, make any attempt to remove the stains. Was this because he simply did not know what he was doing, or because he realised that such an attempt could do no good now that his wife had seen the stains, or because he really had nothing to hide in connection with them?

"Then there are questions you must ask yourselves, also, about the evidence given by Miss Prenton for the defence. She is a prostitute and one, as you will have gathered, who is not ashamed of her calling. Her evidence, taken alone, does not establish the prisoner's innocence. It does, however, place him in her house from roughly nine-thirty to eleven o'clock. It would have taken him some fifteen minutes to walk back to the spot where Sheila Morton was murdered, and that would mean he did not meet her until, say, a quarter-past eleven or a little later. Mr. Newton argued very forcibly that this left him little time to murder Miss Morton and be back in his room at the hotel at twenty-five minutes to twelve. This argument, of course, only has validity if you accept Mrs. Wilkins's evidence about the time of his return. Mr. Newton also argued that if we accept Miss Prenton's story which places the time of meeting no earlier than eleven fifteen, Miss Morton must have been out walking for more than an hour when she met Wilkins. He said that this was most unlikely, since her father was ill, and she had said she would not be very long. Does this argument seem to you conclusive? Bear in mind that she knew a night nurse was installed, that there was nothing she could do for her father, and that she had been with him continuously since his heart attack on Saturday evening. It is for you to decide whether Mr. Newton laid undue stress on this point.

"But you must consider, further, whether you do give credit to Miss Prenton's evidence. At one point her story is inconsistent with that told by Mrs. Wilkins. She says that the prisoner opened a tin of baked beans for her, cut his thumb, and used his handkerchief to stanch the bleeding. According to Mrs. Wilkins there was no handkerchief round the prisoner's thumb when he arrived home, and no blood-stained handkerchief in his pockets. Then there are other curious features of Miss Prenton's story. In spite of her professed sympathy for the prisoner she did not come forward immediately, not until a private investigator employed by the prisoner's family had called on her. She said that this was because she feared the effect of calling police attention to her occupation, a statement which somewhat lost force when Mr. Hayley pointed out that she had several convictions, the last only a few weeks ago, so that she was already well known to the police. The prosecution suggested that she had been moved solely by a desire to be the centre of interest, and that her story bore the stamp of falsehood. Is that a sufficient motive for her action in coming forward into the glare of publicity? You had the opportunity of seeing Miss Prenton in the witness box, and you must decide. Does it seem credible to you that this prostitute should take a man home for an hour and a half, refuse to accept money from him, and even cook him a snack meal? And if you do not believe this part of her story, can you believe the rest of it? Can you believe her account of the opening of the baked beans, and the cut thumb, and the handkerchief wound round it, which so strangely disappeared...?

"I come now to the prisoner's attitude when interviewed by the police. On Tuesday morning he had gone again to the

Langland Hotel and had been told of Sheila Morton's death. Inspector Kenning has said that Wilkins showed anxiety at once when the stains on his jacket were pointed out to him, and mentioned that he had cut his thumb. Was this a perfectly natural anxiety, since he knew Sheila Morton had been murdered, or did it show a consciousness of guilt? You will remember that he made no attempt at any time to expunge the marks from the jacket or trousers. Then there is the remark he made at the time of his arrest—'I loved Sheila. I would never have hurt her if I'd been in my right mind.' Was this the remark of a murderer who knew he had been found out, or does it simply mean what the prisoner said in the box—'I had a blackout. I didn't know what I might have done.' You are confronted all the time with the fact that the prisoner says he can offer no help in relation to the events of that Monday evening after he left Lonergan. He is saying in effect, 'I do not know what I did that evening. I cannot help you. I must leave it to you to find out the truth.'

"Lastly, I must say to you something about the question of motive, which was so much stressed by Mr. Hayley in his closing speech. The motive attributed to the prisoner is that of frustrated passion. He had developed an extravagant fantasy about Sheila Morton, of that there can be no doubt. You have heard how he pursued her at the tennis club, you have heard how he induced his wife to come down to Brighton when he heard that Sheila Morton was there. What did he hope to achieve by this? You may think that he hardly knew himself, that he hoped for some extraordinary combination of circumstances that would enable him to carry on an affair with her even when his wife was in Brighton. Of course, such a combination of circumstances could never have occurred, and if it had come to pass we may be sure that Sheila Morton would not have accepted his advances. But still, consider the effect upon such a mind as the prisoner's of the sudden discovery that she was engaged to be married. He does not deny that this was a shock to him, and that it set him off on an evening of drinking. You may think that there is a pattern suggestive of the fear of violence in his actions, and it is certainly very striking that he preferred to visit a doctor he did not know, like Doctor Glenister, rather than his own local doctor. Was this, perhaps, because he was afraid of what he might learn about his own nature...?

"In his closing speech for the defence Mr. Newton suggested, if I followed him rightly, that the prisoner's psychological make-up was of such a kind that had he murdered anybody it would have been his wife—that their mutual lack of confidence had developed on his side at least into hatred, and that in his mind she stood in the way of his achieving happiness with Sheila Morton. You will give such weight to this argument as you feel it justifies, but you may think it is a far-fetched idea, particularly in view of the fact that Wilkins had just heard of Sheila Morton's engagement. Mr. Newton also suggested that Sheila Morton might have gone from the promenade to the beach, and have been attacked there by a complete stranger. Does it seem to you within the bounds of possibility that such a girl as Sheila Morton would have gone down to the beach on this very dark night, alone?

"I must stress, however, that it is not necessary for the defence to provide an acceptable explanation of the events of that tragic Monday night, or to say how Sheila Morton met her death. The onus is upon the prosecution to prove beyond all reasonable doubt that John Wilkins was guilty of the crime with which he is charged. However strong his motive, that is not in itself enough. Suspicion, however strong, is not enough. You must be certain..."

XXIII

They took John Wilkins down to his cell when the judge had finished, talking to him firmly but kindly, telling him that he must be patient and that perhaps the jury would not be long. The prisoner, however, showed no sign of impatience. He sat down with perfect docility in the cell and, hands upon knees, stared at the blank wall. What was he thinking—or was he thinking anything? one of the prison officers, who was of an imaginative turn of mind, wondered.

The time after the jury has retired in a murder trial, the supreme climax of the case as the uninformed might think, is in fact anticlimactic, a period of waiting during which spectators stretch and yawn, and counsel leave the court to smoke and talk in their rooms.

"What do you think?" Charlie Hudnutt asked Newton, as they sat smoking in the little room provided for them. Hudnutt sat on a table swinging his legs, Newton paced the floor.

"If they're back inside an hour, all right. If it's longer—" He did not complete the sentence.

"That chap second from left, the one with the handle-bar moustache, was lapping up everything you said." Newton grunted. "Old Morland was fair enough. Always is. He was bound to throw that benzidine stuff out, wasn't he? Well, it's over. I'll be glad to get back to London."

Newton nodded to him abruptly, opened the door and went out. Charlie Hudnutt shrugged his shoulders and then, whistling, consulted his diary. He felt entitled to a little relaxation. A telephone call to Gillian now—or should it be Margaret? His whistling became louder.

In the gallery a good many spectators stuck it out, reading newspapers or books, and whispering among themselves. Below them sat a number of people involved in the case. Old Mrs. Wilkins sat with hands folded over her stomach, her heavy features composed. She did not speak to Uncle Dan, who shuffled his long legs on the floor, fumbled in his pocket for a paper, and once or twice put up a hand to hide the persistent tic in his cheek. Mr. Morton sat near them, jaunty in a silk shirt and a black bow tie with white spots on it, his delighted glance twinkling every so often up to the watchers in the gallery as though he would like to say to them: "Here I am, the father of the murdered girl, the sick man who has so triumphantly survived." Putting his hand into his pocket Mr. Morton stealthily withdrew it, conveying to his mouth a custard cream biscuit.

In the row behind him Betty Prenton sat, next to May Wilkins. May's eyes stared directly forward as though fixed, unaware of the disreputable member of society who sat so close to her, only a few inches between them.

The judge's summing up had finished at eleven o'clock. At a quarter to twelve Uncle Dan said, "Disagreement. Must be good for the boy, mustn't it? Odds on a not guilty verdict now, I'd say."

"They cannot find him guilty," Mrs. Wilkins said.

"Of course not," Uncle Dan said hastily. "Think I shall

stretch my legs a minute. They won't be back yet. Might have a cup of tea over the road. Keep my eye on what happens here, of course. Coming?"

She shook her head. He went out of the court into the heat, crossed the road and ordered a cup of tea in a small café. He noticed Betty Prenton at a table farther inside the room, and walked over to her.

"Just wanted to say thank you. You were wonderful in the box. Mind if I sit down?"

"It's a free world, or so they tell me." Her hard, assessing glance raked him from untidy grey hair to scruffy brown shoes, noting the tic, the lop-sided face, the long, twisting hands. "You've got nothing to thank me for. Don't even know that I did any good."

"Must have taken a lot of courage. A damned shame, the way Hayley went for you. Cigarette?"

"Thanks." Her fingers, nicotine-stained, strong, predatory, plucked one from the pack. Across the court she was a good-looking woman, Uncle Dan thought. Close to—well, she was still good-looking, but you could see the coarse skin, and there was a sort of glaze of hardness on her. What was it she was saying now? "He had his job to do."

"Didn't have to do it like that. Damned insulting."

She took a pull at the cigarette, and looked at him. "You're his uncle. Why did you introduce him to that phoney doctor?"

Uncle Dan spread out his hands placatingly. "How was I to know what he'd be like? Just met him in some club, he seemed a pretty smart feller." He took a gulp of tea. "Thought he might introduce John to someone like yourself, woman of the world. That's what he wanted."

"You think he's guilty, don't you?"

"Hell, I don't know."

"He didn't do it. I can feel it here." She put a hand on her stomach. Over at the court there was a small flurry of people. "Something's happening. Let's go back."

They walked over to the court together. Uncle Dan said nervously, "I go this way. Which way are you—"

"I get it. Don't worry, I won't embarrass you. I know my place—on my back." She laughed out loud. Uncle Dan managed a feeble smile as he scuttled away from her.

The time was twenty minutes past twelve. The jury were back in their places, looking solemn. John Wilkins was in his place too, pale but docile still. Now the judge came in, moving like a sleep-walker. Everybody stood up. He sat down. Everybody sat down.

The clerk, a snuffy little man sitting below the judge, said, "Members of the jury, are you agreed upon your verdict?"

The foreman of the jury was a gentle-looking old man, with a long horsy liberal face. He said, not at all as though he were certain about it, "We are."

"How do you find, is the prisoner guilty or not guilty?"

"We find the prisoner guilty."

Old Mrs. Wilkins gave a small cry. Uncle Dan looked down at his legs. Mr. Morton smirked, and bowed his head slightly. A smile quivered at the corners of May Wilkins's mouth. Betty Prenton closed her eyes. Magnus Newton snapped a pencil in two. The prisoner, anxiously watched by the prison officers on either side of him, stayed calm as a dummy.

The judge's clerk placed a small square of black silk upon Mr. Justice Morland's head.

Epilogue

I

Uncle Dan and Mrs. Wilkins hardly spoke on the way back to Clapham. In the train he read the evening papers, with their account of the summing up and verdict. Then, a little furtively, he turned to the sports pages. The furtiveness was unnecessary, for Mrs. Wilkins was staring out of the window.

Back at Baynard Road he said nervously, "Would you like a cup of tea?"

She took off her formidable hat. "That would be very nice."

Uncle Dan opened the windows, made tea and brought it in, with biscuits on a plate. To his surprise she ate several biscuits, and drank two cups of tea.

"I wondered—" he began. The tic in his cheek was very noticeable. "I wondered whether—what you want to do now?"

"What do you mean?"

"There'll be a tidy bill from that detective agency. After all, the chap did find out something. But I mean—do you want to go on?"

She dabbed at her mouth. "What do you mean, go on? They said he was guilty."

"There's the appeal, of course. Still, that's not what I

meant. Are we going to dig up fresh evidence, that kind of thing?"

"They found out that he did it."

"But you believe—only a few minutes before the verdict, you said—"

"They found out that he did it." Her face was heavy, brooding. "There's an end of it."

Uncle Dan fairly gaped at her. She spoke very slowly, her jaws working as though she were still eating. "My son is a murderer, Dan. He killed that woman. They found it out. Now I have a headache, and I am going upstairs to lie down."

When she had gone Uncle Dan sat, with his legs stuck out in front of him, looking at the teacups.

II

"Come to us when it's all over," the Edwards had said to May. "You won't feel like going back to that flat, or at any rate not yet." Mr. Edwards was waiting with the car at Victoria, and there was high tea when they got back to the neat little semi-detached house.

"They were bound to find him guilty," Stella Edwards said with a glint in her eye. "All that about washing his bloodstained hands in the basin, I mean to say, you must have been terrified."

"Not at the time," May said. They were sitting in the garden, which was as neat as the house.

"If you ask my opinion, that girl led him on. I mean to say, I'm not excusing John or anything, but some of those girls really ask for it. Going down on the beach at night, I mean to say."

May did not reply. Mr. Edwards nudged his wife, who said, "May, darling, Harry and I felt—we thought you ought to get away from it all. Why don't you come down next week to Devon. You know, to the Restawhile Guest House. It's awfully quiet, and they're such nice people. We'd simply love to have you. And stay with us till we go down, you know the guest-room's always ready."

"Thank you very much, I should love to." May gave a slight titter. "I wanted to go with you in the first place. I shall be getting my holiday in Devon after all."

"Why, yes," her friend said, a little disconcerted. Harry Edwards pulled his moustache and thought, half admiringly, *My word, she's a cool one.*

III

Mr. Morton got back home feeling just a little deflated after the excitement of the trial, which had kept him buoyed up, on top of his form. The daily woman, Mrs. Kipler, had kept the place clean and tidy, but he was positively faced with the necessity of getting his own supper. That had, however, its compensations, as he felt ready to acknowledge while he put on an apron that had belonged to Sheila, and melted fat in the pan.

Two pieces of fried bread, two large rashers of bacon—what else? He broke two eggs into the pan, and after a moment's hesitation added a third. The fat sizzled merrily. This was better than the slops and fruit juice Sheila had made him take for supper every night. Humming under his breath Mr. Morton put it all on a large plate and sat down in the kitchen to eat it. While he ate he hurriedly skimmed over the apologetic letter from young Bill Lonergan, that had awaited his return: "...sorry that I could not stay... afraid you may have thought me rude... under great stress, as we all were at the time... distressed by the verdict, hoped against hope that the jury would... anything at all that I can do to help... a housekeeper..."

Mr. Morton pushed a piece of fried bread round the plate to collect the last pieces of yolk. A good fellow, Bill, but dull. A housekeeper? Perhaps, but what a bore that would be. He belched, sighed, shifted wearily. He was beginning to feel rather ill.

IV

"No dice," said Mr. Moody to Mr. Likeness, who was back in the office reading the morning paper.

"No dice."

"Newton good?"

"So so. Not really. Anything much doing?"

"Nothing to worry you. Routine stuff on your desk. Have a good time at Lewes?"

"Took a few shillings off Pinkney playing snooker." Mr. Moody left him. Mr. Likeness picked out the winners of the 2.30 and the 4.15, rang up and placed bets for rather more than he could afford, and then turned to the accumulation of papers on his desk.

V

"Come along now, here's your visitor," the warder said. John Wilkins rose obediently, followed the warder down the corridor into a small room, and stared at the woman on the other side of the grille.

"It's me," Betty Prenton said. In this dough-faced man with dull button eyes she hardly recognised John Wilkins. "You remember me, Betty Prenton."

"Of course," he said politely.

She felt at a loss. "They asked you—told you I should be coming, didn't they?" He did not answer. "Is there anything at all you want, anything I can do for you?"

"I don't think so, thank you."

"Is the food all right? Do you get enough exercise? I know what prison's like, you know, been in myself, though it was only for a day or two."

"Everything is all right." He sat with what seemed to her an unnatural stillness.

She said desperately, "I've moved from Brighton, you know. Couldn't really stay after what happened. I'm in London now. Better in some ways, though I liked it by the sea."

Now he showed interest, leaned forward, put his face to the grille. "Have you brought any message?"

"Message?"

"From Sheila." The fat, dough-coloured face trembled, tears showed in the dull eyes. "It's been a long time."

"Sheila? Oh, my God." Betty Prenton put her face in her hands. John Wilkins began to talk quickly.

"I know it's been difficult. And I don't mind waiting, tell her that, won't you, but it's hard without some word. Just a word. I don't understand why she can't write to me. Is it that father of hers? Got to look after him, but all the same—do you suppose they're keeping the letters here so that I don't get them?" A little saliva began to dribble from his mouth.

"I'll see if I can get in touch." Betty Prenton began to back away from the grille. "Good-bye."

"Please don't go." Tears ran down his face. "I've got to talk to somebody about her. You—I don't remember you, but I know you'll understand."

"Come along," the warder said, "it's time." John Wilkins turned towards him an agonised face. Betty Prenton fled, but not so soon that she was unable to hear his animal cry.

VI

Betty Prenton paid her visit to John Wilkins at the end of August. It was on a golden autumn evening at the end of September that Magnus Newton visited Doctor Max Andreadis, and they sat sipping sherry in the small paved garden of the psychiatrist's house in St. John's Wood.

"Wilkins is in Broadmoor," Newton said abruptly. "You know that, I expect. Transferred a couple of weeks ago. Perhaps we should have pled insanity."

Doctor Andreadis smiled. "But under those rules of yours—did we not discuss them at our first meeting—"

"He was sane. I know. Damn." He had knocked over his sherry. There was a little confusion, his glass was refilled.

"Prison life," the doctor said, "makes psychopaths of us all."

"Perhaps. Do you think he did it? None of your damned generalisations, either."

"Are you dissatisfied with the verdict?" Andreadis was looking at Newton curiously.

"I'll tell you a story, Doctor. Early this month I took my wife and young daughter—you remember she was ill at the time of the trial—for a holiday. We went touring through France and Italy with the car. We stopped one night at a little village called Previso, on the Adriatic coast, stayed in one of the two hotels. Next day I went for a walk, while my wife and daughter stayed on the beach. Sat down on a hill overlooking the sea, dozed off. I'd had a lot of driving to do the previous day and for some reason hadn't slept well. I was wakened by the most frightful noise. It was a moment or two before I identified it as a very queer sort of laugh." He paused. "Do you remember one of the witnesses in the case, a stupid old man named Fanum? Remember the laugh he said he'd heard? It was like that, nothing earthly, a kind of wail."

Andreadis simply looked at him. Newton went on.

"I was shivering, felt suddenly cold. I crawled to the edge of the hill, looked over. Below was a little cove, sandy beach, only one person on it—did I say this was a rather desolate bit of the coast? This one person, a man, was lying on the beach reading a newspaper. He was in a paroxysm of laughter. Writhing on the beach there as if he were in a kind of fit. At one point he stuffed a handkerchief into his mouth to stop the noise, but then he took it out, and the noise started again." Newton shuddered. "The cause of it all seemed to be this paper. I couldn't, of course, see the date of it, or the item that amused him, but when we got back to Previso I looked up the English papers, which are on sale there a couple of days after publication. I found a report that old Morton, Sheila's father, had died of a heart attack. Apparently the old man had been eating all sorts of unsuitable foods, and his doctor wasn't surprised."

"And the man you saw on the beach?"

"The man on the beach was old Morton's next-of-kin, his nephew, William Lonergan."

"And Lonergan inherited?"

"No, he only got a couple of thousand pounds. The old

man had made a new will and left most of his money to some home for old people."

"What then?" Andreadis was looking at Newton very carefully now.

"Don't you *see*," Newton asked now, in a burst of speech that seemed as painful to him as the lancing of a boil, "don't you see how it all fits in? We thought nobody else had a motive for killing Sheila. But consider Lonergan. Old Morton was thought to be certain to die, the doctor said so himself. Sheila would get the money. Lonergan had been more or less engaged to her, remember. He would have come down from Birmingham with the idea of proposing again, to become the husband of a rich woman. What does he find? She has suddenly become engaged, no doubt she will marry soon after her father dies. Think what a shock it is to him. And besides, he has been engaged to her himself, he doesn't want to see her married to another man. Think how angry Wilkins's insinuations made him. When Sheila comes out for her walk he meets her—perhaps it really was by accident. He is a man she knows and trusts, her cousin. They go down on the beach together. He kills her. Now the money is Lonergan's, as next-of-kin, as soon as the old man dies. But the old man doesn't die. Lonergan doesn't dare to kill him, because that would certainly cause suspicion. As it is, he goes quite free of suspicion, and is able by his evidence to make Wilkins's guilt seem more certain. If he was really a friend of Wilkins he had no need at all to make that little conversation so damning." Newton stopped abruptly. "Could I have some whisky?"

"Of course." While Newton splashed whisky in his glass Andreadis said, "In the end Lonergan didn't get the money, or only got a little of it."

"Yes. But he couldn't tell the old man would make a new will. What do you think?"

"I think that the holiday did you little good."

"No, man. About Lonergan."

Andreadis sipped his sherry. "You have become hysterical about this case. I saw the seeds of it at Lewes."

"Lonergan, what about Lonergan?" Newton's face was red, the veins standing out on it. "Don't you believe he did it?"

"No. Do you imply that he murdered his uncle from Italy?"

"Of course not. Simply waited for him to die. He knew he wouldn't have to wait long, couldn't tell about the will. You said yourself that you weren't sure whether Wilkins was guilty."

"Did I say that? If so, it was merely to avoid an argument."

"Then you think he did it?"

"Certainly. And so do you. All this is merely a justification of what you feel to have been your own uncertain handling of the case."

"Lonergan had the motive, an overwhelming motive, once you see it. He had the opportunity. Nobody ever checked on him, why should they?"

"You must face reality." Andreadis stood now, tall, commanding, for a moment austere. "This fantasy has been evolved by you out of a laugh you heard on a beach, when you woke from sleep. That is its only connection with what happened at Brighton. The rest is in your own mind."

The sun melted below the rooftops in a mess of red and gold. "If I cannot convince you I shall convince nobody," Newton said. He stood, a head below Andreadis, and drained his whisky. "But you were not on that hillside, Doctor, you didn't hear that laugh as I did. I tell you I know now what that old man meant by saying it was a murderer's laugh. I know what he meant, I tell you, by saying that the laugh had in it the colour of murder."

The sun suddenly died. The two men stood looking at each other in the twilight.

To see more Poisoned Pen Press titles:

Visit our website:
poisonedpenpress.com
Request a digital catalog:
info@poisonedpenpress.com